Maui on the Rocks

Oliver Gold

Oliver Gold

This is a fiction novel based on Oliver's true story. Only the names have been changed to prevent the guilty from coming after the author.

Maui on the Rocks

© Oliver Gold / Aloha S. T. Entertainment

First published 2016
Second Edition 2018

ISBN-10: 151464911X

ISBN-13: 978-1514649114

"No alien land in all the world has any deep charm for me but that one, no other land could so longingly and so beseechingly haunt me, sleeping and walking, through half a lifetime, as that one has done. Other things leave me but it abides; other things change, but it remains the same. For me its balmy airs are always blowing, its summer seas flashing in the sun."

Mark Twain
Honolulu, Hawaii, 1866

"Sam, I wish you could abide a while, on the island of Maui today. You would be delighted to feel the fair wind, soft as a passing bird, the seas still sparkle in the sun, the surf forever ripping away and returning the sand. The Maui sunrise still fires the imagination, the sunsets haunt the soul like no other land in all the world."

Oliver Gold
Lahaina, Maui. 2018

Oliver Gold

Books by Oliver Gold

Maui on the Rocks
Maui Leis an' Lies
Maui out of Body

Available on Amazon.com

1

Booze Flight out of Seattle

It took four 'Cuba Libras' and one complimentary Mai-Tai to endure the five-hundred and seventy-two-hour flight from Seattle to Maui. Uncle Ole was a little fuzzy on the exact numbers. The Mai-Tai tasted like Kool-Aid, but the big Swede drank it anyway. He told himself that all this drinking was a celebration, not an escape from heart-break. This was his one-person, retirement party. It wasn't about Tanya. After years of planning, he'd finally bought it; a one-way ticket to Hawaii.

"Here's to re'fier'ment." He finished the Mai-tai with a congratulatory slourish. The rum drinks were ramping up his confidence so much that he pressed the button for the flight attendant. She hovered over him immediately. He was her friendliest customer and her best tipper.

"Take a message to the pilot for me." He commanded.

She backed up a pace, as if her suspicion alarm went off, perhaps wondering if Mr. Friendly here, was a terrorist.

"Tell the pilot that if he want'za catch a nap or somethin', I'm a licensed pilot 'doo, an' I would be happy to fly 'da plane for a coupla' hours. I've alwaze wanted to fly one of these Boeing 7-297's."

Fortunately for everyone aboard, the flight attendant talked him out of it with another free Mai-Tai. Ole nudged that Kool-

Aid for a while until he began to feel the plane loose altitude.

"It won't be long now," he said to the old man sleeping next to him by the window. There was no reply, so Uncle let him be.

The jet continued to descend gracefully and the excitement of nearing Hawaii spread through the passengers like a sunny morning in Seattle. He could smell the tanning lotion being applied liberally on the white skins all around him. It was a happy, vacation smell.

Suddenly, the plane dropped like a broken elevator, straight down. His empty plastic cup went flying out of his hand, spilling ice all over the ceiling. His stomach lurched the same direction. The passengers screamed! Spastic, horrible screaming that wouldn't, couldn't stop. Frantic prayers shouted desperately in Spanish, Hawaiian and English filled the air along with the ice and the flight attendants. Everyone else had been wearing their seat belts.

Uncle Ole closed his eyes and escaped the panic with a disciplined, slow breath. He knew it may be his last and he took time to remember the impermanence and sweetness of life. Though they were still falling, his own mind was surprisingly calm amongst all the screaming. Life had been long and happy. He trusted in Death to provide the same.

The jet fell faster than the drop of any roller coaster. He thought of the word, 'fear,' but it held no power over him. He was excited yes, like the other passengers, but with patient acceptance. Planes go down from time to time. Today, his number was up, or down, it really didn't matter at this point.

The bizarre screaming was getting crazier with every falling second. The old man next to him wasn't screaming; just yawning and looking out his window at the clouds racing straight up.

Ole thought of religion. He'd always believed in a 'Holy Spirit' and the wisdom of Jehovah, Buddha and Jesus, but he was a chemistry teacher. Life on this planet was complicated. He knew things and taught things that those Great Masters from long ago, never chose to share with their admirers. His thoughts sobered a bit as he recalled the ABC's of Chemistry: Energy is neither created nor destroyed, but it's always changing. Ole figured his atoms were about to be changing very soon, like in a few thousand feet. He tightened his fingers in a vice grip on the arms of his seat. Maybe he *was* afraid. The jet was going down, going down! The screams were piercing his ears along with the painful plunge in altitude. The big broken bird tipped forward; throwing everyone back into the hard cushions of their seats with teeth pulling 'G' force. The plane was falling in a nose dive!

"JESUS, MARY, AND JOSEPH!" Ole screamed.

The old man sitting next to him reached out and held his hand like any dad would for a frightened child. That brought him half-way back to his senses. Ole thought of his parents. He owed them everything. They had been good parents. He thought of Tanya, and his three daughters. At least he had loved and been loved in dis life. He thought of IZ Kamakawiwo'ole and his version of 'Over the Rainbow.' Ole gripped the old man's hand and hummed the melody figuring all his rainbows will soon be, over.

The plummeting jumbo jet was starting to spin. His seat belt was sawing him in half. Then somehow, the falling pig spread her wings! Everything went right back to powerful, level, almost-controlled flight. The jet accelerated like a rocket. Turbulence continued to play the screaming passengers like a calliope on a merry-go-round. Even when the flight smoothed out, the shrieking dropped only one octave into a loud chorus of panic and confusion.

Uncle Ole held his nose and tried to relieve the stabbing knives in his ears. His head was a balloon that would feel better if it could just explode. Both ears were popping a fresh batch of corn as the plane descended on its crunchy approach to the islands.

He reflected on the last few minutes. *Did he really expect Jesus and his family to save the jet from crashing?*

Maybe they did, a voice inside his head answered.

Anyway, he was mighty glad the plane wasn't smashing into the ocean about now. This was his first week of retirement, he wanted to spend some of it on Maui. He turned to the old man, but there was no old man. Uncle Ole had the window seat. *Who was holding my hand?* He shivered, closed his eyes and tried to tell himself it was the rum, but it felt like an hallucination or a miracle.

As the Jet approached the airport, it started shaking violently again; so the passengers started to scream again. He looked out through his window, the sugar cane fields were blurring by, bent flat by the gusting winds. Too much runway was already history. The wide-body, A 330 Airbus was coming in too high and too fast.

"Set her down NOW, Captain!" He shouted. He wasn't philosophizing anymore.

He saw dozens of fire trucks and ambulances parked in a hanger off to the far side of the runway. It looked like the emergency crews had all gone to lunch.

The jumbo jet dropped the last hundred feet in three seconds; its big tires suffering a tremendous, "whompa-ka-whomp!" Both jet engines screamed into reverse, to stop Newton's Law of a body in motion stays in motion, until it hits the ocean at the end of the runway.

Just in time, the pilot slowed the hurtling jet down to about fifty miles an hour and yanked the steering wheel to the left. The starboard wheels came off the ground as the plane swung sixty degrees to port. The big, smoking-hot tires cleared the ocean by a good four feet, but the jet was heeled over like a sailboat running downwind, straight for the terminal. The pilot got her to a slow roll before they hit the building and pulled up the parking brake, full stop. The 'Fasten Seat Belts' light went off with a happy,

"Ping!"

As the plane continued to shudder, "Hawaii Five-0" began to surf through the interior speakers,

"Bah-pah-pa-pa-pa bah, bah pa bah bah bah,"

Everyone cheered the pilot! The applause was a roar inside

the plane's economy cabin. Nervous tension on every face drained away from, 'Oh God, we're all gonna die!' to 'Oh Boy, we're in Hawaii."

The rumpled flight attendants that were sort of matronly looking at the beginning of the flight, were starting to look like cover girls; their makeup smeared and their hair tossed wild and sexy. They were all smiling at Uncle Ole. The truth is, they were smiling at everyone. He could hear them way up there by the front door saying nice, normal things like,

"Aloha, welcome to Maui," to passengers hurrying off the plane.

The young mother and the two horned-children from Hell that had been crying and kicking his seat for the last one-hundred and fifty-thousand miles were slow getting up, so Uncle got into the aisle while there was still room. He managed to stand without banging his head on the overhead compartment, but he nearly passed out from rising too fast.

The rolling barrel of Caribbean rum he'd consumed was making his vision slosh from wall to wall as he tried to convince his carry-on to follow him down the narrow aisle. The thing had a mind of its own, bumping into new friends along the way. When he passed the pretty flight attendants he smiled his goodbye. They both gave him a wink and said,

"Aloha..."

He tried to repeat the word, but his teeth got stuck together with the same piece of gum he had been chewing all during the roller coaster landing. His ears were still machine gunning their way down to sea-level. Uncle Ole heard his voice reply to the flight attendants, something that sounded like,

"Marimba..."

He found himself stepping into the jet-ramp thing. It was a ninety-degree tunnel of hot. It felt *so* good. Years of Seattle chill and six hours of jet air-conditioning, had built an igloo around his bones. This metal oven felt just right. He needed a good baking

HAhhhhhh waiiiii, was all he could think.

He wanted to stay and roast in the oven, but the school of shoving, agitated, tourist fish behind him, kept pushing him up stream. Uncle Ole swam with the fish and popped out of the oven only half-baked. He got a splash of cold in the waiting area of the Island Wings Gate. He felt like a salmon in some mad migration as he swam with the colorful tourists. They swirled around a dangerous reef of chairs, and balled up inside the arrival holding tank. It was a surprise when one whole side of the glass aquarium slid open and all the fish spilled outside onto an outdoor walkway.

Uncle Ole fish slowly swam counterclockwise to the race of the school and found a quiet eddy to rest in. He was feeling pretty good about his progress so far; he hadn't fallen on his face yet. He had just congratulated himself, when he was smacked up the side of his head by the powerful trade winds and almost knocked flat. The wind slap on his face reddened his blue complexion up a few shades and his ice cold-bones began to thaw. With the marvelous heat, his spirits began to soar.

12

Now Hawaii, now! His inner-Zen declares.

He's about as Zen aware, as 'way too much' booze will allow. At least he caught the right plane out of Seattle. Of course, he was sober then; things were more complicated now. He gazed out beyond the identical-looking, rental cars. The 'vacation palms' in the far parking lot were gesturing like hula girls welcoming him to the islands. As he watched them dance the winds increased, making the palms shake faster than Tongan girls.

The trades blew wild across a sky of blue, deep, rich blue. Two puffy-white clouds were holding hands and skipping merrily out over the ocean. It was a beautiful moment. He was sooo glad to be here, a tear formed in his good eye. Uncle figured it must have been the girly Mai-Tai. He's not a crier. Maybe, it was a tear of joy, or maybe it was about Tanya after all. He felt that heartburn again. Hawaii looked great, but it would have been perfect, if his wife had come with him. He missed her already. Within three seconds Ole remembered how she drove him to the airport this morning, kissed him goodbye and told him she was filing for divorce. He looked back at the Hawaiian sky and got all happy again.

See those trees doing the hula? His inner voice was the tour guide. *Those ar' your dancers now.*

This was not Uncle Ole's first time to Hawaii. Right after he married Tanya, they moved to Honolulu so he could take his first teaching job at UH. Back then she loved everything about Hawaii, the climate, the mix of cultures, even him. Those swaying palms of his were starting to look kinda red through

13

his bloodshot eyes. The blue sky was tinting green; it was hard to keep his balance.

Ole had found the rainbow mix of cultures, inspiring. All his students called him 'Uncle.' It's a term of respect, part of the family, melting pot style of Hawaii. Like a 'social-glue-stew' in the pot that reminds the different races of their common humanity. *If it were a worldwide custom, people would get along better.*

All this remembering and thinking was about to give him a nosebleed. But, thinking is such a stubborn, busybody habit for a teacher that it's hard to stop, even after retiring.

The mountains were beginning to look pink with green polka dots. The colorful tourist fish were still swimming past; some of the little ones leaping for joy. He felt so good he wanted to leap with them, but he felt safer just slowly turning in his warm eddy.

When he took the teaching job at Stanford and then landed the head of the department position at University of Washington the name 'Uncle' stuck to him. Over the years, he documented a growing sense of, family forming as he spread the term's 'Auntie' and 'Uncle' among the faculties of both universities. He'd written a paper on it which was published in Psychology Today.

Speaking of today, why not occupy the 'now', of your first day of retirement, remember? You can forget all that teaching stuff, its history. His inner beach bum reminds him of what's really, important here.

The palm trees were doing the 'loco-motion' even wilder now in the gusty wind. He decided it's a good thing he didn't fly the big jet after all. Landing in this fierce gale would have been a little too exciting even for him, ultralight-pilot, first-in-his-class, at the Mt. Vernon Flight School.

Uncle Ole had been away from Hawaii for too long. Something like twenty-seven years, two months and nine days, but it was hard to be real accurate this afternoon. How many Mai-Tais? No matter, no reluctant wife could stop him from retiring on Maui someday. Today, was a someday as good as any.

He leaned his fish tail on the chest high wall of the airport walkway for support and drank in big pulls of warm, tropical air.

"Hello Hawaii… Goodbye 'bite-me,' cold Seattle." He heard his voice speaking out loud this time, in sync with his mind once again. The tourists behind him laughed. Everyone from the Seattle to Maui flight seemed a little giddy. Maybe because they'd all survived that horrible landing. He turned and watched them swim out of the cold aquarium and into the hot air. Some fish wore expressions of excitement; those happy, vacation faces. Others had the beatific fish-eye gaze of saints. Their faces were lifted toward heaven like he'd seen in Renaissance paintings, only these faces looked like fish heads with halos. They were among the redeemed; Angelfish like him that finally made it back to Heaven. He lingered in his quiet pool out of the main current, and watched them enjoy their first tropical orgasm. Ole managed to stay in one place by doing a slow backstroke with his pectoral fins. He was in no condition to hurry. He planned to stay here for the rest of his fishy life.

See tha' ocean over der', thaz's your ocean. See thoz' mountains, doze 'er your mountains now. His inner Columbus was claiming the world around him. He just happened to be from Earth; Hawaii is part of the Earth, so Hawaii was now his to claim. He held a colonial view of geography. Not that he wanted to be a king or anything; but he was determined to make Hawaii his new home and a happier place for everyone already here.

The colorful fish were still rushing past. Some of them were starting to look like people, but most looked like smiling rainbow trout.

Fish smile? He heard his inner thoughts wondering. *Better wait a little longer.* Leaning on the airport wall was enough of a challenge.

Eventually he remembered he had a guitar and some luggage. That's all he owned now. Finding his stuff would be the logical next step, if he could remember how to do steps. He smiled again.

Would that be, a 'two-step' or a 'polka'? His inner dance coach is trying to figure the next moves here. The flow of passengers was schooling past just a little slower. He saw an opening, signaled with his arm like he was on a bicycle, and merged into them, becoming one with the fish.

Uncle Ole tried to concentrate as he approached the top of the down escalator. Its metal blades looked dangerous. Even

16

trying to be careful, his right or left foot was too far forward on the first battle axe that slid out to be stepped on. It moved so fast he feared it would cut off his feet. When he looked down, everything started to spin like a hula-hoop. He grabbed for his carry-on handle behind him and all he caught was vertigo. He was a big man, six foot-two and he fell forward, hard against the back of a larger man wearing a white t-shirt and a Panama hat. The man's hat flew off and over the heads of the people further down the silver waterfall. It looked like crocodiles ate it down there in the river, far below. The hat-less man fell right on to the back of giant boulder of a guy in an extra-extra-extra-large t-shirt. This was a three-hundred-pound, local guy that stopped the dominoes right there. The big Hawaiian turned with a frown. But, instead of being angry he simply said,

"You Okay, brah?"

Those kind words were Uncle Ole's first impression of the native, Maui people. He never forgot that gentle man's kindness. The now hat-less man was also mellowed by the 'Aloha' and turned to help Ole take a firm stand on the shiny knife blades. Ole sincerely apologized to them both and tried to keep his balance on the rest of the stairway's descent.

It wasn't too hard to find the baggage area. The fish were changing shape, running on four legs, like hunting dogs after a fox. Uncle Ole trotted along as best he could, considering the rum-blur he was in. He stopped when all the other dogs stopped, to wait by the luggage carousel. This looked like a big, metal dog-food dish. The hungry dogs paced back and forth waiting for a fox lunch. Nothing happened for about a week. Some hounds got so tired of waiting they sat on the floor with their tongues hanging out. A couple of young pups pulled out ukuleles and started baying something that sounded like a hula song. A day later, a blue light on a ten-foot pole in the center of the food dish suddenly started blinking like a strobe light... 'supper-time, supper-time, supper-time,' it seemed to announce.

The light was a real pretty, blue. That bright police-blue so full of authority, sending a message Uncle thought he could decipher: 'Congratulations! After days of official TSA interrogation and considerable torture, your luggage is now being released into your custody.'

Then, extremely loud blasts of a horn began to blow. They sounded like the harsh trumpet notes of a washed up, jazz musician, hiding somewhere up above them. Maybe it was the Most-High, Maui 'Airport Angel' announcing the glorious 'Second Coming,' of the luggage. Either way, it was a marvelous moment. All the dog-people stood with their full attention on the food dish. There was a loud bang and the silver carousel began to move. It turned very, very slowly. Another two days went by with every dog wishing he was fed and running on a Maui beach somewhere.

'Turn, turn, turn, 'ders a time fo' Bethany' suitcase un-der heaven,' his inner juke box was sounding a little strange.

Black suitcases started crawling down the chute into the food dish. Someone saw them and barked! The luggage came all bunched up, like a live caterpillar inching down a kid's slide. Everyone howled and cheered! It was exciting to watch the jumble of black bags ride slowly around the edge of the dog dish. But after another hour, it wasn't so entertaining.

At last, Uncle saw his two blue suitcases and his guitar come slowly down the slide. He ran over and wrestled them onto a push cart. He walked out into the Maui sunshine and waved 'shaka' to all the taxis. There was a rainbow of cabs passing by on the street: purple, blue, green, yellow, red and orange. He wanted a green one, but yellow got him first.

2

A Psychic Cabbie?

"Let's go to Five-Z-Storage on Kapa Street," Ole said to the cabbie.

"Sure t'ing, buckle-up Uncle," the driver said, as he pulled slowly out into traffic.

"Thanks." Ole smiled some more. It felt so good to be back in Hawaii and hear someone call him Uncle again. He tried without success to fasten the various seat belt ends together. As the cab picked up speed, he tied the two belts into a square knot over his lap. It might have been a 'granny'; he let it be. Some wonderful, quiet minutes of time went swushing by. It was kind of hard to focus on any one thing. Through his open window, the city looked more like a town than a city, but this town had palm trees. They were those 'vacation palms' you see in the brochures. He knew they were coconut palms, he was a teacher. Well, up until last Friday, he was a teacher. *That was then, this is now, now in Hawaii.* Uncle's mind reminded him. He smiled some more. He'd never been to Maui. The mountains were taller than he expected. They had white cut-out clouds taped to them and of course a felt pen, smeared looking, paper rainbow was bouncing from a string tied up in heaven somewhere. It looked like an animated movie set for a film called "Hawaii, Moving There and Starting Over". Tanya wouldn't like it. But to Uncle it was paradise. He was so happy he was about to cry again or sing. He tried to sing,

"Uh huh Uh Huh, I like it," Oliver thinks he's singing quietly to himself.

"Let me guess… " said the cab driver, "yer' movin' to Maui from Seattle."

"Whoa… " Ole's taken back pretty hard. "You tell fortunes while you drive cab?"

"Been drivin' long time, I've seen 'dis befo,' brah."

"What was the give-away?"

"Layerz,"

"Layers?"

"Yah brah, you're layer'd with a t-shirt, 'den flannel shirt, layer'd ova with a fleece vest and 'den one windbreaker ova 'dat." Up Seattle way, eva'body dress 'da kine."

"Okay, but why Seattle? Why not Boise or Portland or Ferndale?"

"The Sea Hawks cap and the yuppie leather shoes, probably imported from Italy. So, you are from a rich 'burb, like Bellevue or Kirkland or Mercer Island."

Uncle forgot he was wearing his team's cap. "Good guess Sherlock. It was Bellevue."

"What else gave it away?"

"Brah you're packin' way too much luggage for one guy. You

got two humongous suitcases and a guitar and a carry-on?

"Most guys travel lighter 'dan 'dat, brah.

"You should be a detective, dude." Uncle was getting cab dizzy

"Oh an' yer' smilin' too much. Way more 'dan mos' tourists."

Ole tried his best to frown a little. He couldn't do it.

"Hah! Welcome to Maui, brah."

Oliver shut up for a while. He was too happy to talk. As they pulled into Five-Z- Self-Storage, Ole asked the cabbie to wait.

"Yah, I know 'da drill. My idle-meter keep running, brah."

3

Self-Storage Prison

Uncle Ole signed up for a four by four-foot storage bin with a combination lock provided. The day warden of the dreary old place looked as scary as any prison guard he'd ever seen in the movies. He had a scar on his chin, skull and dagger tattoos on both arms and walked with a limp. The warden led Uncle down a sad, plywood corridor with heavy chicken-wire cage doors. Glancing from side to side, Ole felt sorry for all those incarcerated suitcases, lamps and TV sets doing hard time here in the big house.

They came to his cell block. The old warden looked at the number above the cage door, #117-A. He looked at the clipboard he carried and had uncle sign for the combination lock. Then, he limped back to the main gate. Uncle carefully stored his two suitcases. When he lovingly placed his guitar in the cage he noticed the damage. It looked bad.

"What the heck!" He didn't like to cuss. His guitar case had a long crack in it. He opened it quickly to see how bad the guitar was smashed. It appeared to be okay. The hard case had made the ultimate sacrifice.

"Damn-it, Island Wings Airlines! If it's shaped like a guitar, it's a guitar. Don't throw it or drop it!" Ole is so mad he's ranting out loud. He heard himself about to cuss again and stopped. He didn't come to Maui to cuss. He tried to focus on the good stuff. He came here to retire from another life. To live out the rest of his days in full sunshine, work on his Zen mind, volunteer sometimes, beach bum, surf, snorkel and maybe fall in love with a hula girl.

Inhale, buddy. That's it, nice and calm, slower… yoga breathe, one, two, three, four, five. Slower now, exhale… one, two, three, four, five, six, seven, eight… It worked. He felt a little calmer. Control your breath and you control your emotions. The dharma wheel has already turned past this. It's history, nobody can change history. Take the middle path, accept it as it is. His inner Buddha is always there for him.

That's when he remembered the horrible turbulence of the rough flight and scary landing. It was easy to forgive a little damage; he and all the other passengers were still alive. Ole gently placed the guitar back in its damaged case and set it in the cage. Uncle addressed his luggage as if they were his only friends on Maui. So far, they were.

"Zorry boys, but don't yoo fret. I'll talk to the judge, post bond and get shoe all out 'ta here in few days. I promizzz." He went out past the warden's tower and once clear of the main gate, he got back in the yellow cab.

"Mango Bungalow Hostel, Wailuku," he grumped. Then shocked at the anger still growling out of his own voice; he spoke to the driver in a gentler way. Ole looked out the windows of the cab and saw another rainbow playing hop-scotch over the mountains. This one looked real and full of hope. Uncle's heart started hoping he and Tanya could somehow work things out. But that wish gave him that same old feeling of falling down the well of wishes that can't come true. He saw a green taxi drive past. There was a guy in the back seat that looked kinda like him, all layered with clothes and wearing a Sea Hawks cap. *He got the green taxi you wanted. Could that be you? If that's you over there, then Whoooo Are You.* Now his inner voice sounds like the hooka-smoking caterpillar.

Some more vacation palms blurred by. After he thought he saw a winged-monkey fly over a house with a space ship in its backyard, he closed his eyes for a while. The ride in the dark was as much fun as with his eyes open. With his tongue hanging out like a dog, the warm air tasted delicious, kind of like what flowers might taste like with a light hint of rum. When he did open his eyes again, he looked for the tall buildings in the city center, like the ones in Honolulu. There weren't any. There were a lot of high-end car dealerships: Acura, Mercedes, BMW, Lexus, and Cadillac. *There must be lots of wealthy people here.* He guess-timated, that would include almost everyone on Maui, except him. They drove past a music store called Bounty Music, then past the waterfront. There was a cruise ship tied to the pier straining her lines against the howling wind. They drove past a couple of shopping malls with more palm trees. The cab driver was quiet as he negotiated the five cars of lunch hour traffic on the street ahead of him. It was all a bit blurry. Uncle Ole's random thoughts kept surprising him: *Would a heavy person sink faster in quicksand than a light person? What if you never cut your hair again? What would you be worth today if you'd bought ten shares of Microsoft in 1986? Will Tanya miss you in a week? Maybe miss you in a month… or never? Too bad you don't know even one person living on Maui. Like perhaps a sexy Asian widow with a flaming crush on you, plenty of money, a big house, a Mercedes convertible and... she owns a liquor store.* His imagination was working perfect, even if the rest of him was a few sheets to the wind. Getting this 'intoxi-duplicated' kind a surprised him.

Oliver felt like a kid again, embarking on a grand imagination-adventure. He felt like a ten-year-old monkey with a new set of wings. Since nineteen-fifty-five when he first saw the movie, 'Wizard of Oz,' he'd dreamed nightmares about those flying monkeys. They terrified him, yet he'd always longed to be one, only not mean, and not a slave to some wicked witch.

Flying primate kids like you shouldn't be allowed to drink rum. Now his mind's his own parent.

Somehow, Ole-monkey would get along. He was determined to find a home and be a blessing to others, as soon as he sobered up. *But falling in love again?* He wondered if that could ever happen. He would try to find a new girlfriend with or without the Mercedes and the big house and the liquor store. *But after thirty years with one woman, how do you start dating again? Could he?* It all felt crazy-sad... without Tanya. He still loved her. Legally he was still married. But in the drunken daylight of reality, he knew it was over. His wife, of twenty-seven years, had made it perfectly clear. Since he started talking about moving to Hawaii again, she had started letting go. She told him over and over, she was never leaving Washington State. She told him she loved him less each day. His stupid heart seemed to love her more each day. He'd beat himself up over this, a couple thousand times.

Why does it have to go that way? One person in the marriage wants to make it last, the other can't wait to get it over with. Even his inner counselor couldn't think of something clever to think.

"Just my luck…. " he mumbled, "married to one of the three women on earth that doesn't wanna live in Hawaii."

"What's zat?" Asked the cabbie.

"Nothin', it's just me, remembering stuff."

"Let her go brah."

"So you did hear me?"

"You're kinda louder than you t'ink. How much ya' drink on 'da plane boss?"

"Los' count, maybe a hun'red… why?"

"Sure boss," the driver was still chuckling as he parked the yellow cab in front of the Mango Bungalow. Uncle paid him the thirty-eight-dollar fare and gave him another ten-spot for a tip.

"That's for the psychic advice. What I really need is new girlfriend." *Now that didn't sound right,* whisper's his inner coach.

"Sure 'ting boss. I know 'da kine, a strip bar wi' easy cuties 'dat wear almost nah'ting, brah… we go?" The cabbie grinned.

"No, not like that. Forget it." Uncle waved his good-bye.

27

4

I Pay in Advance?

Uncle Ole wrestled his wheeled carry-on up the two stairs of the Mango hostel and rolled it over to the front desk. Behind the counter a worn sign hanging from a nail in the wall said, "Welcome, I'll be back in a while, make yer' self some tea."

Clazzy. That's just what you need, a spahtt of tea. You need to sleep for a week. His inner logic is shining dimly through his Bacardi fog. With no sleep possible, Ole started thinking about maybe another drink. He looked up and down the street, but there were no bars in sight, just a few diagonally-parked cars and some plastic bags blowing in the fierce wind. It was a scene from a sci-fi movie, 'The town where time stood still so long, it fell over.' A large dog slept in the shade of one of the parked cars.

Uncle turned and sleep-walked past the front desk. There was a broad door or maybe they had knocked out one wall of the old place. He was outside again in a mowed private courtyard with some swaying vacation palms. Ole caught his breath with a gasp. There was an African Lion sleeping in a hammock. He had blood on his face and teeth. One of his long front legs was hanging down to the ground through the netting. He was snoring loudly and looked too dangerous to be moved. There was no one else around, maybe he ate everyone. In this jungle the lion sleeps by day.

Ole slowly, back-stepped into the lobby to wait 'for a while' like the sign said. There were two dusty-looking, upholstered chairs scratching their fleas quietly by the front door. Actually, there was no door; more like another missing wall. Surfer magazines were rustling in the breeze on top of a bamboo coffee table in front of the old chairs. Since there was no other place to sit, he overcame his Seattle prejudice about dust and bugs. With a grimace, he eased himself down into flea town and picked up a surf magazine. The full color photo on the cover was so amazing he got schemsmerized. He was too tired to turn the page. His ears were roaring with the tumbling surf. He could smell the ocean breaking on the reef. Above the wave was a rainbow, below the wave a Dream Shark was swimming in slow circles. Ole's big head tipped forward. His eyes slowly slid down his face and he was gone. Far, far away, to the happy 'Lah-lah-land' of the amateur drinker.

It seemed like ten seconds, but it was really about twenty-five minutes later, the desk clerk woke him up with a light touch on his shoulder.

"Are you okay sir?"

"How do you spell, O.K.?" He joked. "Yah, I'm okay, just waiting to check in." He rubbed his eyes and tried to focus on her face.

"I can help you with that. Sorry you had to wait. I was cookin' up some chili for supper. Do you have a reservation?"

"Yes, look under Gold, Oliver, Gold." He made it sound dramatic, like he was in a movie, 'Bond, James, Bond.' He got up out of the dusty chair with considerable ease considering the short nap and the tall drinks, and his age. The clerk was

29

early twenties. She went behind the counter. She was very cute in a green t-shirt and very tight jeans, but there was a breeze of stink that followed behind her as she walked. She needed a shower and some deodorant. Uncle backed up a pace. He watched her though, she was pretty. He expected her to start typing on a computer. There was no computer. She bent over the counter in front of him, looking down a list of hand-written names in a spiral notebook. Uncle didn't mean to, but he found himself looking down the front of her t-shirt to her perky college-girl boobs. He didn't intend to stare, but there was nothing more interesting to look at. It took her longer than it should have to find his name on the one page of names.

Maybe she likes men looking down the front of her shirt? His inner coach trying to explain the delay.

Finally, she found his name on the list.

"Yes, here you are, three nights, correct?" He looked. There was his name on a very short list of eight hand-written names.

Uh huh, she likes men looking down her shirt, whispers his coach.

"Yes, here I am, and I'm very tired."

"Will you be paying with cash or credit card?"

At least they've modernized that far into the twenty-first century.

"Credit." He didn't want to flash any cash in this place. He handed her his card.

"I pay in advance?"

"Yes sir, and no cancellation refunds. We've had some 'sleep and runs' so now, we ask for payment up front. Three nights, private room, forty dollars per night, four-point-two-percent tax, that comes to one-twenty-four and seven cents. Oh, any extra person staying in your room, we will require an extra ten-dollars per night."

"It's just me. I just got here and don't know anyone on Maui."

She looked up at him with her pretty face, appraising the rugged looking old Swede with the Sea Hawks cap. Maybe she was judging him on a scale of one to ten. He felt like a three.

"Oh, it won't be long, Maui is a romantic place," she said with an inviting wink. Uncle held his tongue, he was thinking,

Jeez, take a shower cute exhibitionist, stink woman.

She handed him the key to his room. He realized this was the only key he had in the whole world. It was another almost fully Zen moment. Except for this three-night key, he was homeless. It was like being Shakyamuni Buddha before his enlightenment, John the Baptist in the desert, or Jesus teaching love from town to town before he got busted. Uncle Ole was now, one of the millions of homeless people on this planet, un-plugged from society and routine, and paychecks. It was a wonderful feeling. He now had a treasure greater than routine. He had time. He took inventory: he had time and a little dust in each pocket and one key. He felt rich.

He held his nose as he followed the tight jeans of the young clerk to his room. With some difficulty, his key turned the lock and he swung open the door to his new Maui home. It was another oven. He gave a big thankful sigh and started peeling off some of his 'layers'. The cute girl stood in the doorway for a moment watching him. Her perfume was garlic and white vinegar; he closed the door.

Ole had one big advantage over the millions of homeless people. He had worked for twenty years and built a pension fund with Washington State. At the end of this month he would receive his first check. Until then, all he had was his Key Bank check book with four-thousand bucks, plus or minus a dollar, some credit cards and that precious vault of treasure called, 'time.' It was enough.

He did have a few other things. He owned his wind breaker and his fleece vest, both now on the floor and his carry-on bag. Then he remembered his luggage and his guitar down at the self-storage prison. They were locked with a padlock combination of numbers that he was pretty sure he could remember, though he couldn't think of them right now.

He was all done-in from the flight, so he washed up in the surprisingly clean bathroom down the hall, stumbled back to his little oven and took a long nap in the tropical land of hot. Even the sugar from the rum and the caffeine from the Coca-Cola couldn't keep him awake.

After several hours of dreamless snoring with no wife to poke him in the ribs, Uncle awoke in a magnificent sweat and

32

smiled. It was a wonderful moment in time. He lay there for a while, comfortably too warm with nothing to do. Retired. Oliver felt like James Cagney in 'Casablanca.' All he needed now was a drink, dinner and a dame. Okay maybe skip the drink.

He walked to the outdoor area of the hostel. There was the hammock hanging between the coconut palms. The bloody old lion had mysteriously shrunk to the size of house cat, but was still the undisputed king of the hammock. One gigantic Mango tree shaded most of the green lawn. There were sunburned paths of red dirt leading in different directions. Uncle walked the shortest path to the communal kitchen where he saw a few people gathered. Above the kitchen's rusty electric stove there was a large hand-made sign:

~Chili Caliente Tonight / $2.00 bowl~

Uncle lifted the lid... the curry-garlic, peanut-butter, cauliflower-broccoli aroma steamed up in his face like he had opened up a manhole cover. He dropped the lid on the stove but quickly replaced it on the chili pot, just before he passed out. There was a matching rusty, old refrigerator, a clean sink and a roll of paper towels. Above a woven basket piled high with ripe mangos, there was another sign.

~Free mangos ~ Help us keep our yard clean ~ Eat mangos ~

Uncle Ole found a knife and started cutting into a beautiful Hayden. Some college-age kids were making sandwiches and talking about hiking in China and Europe. Uncle sat down at a picnic table, savored each bite of the delicious fruit and listened. He'd never stayed at a hostel before. He kind of liked

33

the place. He could have booked the dorm room for fifteen-bucks a night. It was eight beds in a room that looked clean, but with a very earthy smell to it. None of these people wore deodorant. Uncle felt old and opinionated among these aromatic young leaders and business tycoons of the future.

5

Ms Seang Thai

Back in his private room, Uncle Ole unzipped his carry-on and took out his flute case. He opened it and carefully put the three sections together. He lay back on the bed and played a few soft notes. It sounded good, he must be sobering up. The ceiling fan was still on high, turning its wooden propellers very, very slowly. He whispered a few more full tones. He had played this same flute in college band. The next thirty years he played it for fun and meditation. Perfect soothing notes are the result of deep slow breathing. He'd overcome his childhood asthma with years of flute playing and yoga. There were moments when the Zen took over, and his mind evaporated away into a musical trance.

The ceiling fan had a trance-like wobble in it as it slowly turned, but it didn't click or squeak. Probably a good thing it turned so slow or all those years of dust on the blades would go storming across the hot desert of his room.

This silver flute was a treasure he'd held on to most of his life; longer than his marriage to Tanya. He bought it with five dollars down and five dollars a month at the University Avenue Music store back in the days before credit cards. He was eighteen then, a freshman at Drake, the same year he met Tanya. She played guitar, so they used to find a city park after their classes and jam jazz and cover tunes together. She wrote songs and so did he. They felt like soul mates. Their first gigs were at nursing homes out in West Des Moines.

The wobble in the ceiling fan seemed to be evolving as well as revolving. There were two wobbles to the trance now, one at twelve o'clock and then slowly turning to a worse shake at around seven. It was hypnotizing.

He saw a vision of eighteen-year-old Tanya. She was the cutest of the mini-skirted girls he had met at college and because she played guitar, she was the most fun. Tanya introduced him to Tom Lee, the school's band director. Tom's passion for music matched Ole's so he joined the marching band and the orchestra. Tanya also convinced him to smoke grass. She was a risk-taker. She risked marrying him.

Why couldn't she risk moving to Hawaii with you dude? Coach was stumped. *Betta' to just leave the rain people in Seattle yah? They like it there.*

Uncle put her memory and baggage out on the station platform and stepped back on the train of, 'Now.' But he could not pretend he didn't miss her.

He was very fond of the Moody Blues so he stretched out on the bed, watched the fan wobble and tried playing 'Tuesday Afternoon' on his flute to gain some sobriety. Clear notes buttered the hot Monday afternoon like an ear of Iowa sweet corn. He was born for this moment, his first day of retirement, in Hawaii.

Ole was getting hungry, so he re-packed the flute and took a long look in the room's mirror to see if he looked okay. He wasn't all that surprised to see a large, brown-furred, winged-monkey with grey molting wings and a stupid grin, looking back at him. He blinked a few times until his normal reflection came into focus. There stood a tall well-built human primate with a stupid grin looking back at him. His brown hair stuck out all around his head like a fuzzy aura. He looked like a character from the documentary video, 'This could be you if you drink for six hours on a jet.' Uncle put some sun block on his hands and rubbed it through his hair to hold it down. He found his sandals and put on a clean shirt before he took another look in the mirror. At fifty-four-years-old, his eyesight was getting so bad he actually thought he was getting better looking every day. Maybe because of his happy grin, he thought he looked really-handsome today. If clothes make the monkey into a man then he looked good enough to go out there in the uptown jungle and find some dinner.

He told himself that with or without Tanya, he was retired and good looking, and almost sober. That gave him the confidence he needed to pack his flute in its case and take it with him. He walked the sidewalk uphill to Wailuku's sleepy downtown. He turned right on Vineyard Street and saw another rainbow circling one long bow down from the mountains. There was no pot of gold at the end of this rainbow, but there was a Thai restaurant called Saeng Thai. It looked like palm trees were growing inside it. Or maybe the restaurant was built around the trees. Accepting the omen from the rainbow, he was sure that this was the place he was supposed to find. The food smelled good. He introduced himself to the bartender and balanced himself on a tall bar stool. Ole was the only customer so far. Out of habit, he asked for a Bacardi rum and Coke and to speak to the manager. He totally forgot about his '*no more booze today' plan.*

Over that first drink he chatted with Edgar, the bartender,

37

who had taught Ag Science at Iowa State University. Ed finally had enough shoveling snow, so he packed up and moved to Maui. This is a common theme among mainland transplants to Hawaii, none of them like snow. College teacher jobs were scarce on Maui, so Edgar decided to go into psychiatry and became a bartender. He promised Uncle that if he could adapt here for one year, he would grow some new roots and survive the transplant.

"Here's to a year from now," Uncle raised his almost empty glass and started dreaming about finding a cute girlfriend with big house and a Mercedes convertible. The rum made him belch a little too loud. *Okay maybe without the liquor store,* his thoughts are still sobering up from the flight.

Quite a few evening diners had come in, and the manager was slow to come out of the kitchen. Uncle realized that back on the mainland this would have annoyed him. But here in Hawaii, his disregard for time was beginning to feel good. 'Island Time' on Maui was turning out to be just like 'Island Time' in the Caribbean. Only here in Hawaii there were better roads and happier people. Uncle knew rum drinks could slow time down... fast.

Is that possible? He's wondering. *Can you slow Time down... fast?* Isn't that what Einstein was working on? He would need to meditate or drink on that someday.

Miss Kea Saeng finally came out to greet him. She was tall, slim and beautiful. Even sweating and dressed all in white, with a chef's apron she was an enchanting vision of a Thailand woman. Uncle stood to meet her but his knees went slack.

She spoke fair English, nicely accented in her mysterious way. Uncle explained he had arrived on Maui, today. He was a traveling musician and would like to play his flute tonight as trade for his dinner. He pushed the three sections of his flute together and gave her a jazzy sample of, 'Taste of Honey.' She extended a graceful hand and said,

"Okay, Deal. Tonight only." She smiled sunshine and went back to the kitchen. She must have this sort of request often from drifters like him; there were three youth hostels nearby. During the two hours of light jazz that he played that evening, Ms. Kea peeked out of the kitchen doors to listen and smile. When he was done, she brought him a fantastic shrimp dinner with Oolong tea. He left a ten-dollar tip for her from the thirty-seven dollars in tips he received from her customers that night. There is a pot of gold at the end of some rainbows. Uncle Ole also left his phone number for Ms Kea; optimist that he is.

6

Cadillac For Sale

Ole slept well that night and awoke without any hangover at all. It must have been the delicious food and health-restoring tea. Now it was 'Day Two' of his plan to settle in Hawaii. For over a year he had subscribed to the Maui Sunday newspaper. It arrived in Seattle by mail, a week after its printing. For the last five months there was a nineteen-eighty-eight Cadillac listed in the classifieds for twenty-five hundred dollars. It was still for-sale in the newspaper he found in the hostel kitchen. He used his cell phone to make the call.

"Sid speaking,"

"Do you still have that old Cadillac for sale?"

"Yah, I sure do."

"I am interested in buying it. I'm at a hostel in Wailuku, the Mango Bungalow. If you drive it over here and I like it, I'll give you fifteen-hundred cash for it today."

"I'll be there in twenty-minutes," said Sid.

7

Hey Singer Man

Once Uncle had a car he was able to keep his first commitment. Before he even flew to Maui, he had signed up online to volunteer at the Maui County Fair. It was a short drive to the fairgrounds from the hostel and the Cadillac drove smooth as a land yacht. It looked light pink from all the red dirt covering the white finish. As he drove to the county fair he thought about how he would detail it with a soft toothbrush until it shone like a new, old, white car again. It was a classic diamond in the dust with no rust.

Uncle Ole Gold was scheduled to play music on stage, as part of the entertainment line-up for 'Special Needs Day.' Handicapped people get to enjoy one free day at the fair including transportation and free lunch. Uncle meant it when he planned to 'give' not just 'take' when he got here. For thirty years he had played music in rest homes. The old adage is true, 'to make friends you need to be one.' He made some people happy that day at the fair. His thirty-minute gig on the main stage was a hit. They asked him to play again over in the food tent. There were smiles all around, many people reaching out to shake his hand or give him a Hawaiian-style hug. He played his guitar and his Irish penny whistle and some bamboo flutes. He sang with his whole body and with all of his passion. They gave him a free Bento-box lunch.

"Hey singer man, I like you," a frail looking lady in a wheelchair was reaching out to him. Ole bent down and gave his new fan a soft hug. He could see stories written all over her aged, lovely face. This is what he remembered most about the islands, people sharing the aloha with each other because they, well because they can.

Aloha from Hawaii should be bottled and exported around the world to cure all the loneliness and hurt. His inner-entrepreneur has ridiculous ideas sometimes, but means well.

"Give and you shall receive," works in mysterious ways. One of the people at the fair that day was Mark Chaffin, the manager of the Pioneer Inn, over in Lahaina. After a brief conversation, Mark hired Uncle Ole to entertain two nights a week at the famous old hotel starting next Tuesday. Ole was not too surprised by this stroke of good fortune. He had envisioned entertaining in a beach bar or restaurant for some fun and part-time income.

Ole drove his Caddy straight over to the music store he had seen during his psychic taxi ride. With the help of the friendly but weird musicians working there, he pushed one of his credit cards near its limit buying an amp, a mixer, two speakers, cords, mics and boom stands. While he was there he bought a new hard-shell guitar case. It all fit in the trunk of the Cadillac and Ole headed back to the Mango for his last paid night. As he passed the fairgrounds he wasn't too surprised to see another rainbow's end curving down onto the huge lunch tent with all the special needs buses and vans parked alongside. There's a lot of love in these islands. He felt it as well as the natives felt it. Now, it was time to find a place to live. Three nights at forty-bucks a night had been a perfect start. But that was way over his budget, time to find a place to live.

8

Single Room for Rent

His last morning at the hostel, Uncle found the same three-day-old newspaper and circled several 'rooms for rent' in the classified ads. The first number he called was the only number he called. It was a listing on the west side, in an area called Kahana.

"Hel'ro," an Asian woman's accent.

"Good morning, I'm calling about the room for rent?"

"I home today. I show you, what time you come?"

"I'm over in Wailuku, how do I get there?"

After she gave him directions, she said,

"Could you bring me half and half from store, one quart? I am cooking and no have."

"Ah, sure, I can do that. I'll come over right away; should be there by ten-thirty." Ole figured this woman was clever, for now he was committed to coming to see her rental today not tomorrow or maybe never.

The scenic drive over the Pali Highway was so amazing it was difficult to keep his eyes on the road. The Caribbean green ocean and the west-side beach went on for ten miles. There were bikini-clad surfer girls on perfect waves. He saw guys with dogs on their surf boards and children running along the shore.

On his right, the West Maui Mountains looked like powerful knuckles of some green giant pushing up three-thousand feet or more. Loose sponges of rainbows lived up there in between the knuckles, in perpetual rain. These mountains are the second wettest place on earth. Ole knew that Kauai was the rain champion on earth with 430 plus inches a year. But everyone he talked to, said Maui was the best place to live, 'Maui no ka oi' ('da best), in every other way. That's the reason he chose this island. If he didn't like this one, his next choice was gonna be the Big Island, the one they call, Hawaii.

As he slowed down and drove into Lahaina, he turned onto Front Street and was surprised it was so busy for such an out of the way town. There were hundreds of tourists on the sidewalks, poking in and out of the shops and art galleries and restaurants. He drove slowly by the grand old Pioneer Inn where he would be playing his music next week. It filled a whole block of downtown. Across Hotel Street was the courthouse square with its famous Banyan Tree. There was a marina filled with yachts and tour boats. Ole felt right at home when there were sailboats in sight. He missed his little sloop already. But it wouldn't fit on the plane and moorage on Maui was scarce. He had sold 'Amazing Grace' his 27-foot Cal after loving her for almost three decades of fun. Chapter closed.

Uncle continued north for seven miles on Highway 30 to Kahana. He was counting his fifth rainbow of the morning when he found Makahiki Street, a residential neighborhood of beautifully landscaped, million-dollar homes.

The landlady, who answered his ring of the front bell, was a lovely Asian woman. She was Chinese maybe, he wasn't sure. She spoke good, if not perfect English and was about his own age, but still the proud occupant of a lovely young body. She was probably a yogi, to look so good at fifty-something.

"My name is Oliver Gold," he introduced himself; "everyone calls me Uncle Ole."

"Hel'ro Uncle, my name Yu'layne Njang, p'rease come in."

Uncle liked her right away. First impressions are important in all relationships. She appeared to like him too. She led up the polished wood stairs to a red-carpeted hallway. Expensive looking oriental paintings graced some walls, with nothing at all on others. This gave the place interest and yet a peaceful uncluttered calm. His Zen meter was feeling balanced. She led him through the kitchen.

"Tenants on this floor share kitchen," she said.

"Oh, here's the half and half you wanted."

"Aha, you remember, thank you." She opened the large refrigerator and placed the cream on a shelf marked "Yu'layne in black marking pen on a strip of masking tape.

"There is space in fridge for each person's food. No one eats other's food. Kitchen clean, everyone must clean." The kitchen had every appliance necessary, except a dishwasher.

"No dishwasher?" Ole asked the obvious.

"Too noisy, some people work nights. They come home, sometimes cook in the middle of night. We expect quiet from all the people who live here. Are you quiet?" she asked.

"Yes, I am." Uncle was telling the truth.

"How many people live in this house?"

"Thirteen in house, some live downstairs, have own kitchen, plus one couple in Ohana (guest cottage). I show you room now vacant."

She led out the kitchen door to the large lanai. It was big; fifteen feet wide and stretched across the entire north side of the long home. There were potted palms, ferns and orchids all over the place with a suburban-neighborhood kind of view. It was like being in one of those homes that you see from the Beverly Hills tour bus. She opened a sliding glass door on a room built out on the lanai deck. It was an add-on, he could tell, built for additional income but it was wonderful. Next to the full-size double bed, was a large picture window with a sweeping view of palm trees and the ocean about a block away. It was truly an amazing picture post card kind of window. There were three more large windows around the right side of the bed so the trade wind was blowing cool through the room. There were no screens. He had been in Hawaii for four days and only seen two mosquitoes. It was paradise. There was a free-standing wardrobe for his clothes, a desk with a chair and a TV on the desk.

"How much?" Ole asked, trying not to show his approval or his desperation.

"Six hundred a month, includes lanai, kitchen, share bath and basic cable TV."

"When can I move in?"

"Anytime, lease agreement in kitchen."

Ole wrote out a check for the first month, last and a cleaning deposit. Eighteen hundred dollars was about what he had budgeted for this. After two copies of the palapala (legal papers) were signed, Yu'layne handed him two keys and five dollars for the half and half.

"This key to glass slide door, your room, this one opens gate, far side lanai. Private entrance for you is gate. Make sure stays locked. Cost ten dollars if lose key and I need make duplicate. Never lock kitchen door. Other tenants use lanai and I do too. There is a half-bath with shower out on the lanai that you can use."

He went out to look. The half-bath was walled in under the eaves of the overhanging roof but it had a frosted glass shower door which allowed some privacy. There was no lock. It wasn't funky, it was amazing and classy. Yu'layne went on,

"One person only in room, occasional guest okay, cost ten dollar a night, three nights only. It's in contract. You have storage closet out on lanai. You buy padlock for closet."

"You are going to give me the keys to your house, just like that? No background checks? No references required?"

"I know you good man, you remember half and half for

Yu'layne she smiled a beautiful smile.

"That's it? You trust me because of that?"

"Also hear you sing for kupuna at county fair. My mother in wheelchair, we there and hear you sing at lunch. You gave mother hug when you chat with old people. You not notice me, I sitting with friends near mother's table. I can trust a man, good to elders."

Love one another, give compassion and the sanctifying grace of karma comes back to bless you. His inner Jesus and Buddha are holding hands and smiling.

It surprised him that he missed seeing Yu'layne at the fair. He usually notices pretty Asian women. Uncle got truthful business vibes from this lovely woman as well as respect.

"I'll go get my stuff and move in now, if that is okay with you."

"Welcome to my home Mr. O're," and she bowed.

"Thank you Miss Yu'layne he bowed in return. He thought he felt some subtle sexual innuendo from her.

She's your landlady dude, forget it. Coach thinks he knows everything.

"Do you own a Mercedes Yu'layne?"

"No, my old Toyota is in shop being repaired, why?"

"Just wondering," said Uncle Ole.

9

Hea-eh-ven

Uncle drove the Pali Highway back to Wailuku and moved out of the Mango Bungalow. The cute girl-clerk was wearing a wistful look on her face when she said goodbye. She was also wearing the same jeans and stinky loose shirt. Next he drove straight to the Five-Z-Storage Prison and paid the 'bail' to free his guitar and his luggage. The mean looking warden didn't say a thing. It felt real good to drive away from that place.

Ole figured he'd just won 'The Coolest Place to Stay on Maui Lottery' moving from a hostel to his new room with a view in Yu'layne's beautiful home.

"Ahhhouuum." He started singing. He thought he sounded like the Moody Blues... "Hea- eh- ven".

10

FREE ELECTRONS

Ole's father taught him discipline. His mother taught him perseverance. She used to sing a little determination poem that her mother's mother had sung to her,

"Good, better, best, never let it rest... until your good is better, and your better best."

Ole dearly loved his parents and still sought their advice often. The reason why he was born was to meet them. But he developed 'social chemistry' on his own. He was a chemist and a teacher of chemistry for thirty years. He was no longer surprised when good things happened to him or when he met good people. He came into this life to be happy. To be happy, people of similar energy levels are attracted to each other. Good or bad energy, the attraction principle works the same. In basic chemistry free electrons spinning around some elements are attracted to elements lacking electrons in their neighborhood of the Periodic Table. New combinations are thus formed. Sometimes, a whole new element is created.

New friendships form this way too. Bad apples, ruin other apples in the barrel, which draws flies that lay their cute little offspring called maggots and the whole mess turns to stinking vinegar. Good apples get polished all the way to school on flannel shirt sleeves and are shyly given to pretty fourth grade teachers. The really-good apples get baked into homemade pies. Comparing apples to people was maybe not fair. But the message was in there somewhere.

Uncle Ole knew that everyone manifests free-electron energy whether they are aware of it or not. When people of similar energy fields meet, 'social chemistry' kicks in and they are drawn together. Friendships are seeded, relationships grow and opportunities bloom like plants nurtured in a greenhouse. So far, he had meshed electrons with a psychic taxi driver, a wise bartender, the Thailand restaurant lady, the manager of a world-famous hotel, Yu'layne and her mother.

11

First Friday Night

Uncle decided to celebrate. He hadn't been drinking since the booze flight to Maui four days ago. It was Friday night, he had a beautiful place to stay, a Cadillac and a music gig at a famous hotel.

Striving for a pure mind leads to pure surroundings. His inner coach is big on Buddha sutras.

Tonight, his mind isn't all that pure, thinking of women and rum. But he rationalized that he is 'striving' in that direction most of the time. Pulling his shorts on over his swimsuit he grabbed a beach towel and left by the lanai gate and down the stairs to Yu'layne's manicured side yard. It was almost time for sunset. He left his car parked in the driveway and walked the short half-mile down to the beach. The sidewalk was lined with tropical landscaping. Fan Palms on people's lawns were already lit by spot lights at their base. The lights gave the neighborhood the look of a movie set from the blockbuster hit, 'Homeless Guy Finds Maui Mansion.' Oliver felt like he'd died and gone to Hollywood. No more rainy Seattle nights, shivering in layers of long johns. No more wool sweaters and socks. It felt great to walk outside at night wearing shorts and sandals.

Ole found resort row on Kahana beach. One was called, 'The Sands of Kahana' and walking around like he owned the place, he found the swimming pool and hot tub area. There was an adjacent restaurant with a bar and he had a thirst. Time to celebrate. He walked into the bar like any rich tourist might, but service from the one bartender was extremely slow. Uncle used some of his celebration time practicing the discipline of patience. His reward for waiting, was a treasure called a West Maui sunset. He could see and feel the earth turning away from the sun. The island of Lanai rose up out of the ocean and blocked the light. Soft, red, sky paint was all that was left of today. The bar and its patrons, the swimming pool, the palm trees, the sky, everything was glowing with a pastel pinkish-blush.

Looks like Hawaii through rose-tinted glasses, remembering an expression from a poetry class he took long ago. *The reason I was born was to see this,* he reasoned.

The busy bartender finally served him his tall Coca-Cola and rum, but didn't greet him or smile. *How could you be so unfriendly working in a beautiful place like this?*

Once that plastic glass of sugar and booze was in his hand, he stood up next to the bar, raised his cup and in a deep voice he gave a toast,

"Here's to me!" and he tipped most of the drink down in one draw.

The noisy chatter of the twenty or so people in the bar suddenly stopped. They all stared at the lonesome stranger. Then, as if they had practiced every day for a week, they all toasted at once,

"Here's to you!" They cheered and drank deep.

Everyone wanted to hear his story. One guy bought him another round and then someone bought him dinner. Uncle didn't buy another drink all night. All of his new drinking buddies were tourists who only dreamed of moving to Maui, someday. Here was a guy who did it. More free drinks followed the 'talk story.' He tried to buy drinks for the crowd. They wouldn't let him spend a dime. Ole didn't have enough money to buy twenty people a drink. They probably knew this. The grumpy looking bartender, whose nickname was, 'Dollar,' put on a slightly happier frown, selling more drinks than usual. Time slowed down... fast. He couldn't explain it, but he was here to witness it. Time seemed to get down on its hands and knees and crawl like a sloth.

Uncle Ole was satisfied. He had some new friends from the local chapter of the, 'Neighborhood Falling-off-the-Welcome-Wagon-Committee.'

The free drinks kept coming. The next thing he knew he was in his swim trunks and leaning back in the soothing water of the resort's hot tub. *So, this is what it's like to be retired on Maui,* his thoughts sounded far away but more-sober than he felt.

Thirty years you work to get to this moment. Smart you took the early retirement and a small pension. You stay frugal buddy and you never have to work again.

The one-hundred and four-degree water and the rum drinks were softening his thoughts toward the sentimental. He saw his wife Tanya smiling in a memory. It made him smile and then droop to think she would rather divorce him than sit here

54

in this hot tub on a starry Maui night. She was a big part of his life. The whole idea of a possible divorce hurt him deeply.

Don't think about it. Occupy the spa around you, that wise Zen coach again.

But, he did think about it, all the time. He had planned his life very carefully. He had planned his retirement with Tanya. Being here by himself was not going to be easy. He missed her and she could have easily gotten a part-time job. She was a CPA. These island companies need good accountants to count all the money they're making. Her income along with his pension and a few music gigs; life in Hawaii could have been so easy. Without her help he could get along on a shoestring budget, but he would have to be very careful.

You won't need shoestrings, you won't need shoes. Coach has a sense of humor.

Three couples arrived and stepped carefully, drunkenly into the hot tub. They were all speaking something that sounded Slavic-European but more intoxicated sounding than Slavic, if that's even possible. He listened for a while to their excited voices and then asked,

"Russia?"

"Ukraine," replied a tall, broomstick man with no eye contact and a drunken smile. The noisy rumble of water jets pushing into the tub made conversation difficult so Uncle just smiled and said,

"Aloha."

55

They all tried to say the same word with their Ukraine accents but started laughing and then in unison they smiled and said, "Vodka!"

It was fun to see people from so far away, enjoying Hawaii as much as he was.

These couples must be real movers and shakers back home, to afford a vacation in Hawaii. He wondered what they did for careers, but he didn't ask.

The three women were all gorgeous. The brunette across the tub from him winked whenever he happened to look her way, which was only about every five seconds. He laughed out loud, louder than the bubbling jets of the hot tub. Maybe he still had some mojo working. He was a rugged looking guy with a good physique. No beer drinking since he was forty, and years in the gym, yoga, Tai Chi and a 'no-hamburger' diet had kept him muscled and trim. Tanya used to tell him he was, 'easy on the eyes like Robert Redford.' He could not recall her saying anything like that for the last five years. He looked back at the bikini-clad brunette. She had beautiful green eyes and she winked one at him again. One side of her bikini top was slipping and revealing more and more of her seductive bikini boobs.

Uncle tried to look away and make his rum-soaked brain think of something else. He went back to his slim financial plan. It was hard to think with one half of his brain keeping his heart and lungs working and the other half as drunk as a Ukrainian. He had to find the ends and make them meet somehow. Happiness is as happiness does. He remembered

Forest Gump saying something like that. He was happy tonight and thanks to all the stars in heaven his first pension check would arrive in twenty-six days.

He was starting to take better care of himself. Well except for special occasions of excess drinking. Every month he stayed alive from now on, he'd get a check from Washington State. Uncle ran the math through his less than sober, right-side brain-calculator. He figured that after he paid his monthly bills; six-hundred dollars for rent and four-hundred dollars to Tanya to help support their youngest daughter still in school, he would have about thirty dollars a day to live on. It wasn't much, but it was something. If he was very careful, he wouldn't have to get a job. He could be a retired, thirty-dollar-a-day escapee from the working class. It made him feel like a millionaire.

The brunette was staring at him with a look that he hoped her husband sitting next to her, didn't notice. This hot-tub-crashing life could take years of practice to perfect. He stopped looking at the brunette and watched the spa bubbles. It looked like they were popping on the surface and flying away like little monkeys with wings.

"Ahhhaouuum," he sang like the Moody Blues and thought nobody heard him. Uncle leaned back in the steaming tub lightly spiced with rum-scented chlorine and smiled up at the night stars.

There was another pretty Ukrainian women sitting next to him in the hot tub. She heard him sing and leaned over toward him and sang back,

"Vaaah-Vooom," and she put her long leg over Ole's and started rubbing against him in a very suggestive way. Her large husband next to her could not see this inviting touching under the opaque surface of bubbles.

Time to go, his coach advises.

Stumble-walking carefully back to his new room at the Makahiki Street mansion, all he could think about was the thrill that young woman had given him with her leg and the flirting looks of the green-eyed brunette. Tanya didn't want him anymore. She had kept her distance from him for the last two years. He needed a girlfriend, someone cute, who wanted him, someone with a liquor store and a big house, and Mercedes.

Yah, like that's gonna happen, coach has his doubts.

"Hey, zo' why not? Ya gotta dream. That'z what I think I always zay, bream dig."

You're an idiot, laments the coach. *Why am I stuck in here with you?*

Arguing with himself wasn't easy after he'd had enough rum to wonder if he knew what he was arguing about. He knew he was lonely. He was used to being with his wife, even if she was colder every day. She was somebody to be with, somebody to take care of. So far, the only attractive women he had met were the cute stinky girl at the hostel, Saeng the owner of the restaurant and lovely Yu'layne, his landlady. Three warm smiles, yet all of them unapproachable for different reasons. He began to visualize a girlfriend in his dizzy walk home. Uncle was such a dreamer that he expected a girlfriend miracle to be just as easy as finding a Cadillac and a music gig and a great place to live.

Ole found the right street and wove his way home through his new neighborhood. Somehow, he found Yu'layne's house and his private entrance, unlocked the wrought-iron gate at the top of the stairs and slid the glass door to his room open as quietly as he could. It was a miracle that he missed the floor and landed on the bed.

12

One Happy Hangover

It was a dark Maui morning, maybe five, am or so. Outside Ole's bedroom window something pounced hard right next to his head. He woke with a start, but he couldn't pull his eyes open. It was his first sleep in a new place, so disorientation plus last night's free booze party were adding to the blindness of it all. There was a dim glow on the stretched drum-skin over his eyes. No matter how hard he tried to blink them, his eyes would not open. Neither would his mouth, glued shut with sleep. His tongue felt thick, like a wrung out, day-old bar towel. It had a cheap tequila taste, maybe it was a floor-cleaning bar towel. He tried to smack his lips, no way. They felt like they were sewn together.

Uncle tried to move one hand, not possible. It was locked in some kind of steel trap under his hip. The other hand could move a little and he sent it searching under the bed for his water bottle. Ole rubbed his eyes on the sheets with no success. The sheets smelled bad too, like a tavern at closing time. His eyes were locked down like two garage doors. He laughed out loud. The voice in his head laughed along with him,

Wah, ha hah, you gonna love this island dude. O'kay, wher'z 'da remote-control button for your eye doors? If you can't look, you can't see what pounced.

His good-natured laugh freed his mouth, but his are lips

covered with number-four-grit sandpaper. His teeth felt wooden, his muscles stiff, but there was no headache at all. Just another happy hangover.

Ole was about to roll over for more guiltless sleep but a quick shake in the leaves by his open window gave him 'chicken skin.'

"What?"

The predatory something that pounced is moving a little closer now. Ole still can't see, but he can sense it. He felt it rushing up to him, moving fast, maybe about to pounce again?

Could be dangerous, wake up! There's some panic in coach's voice. *Gotta get your eyes open, wherz 'da remote control?*

No use. His eye-doors stay down, locked and double bolted. Inside his eyelids, he sees a vision of tiny, bright spotlights. They swirl into an image of a lovely Hawaiian hula girl wearing only the grass skirt; her coconuts have gone missing, so her black hair is all that's hiding her dreamy, brown breasts. She's a vision of, 'Our Lady of the Dreams of Retired Fools,' singing the Hukilau and throwing a silver fish net over him. She captures him and lowers him down gently, lower and lower. Somehow, the net and his atoms dissolve right through the bed and even the floor melts away like butter. The net opens and he has atoms back in his body again, so he falls away into an ocean of dreams.

13

Dream Shark

Wahoo! He's surfing a green giant of a wave on his long board. It's a hundred feet high and he's in a controlled fall, dropping down the face of the wave. Sure, it's dangerous. Mess up and you're on the coral grindstone that turns healthy flesh into stew meat. Worse than that, you could be held down under that monster wave, playing, 'Five-Card-Hold-Your-Breath' with the Dream Shark.

Uncle grips the board with his big feet as it falls. He's got this wave; he's looking good, a surf-dude movie star. He ducks his head and rides his board into a perfect tunnel. Smile for 'da helicopter cameras, give some 'Shaka'.... Yee-haaaa! It's a Magic Maui Moment. He hears the Beach Boys singing in his head about everybody having an ocean, Lah Lah, Lah do, do do something... Suddenly, there's something rushing past his face again. Oops! His weight is too far up the board, the tip digging under, going submarine.

Aaaak! He's lost the ride and takes a spectacular wrong-way, head-first wipeout. His board goes flying up, yanking his leg by the leash. It was so ugly it should a hurt, but somehow it didn't. Ole rolls deep under the dream wave. He's twisting and holding his breath while the gigantic surf tumbles him like a chunk of sea glass on the sandy bottom. Somehow, his dream eyes are wide open underwater. He can see some hands swimming, must be his hands. He's dog paddling.

Wroof, wroof, which waz up? Wahhhh…Wroof, reed air!
Coach's canine voice sounds like Scooby Doo in a real cartoon-panic now. Looking around, he sees Brain Coral.

Is z'rat your brain, r'uncle?

His busted long board goes tossing around him.

Is z'rat yer board, r'uncle?

Why so many questions from Scooby-coach? Is his brain just nosy or writing a book? No answer.

There's a lot of junk in the sand, like empty beer bottles, lost fishing lures, a barnacled bicycle.

Okay, dat way's down, so r'up must bree… a b'ricycle? He turns to look at the bottom again.

No dude 'roo reed air 'rot a b'ricycle. Scooby with common sense.

A shadow swirls past his head. It's grey and long and he gets a chill. It's the Dream Shark. sinister, sleek, hungry, always waiting, staring at him with that cold, patient, unblinking wait. *Maybe thinking of a hot-dog surfer for lunch.*

"Five-Card Stud or Black Jack?" Vibes the Card Shark.

Swim dude, get outta here! You need to breathe, you need to wake up. His lungs are a stopwatch reading three minutes elapsed... and ticking.

Gotta breathe soon. Hoo'yah, there it is! The remote control, oh no! Why there? Please not there!

Yah dude, Shark's chewing it in his teeth. Coach in a panic attack.

He sees the shark's white teeth grinding away on the plastic remote. Ole's lungs are crushed to nothing. The stop watch is ticking faster toward 'mak'e' (dead). Dream Shark swims too close to him and Uncle wraps his arms around the 'mano' and slows it down like a rodeo steer. He tries to pull the plastic remote out of the shark's teeth.

"Gimme that remote!" He can't shout under water but he hears these words coming from somewhere.

It's a breathless struggle. Dream Shark rolls in a mad thrash. Ole's lungs are empty. He's about to breathe saltwater. He punches the shark right in the gills, yanks the remote out of the shark's gaping mouth and pushes the only button. He hears some terrible grinding sounds.

Oh! Hey yah! Uncle reaches the surface. He spits out the pillow that had gotten stuffed in his mouth and pulls in long drafts of delicious gasps of air. The remote button is working. His left eye is lifting open on sandy tracks, making a grinding noise or is that his teeth grinding? He looks out through the open slot of one eye. It's like looking under a garage door as it slowly rises, showing a large, ghostly-green something, moving closer into focus.

"Whoa!" he shouts. Right there next to his eyeballs and ready for the next pounce is a seventy-foot-long dinosaur! Ole shuts his eyes expecting to be eaten any second.

Maui has dinosaurs? Didn't they film some of Jurassic Park on Maui? He's trying to remember. He blinks his eyes and his hallucination 'poofs' away... there's no dinosaur, just one, tiny, un-scary, lizard with beautiful green skin resting there on the window sill next to his bed, and too close to his face. Maybe he's in a Geico Insurance commercial?

"Thank you, Anole lizard buddy. I think your jumping around just saved my life. That shark pillow almost killed me. Holy fresh air, what a dream!"

If the lizard was listening, he didn't respond. It hasn't moved since Ole opened his good eye.

"Little green buddy ol' pal, just go away. Have mercy on this old monkey trying to sleep. Go jump-jump out there in the bushes." Uncle begs.

Maybe he's a deaf lizard because he runs up even closer to Uncle's eyes. Much too close, like five inches close, and five inches from the tip of his tail to his nose is the whole length of the little guy.

*Whoa, lizards have nostrils? Never saw that before. C*oach is learning new stuff.

The liz holds perfectly still, a green statue with one eye staring at Uncle. It's a prehistoric moment, a stare as old as time; lizard eye to primate eye. The ancient stare question; who's gonna pounce? Who's gonna run? Time stops. Nobody moves. Uncle grins. There it is.

"Hoo'kay little green buddy, you wanna stare down?"

65

Uncle goes, 'Man vs. Reptile' with the lizard. But three whole seconds is a very long time for Uncle's hung-over eye to stare. He just has to blink.

"Ha hah, you win liz'ad," the laughing voice in his head matches the voice he hears laughing out loud. He's getting back in sync. Ole's seeing with two eyes now, breathing easy, no pains.

Lizard puffs out his red chin sack, Victory! He holds that pose for the cameras. Then he puffs out his red throat even bigger, the fans cheer! Lizard keeps puffing and puffing his bright chin bag out again and again like somebody waving a stop sign.

"Hoo'kay you won already. Watchu keep showing me your red chin for little buddy? You looking for a girlfriend too? Wanna make a little whoopie? Why show me? Do I look like a lizard?" Actually, Uncle felt a little green. *Note to self, check the mirror,* his worried inner vanity warns.

Ole may look green, but he feels pretty good. His eyes begin to slide slowly closed. Then his whole forehead shudders with a thump as both eye doors drop shut again. Sleep pulls him close and gathers him up in a dark, sweet embrace. He hears somebody singing 'hello to darkness and old friends,' the haunting melody sounds just like on his stereo long ago.

Uncle Ole is asleep again, playing his dream guitar and feeling so grateful for saint Paul Simon, for giving the world these peaceful, lonely words.

14

Birds Smile?

It was maybe an hour later, Ole's awakened by thunder from above.

"Bang! Scramble! Scuffle! Bang-bang-bang!" There's way too much noise on his ceiling.

It wasn't big foot, it was three small doves, who flew off the roof and onto the green branches outside his window. Ole can see again, both eye doors almost wide open. He watched the little doves sitting next to each other. Doves all look alike, but it soon became apparent which one was the male. He hopped onto the back feathers of the small dove on his left like a rodeo cowboy. He shakes her around like he's gonna kill her while she clutches tightly with both tiny bird feet to the branch below her. Feathers fly in all directions. After a whole minute of this he hops off her. Smiling a little too much, he starts preening his chest feathers. She stays close to him and preens his neck feathers with her tiny beak. Thirty seconds go by. Now his head is bobbing up and down. Then without warning he hops onto the back of the small dove on his right. He shakes her so hard it's a wonder they stay on the branch. Feathers come loose from both birds. It's over quickly this time. Both females snuggle up close to Mr. Lucky and they start cooing and smiling as they all preen each other.

Wow dude, you neva' saw birds smile before. Coach is amazed more than ever. *It's the Discovery Channel right out your window this morning. This Maui is passion fruit, uh huh. It's time you found some fruit of your own. Buddy, you need a girlfriend, or two.* Other birds were starting to yell love calls at each other. This place was noisy as an aviary. The Mango Bungalow in the city was never this loud. He's wide awake, now. Who could sleep through such raucous bird racket?

One by one, little Java sparrows make nice morning chatter. But, they are never one by one. They are always in small flocks of about nine hundred, and this morning one-thousand were right there, two feet away outside his window. The Myna birds stopped by next, adding their noise, but they can't sing. So, they sing anyway, like Bob Dylan, just as loud and just as bad.

Invest in some ear-plugs, brah. His inner coach wants to sleep past five, am.

15

Call Me

The noisy morning birds eventually all flew away, Uncle's vision cleared. He stretched out in his new bed in his new room and felt thirsty, but wonderful. The view from his big picture window was brochure-perfect Hawaii. There were *his* vacation palm trees and *his* ocean with *his* morning sun shining on the tops of *his* mountains on Molokai with a huge rainbow of course. Hawaii must be the rainbow state of happy hangovers. He was off to good start. He woke up in a million-dollar home for just six hundred dollars a month. His mortgage on his golf course home back in Washington State had been three times that amount. He felt lighter than air with no more lawn to mow, no maintenance to worry about and no taxes to pay. He felt about as dumb as a fox.

But, he was a lonely fox. Tanya didn't want him or she would be here in bed with him. The memories of the winking brunette and the pretty Ukrainian woman's leg last night in the hot tub, were still doing jumping-jacks in his mind. Ole truly believed that eventually, his 'Three-D visualization powers' would magically bring someone special into his two-dimensional life. How long would he have to wait?

Forget waiting, you're going on a girlfriend search today. So, get up and get going. His inner coach must be lonely too. Oliver knew the Humpback whales wintered in Hawaii to birth their five-hundred-pound kittens and make humpy-hump-hump for the future of the species. *Maui must be the Passion*

Fruit for birds, whales and humans. Hey-hey, why not take a whale watch cruise while searching for a girlfriend? Maybe he'd get lucky, see some whales mating and meet some cute gal in a similar mood. He'd heard through the 'Coconut-Wireless' that you could buy a preseason book of five whale search trips for only sixty-bucks. He figured he could afford it if he went without food for two days.

Uncle drove his big Cadillac into Lahaina town and parked in the three-hour-free parking lot on Prison Street. He he'd washed most of the pink dirt off the car so it looked white again. Uncle enjoyed the short walk past the humongous old Banyan forest that completely hid the big courthouse and whatever else might be hiding in there. He walked up a flight of stairs into the Wharf Cinema Center looking for the Big Ocean Whale Watch ticket office. Several stores he passed by had 'Help Wanted' signs in their windows. He would go without food for a week, before he would take another job. The pretty Philippine women working in these stores smiled as he looked in.

Cute girls in there, maybe you should apply for a job. Ole ignored the coach this time. He walked up another flight of steps and found the door he was looking for. There was a well-dressed attractive lady standing at the counter. She helped him with his purchase of a coupon book of five boat trips.

"Do you guarantee I'll see whales?" He asked, trying to make small talk. She was very beautiful, a natural blonde, shoulder length, professionally dressed. She had to be mid to late thirty's with a slim figure. Her makeup was perfect in every detail. *It must take an hour to get your make up that perfect.* He thought to himself. She was a very sophisticated looking woman. She answered.

"Our policy is on the back of each ticket. If you don't see a whale during the two-hour boat ride you can go again for free."

"I like that, cool. Have you gone on many of these whale search trips, yourself?"

"Only one so far, this is a new job for me. We did see two whales but it's early in the season. They'll be jumping like catfish in a pond by February or March."

"So, I should wait 'til then?"

"Anytime you have time to go, is a good time to go."

"Good business answer. What's your name?"

"Michelle. And yours?"

"Oliver Gold, call me Ole."

"How can I call you, if I don't know your number?"

Is it this easy on this island? He's trying to think of something clever to say.

"I don't have a card," he said. "I just moved here last week. I can write it down for you. Let me use your pen."

She laughed and handed him her card.

"Here's mine, call me."

"Ok, I will." He said with his most handsome smile.

Other people were now waiting in line behind him so he winked his goodbye and turned to leave.

"Call me." She said again.

Uncle Ole walked across the street, sat on a park bench under the Banyan tree, waited ten, unbearably slow minutes, opened his old-school, clam-shell phone and called her.

"Big Ocean Whale Search Ticket Office, Michelle speaking."

"Hi Michelle, It's me, Ole, still busy?"

"Ole? Ole who?"

"What? I just met you remember? I'm that tall, good looking guy from ten minutes ago."

"Just messin' with ya. Not busy now, whaz-up?"

"Well Ms. Michelle, would you like to go on a whale search trip with me? I suddenly have a lot of tickets."

"I would like that Ole, but I work seven days a week."

"What? The whole week? What do you do with all that money?"

"Well you know Ole, Pakalo'lo is very expensive here. Like two-hundred and fifty-dollars a lid."

72

"You work every day of your life so you can afford grass?"

"How much is in a lid?" Uncle knew, but he was shocked that this professional, middle-aged, attractive woman with the perfect make-up could be hooked on marijuana. He hadn't smoked grass since his college days, a lot of years ago.

"One ounce," she laughed, "don't you know?"

"I've got a lot to learn." He could not hide the disappointment in his voice. He was thinking that he should just forget it and close the phone. But she had started talking two-miles-a-minute. Maybe she was high right now. She talked faster than he could even listen, accelerating to three-miles-a-minute. Soon she got to the part where she lived alone, well not completely alone. She had two dogs that slept with her in her Volkswagen van on the beach near Olawalu.

Uncle Ole closed his phone without saying goodbye. He shook his head in wonder, tore up her business card and threw it in the nearest trash bin. He could not imagine pretty Michelle sleeping stoned in a van, with two dogs. He shook his head again, as if to convince himself that Michelle was off his list.

Oh, remember what? You got no list, brah, coach is such a smart-ass sometimes.

"Poor dogs gotta smell that "stinkin' green smoke," he said to no one.

16

It's Yours

He watched some tourists waddle by. You can always tell the cruise ship tourists, they are all extra-large. A bare-chested man rode slowly by on his bicycle. He had big Amazon parrot riding on his handlebars. He smiled and Ole waved. Down on the far corner of Banyan tree park there was a Hawaiian man with gray-hair down to his waist and a gray beard almost as long. He was yelling at the top of his lungs about Jesus. Ole wasn't sure if he was mad at Jesus or mad at everyone else in town because of something Jesus had said. But he was waving a Bible and yelling at everyone he saw. Ole could hear him preach a half block away.

Behind Ole, a dozen or more local artists had set up tables for a craft fair under the Banyan tree. A musician with a ukulele was singing Hawaiian style over on the old courthouse steps. Ole wandered from booth to booth looking at all the art he could do without. To stay on budget, he could not even buy food for the next two days. There were several flocks of cute tourist chicks looking at the art displays, so he browsed. His assignment today, was to find a girlfriend.

Ole stopped at a table with little glass art things lined up in rows and water color paintings that were recognizable if not well done, standing on end in a wooden box, on the table. He fingered through the box of professionally matted, below-average prints but his thoughts were on the lovely Asian artist sitting in a chair at this table. She was painting on a canvas attached to a table easel. Her painting wasn't terrible. It wasn't great. But she, was a living, breathing "Ten" on his scale of beautiful women.

Try to think of something artsy to say. His mission commander is nudging him to speak.

"How much are these prints?"

Ooo, Lame dude, you didn't even say hello, what an idiot. Coach sounds disappointed.

"They are not prints. Each one is a hand-painted, signed original. They are twenty-five dollars each."

"You should ask double that. They are very good," he lied.

"Ok, I'll take fifty dollars each, just for you, since you're a gentleman who recognizes fine art. By the way I'm running a special today only, two paintings for one-hundred, plus tax," she laughed.

See what happens when you lie. His coach is laughing too.

"Hah! I wish I could. I just moved here and I'm on a survival budget. Some days I can buy food, if the rent is paid."

Lame again, dude, what is this, true confession to the cute stranger? Be confident. Remember your electron force field. You are what you think, be amazing.

"Been there," the lovely artist replied. "Think you can make it here?"

"I've dreamed of living in Hawaii since I was a kid. I finally got here. I'm staying, until I starve that is."

"My name is Setko, I wish you luck. Do you like my art?"

She was very pretty when she smiled. She had that strong assurance that some women wear so well. He figured her for another Yogi. She had to be at least forty-something but still slim and sexy-healthy looking. She was high on Art, not high on grass. He was so busy checking out her curves he forgot to even introduce himself.

"Yes, I do, he answered. You have a gift for getting the colors all wrong in neat sort of way."

That's no lie this time, but don't say anything more stupid than that. Coach is fuming.

"That's just what I try to do with my art. I am so happy you noticed. Pick out your favorite painting and show me."

He found one that sort of looked like Banana trees blowing in the wind. But the trees were red, the sky was green and the mountains in the distance had pink polka dots. It kind a looked familiar.

"This one is wonderful." He said and cringed, hoping lightening wouldn't strike him dead.

"It's yours, no charge, my welcoming gift to a new friend on Maui."

"What? Are you serious, this beautiful fifty-dollar original?

That's very kind of you Setko."

She's flirting with you dude, she likes you.

"You're most welcome. I wish you luck. My husband and I have been here for fifteen years. We left our corporate careers in Portland and came to Maui without job prospects. We were struggling at first, but when we both accepted the lives we had always dreamed of and turned to art, we made it... you can too," she added.

Uncle sighed inside, no ring on her married finger to alert him she was. But she was generous and kind and honest. It was refreshing to meet someone happily married and proud of it. He had felt that way about Tanya.

"I think... ah... oh, my mind got off track. I forgot what I was gonna say." He stumbled in his embarrassment.

"Oh, don't you just love it when that happens? When It happens to me, I follow that new path. It becomes, 'the road not taken,' and It always leads me to exciting new places. That's when my art is at its best, when my mind wanders."

I'm gonna like this island, Ole thinks to himself, *everybody's a little crazy here.*

He bid Setko goodbye and with his new, professionally-matted, original, ugly painting under his arm, walked away. He didn't know where he was going. He just started walking. His mind was slowly turning with the dharma wheel of life. He felt a little high, but he hadn't been drinking since last night, a whole 12 hours ago.

Here he was an average, good looking guy on a romantic island in Hawaii, surrounded by beautiful, local women plus all the cute tourist girls. The locals seemed a little too crazy or unavailable and the tourist girls were all accompanied by their husbands or a boyfriend or they clustered together in small groups. *Where are all the single female tourists?* He's wondering and walking, shaking his head but it won't clear. Ole was beginning to learn that when single women come to Hawaii they travel in coveys of six gal-pals. Always so stuck to each other, it's impossible for a 'los lobo' like him to pull one away from the flock.

17

The Blue-eyed Hawaiian Wahine

Ole still had an hour of free parking left so he kept walking. He came to the Lahaina town library. He's thinking, *tourists probably avoid libraries, same goes for stoned workaholics and busy abstract artists. Chances of meeting a retired local lady that likes to read are much better here.*

Uncle's thoughts were on track and his chick radar was on full scan as he cruised through the rows of book shelves. He did not have to pretend an interest in books. He was an avid reader. But today, his mission was to meet a girlfriend so he didn't even look at the titles. There were only three people in the place. The two librarians were nice looking but had very low energy fields around them. No free electrons there. He was the third person. He found a comfortable chair near the magazines and read a robotics article in the Journal of American Science.

He was only reading for five minutes when his radar blipped an alert. A Vietnamese-looking girl entered the library. She was so cute, wearing black short-shorts that said 'Las Vegas' on the butt and a pink t-shirt. Ole guessed her at about twenty-two years old. A minute later, two tall boys followed their mother into the library. One was about fourteen and the other, maybe sixteen. They were punching each other and arguing. Uncle's radar shut down, false alarm. He went back to his reading. The young mother turned and scolded the boys in the harsh, cymbal-jagged sounds of her language. They both started whining.

Time to go. His boss is reminding him of his purpose here. Ole returned the magazine to the rack and headed for the door.

Outside the library entrance, he saw a slim Polynesian lady carrying too many books. She struggled to keep them in her arms but one was slipping free. Uncle Ole came to the rescue just as she dropped it. He somehow caught that text book before it hit the sidewalk. Since he was down there he noticed she had beautiful knees.

"Nice catch," she laughed.

"Used to play baseball, guess I've still got it." He stood up straight and continued,

"Can I help you with these?" pointing to the stack still in her arms.

"Sure. Grab this one before I drop it too."

They got the all the books inside the library and onto the return counter and just stood there for a moment in time smiling at each other. Uncle could not believe his eyes. She was Hawaiian but with blue-eyes.

Whoa, what a blended girl this is. Coach was giving this one high marks. *Say something wonderful and quick.*

"Are those tinted contacts?"

You need charm school, dude. That was just plain stupid.

80

"I get that a lot. No contacts, my eyes are really blue."

"Sorry, you look so native Hawaiian I was sort a shocked. I'm Oliver, Oliver Gold, recently moved to Maui." He tried to recover. At least he remembered to introduce himself this time.

"My name is Coco. I've been living here almost three years."

"Are you Hawaiian?"

"Half Hawaiian on mom's side, dad is a mix of German-Swedish," she said proudly.

"Since you are returning so many books, my guess is you are a recovering book junkie?"

"Hah! You're so close to right. Are you a detective? I'm an author, and I love to read. I'm researching for my next book."

Think of something clever and not lame this time.

"Cool"

That's it? Cool. Oh that's sooo clever. Coach wants to slap him on the wrong side of his brain.

It wasn't enough for her. She started to move away from his silent awkwardness. She was about to thank him and turn to leave. But just in time he said the right thing.

"If I buy the coffee, will you tell me all about your books?"

Coco's blue eyes turned on him all sunshine and rainbows.

Her smile could have launched a fleet of Hawaiian canoes. She had a Hawaiian Helen of Troy face with a confident smile. She was forty-something and beautiful in a sexy, twenty-ish sort of way, with great knees. Her blue eyes had Fourth of July firecracker-electrons shooting out of them. Uncle went weak in his own knees, but with great effort he managed to stay upright. His heart was burning 91% hopeful octane for the third time today.

What's wrong with you dude? It's just coffee with an amazing, sexy, Hawaiian doll. Show some confidence, power up your Chi.

"Sure, where to?" she asked.

"Let's try the Pioneer Inn."

She followed his lead across the street and onto the wooden sidewalk of the famous old landmark hotel. The saloon in the restaurant has swinging half-doors, like in old Western movies. Uncle had done his homework on the place since he will be playing music here next week. Maybe, Mark Twain and Herman Melville had swung through these same doors. Uncle felt the weight of history as he pushed them open and then held one wide for Coco. He hadn't noticed it before but there was a scent of Plumeria on her that whispered of tropical nights. He noticed it now as he watched her glide by. Her posture was straight and her long black hair swung in a high pony tail. Elegant is the word that came to mind, along with way cool, sexy, cute shorts and nice butt.

The sweet scent was due to Coco pulling a small bottle of Plumeria sun screen out of her purse and rubbing a little in her hair as she followed along behind Ole.

A waitress greeted them and set them next to an open window looking out toward the marina.

Aloha, my name is Gina. "What can I bring you?" she asked.

Coco waited for Ole, but he nodded for her to order first.

"I'll have a rum and Coke, please."

Ole smiled like a kid on Christmas morning. Here was a woman he could like as well as lust after. His hopes were rising.

"Same, Bacardi Gold," he said, and once again they were content to just smile at each other.

"You don't drink coffee?" He asked.

"Not in a room displaying so many bottles of booze," she waved one hand toward the bar.

"Okay... now, I believe you really are a writer. Tell me about your books."

"Only one so far, non-fiction, a travel and entertainment guide to Northwest Washington."

"What's it called?"

"Budget Traveler's Guide to Northwest Washington State."

"I used to live in Seattle. Tell me something I don't know."

"Okay… it costs fifteen dollars to ride the elevator to the top of the Space Needle, but you can ride for free if you make reservations at the restaurant for lunch. And lunch is much more affordable than dinner which is way over-priced."

"Everybody knows that," he jabbed.

"Not tourists from Nebraska. Okay… how about this?" She paused, scrunching her bushy black eyebrows together with such sexy determination, Oliver held his breath. "You can take your bicycle on the Lummi Island Ferry boat for only twenty-five-cents each way."

"I didn't know that. I wanna go. What else you got?"

"Oh, lots of little-known places to go, with fun things to do. Like take a drive up the Mount Baker Highway to find a family-owned restaurant called Graham's Store, in the town of Glacier. In the main bar you warm your feet after skiing, next to a big wood stove. A whole pitcher of beer is only three dollars and you can select a steak and cook it yourself on a grill over wood coals."

"How many of these books have you sold so far?"

"The book has been in stores for three years and has been popular. I've sold enough to keep me writing instead working a nine to five. It's time to publish a new edition. My editor is after me to update ASAP. Prices change, old places close or open under new management, plus there are lots of new places opening all the time. "

"So, before you can publish a new edition you must travel

all over the Northwest again to see for yourself, right?"

"You catch on fast Oliver, just like you caught that book for me today."

"Yah, people tell me I'm a good 'catch,'" he laughed at his bad pun. They smiled at each other some more. Her blue eyes and Hawaiian charms were making him crazy. He was radiating confident Chi in a three-foot circle all around himself. If it were night, he was certain he would glow in the dark.

"What's the new book about?" He asked.

"It's fiction, but based on my true story about moving to Hawaii and dating the crazy guys I meet here."

"What?" I've been thinking of writing a book like that all morning only about meeting crazy women. I even have a title for it already... *Maui on the Rocks.*"

The rum drinks arrived. They lifted their glasses.

"Here's to the crazy people we meet on Maui," she said.

Ole posed like a king. Coco posed like a queen. They drank deep, heads back then their eyes returned to look deep into each other. It was the kind of eternal toast that 'old souls' make when they recognize a friend from long ago, maybe from another life. There was a Zen presence coming from within this blue-eyed, wahine doll.

"So, Oliver, how crazy are you?"

Don't blow this, whispered coach.

It sounded wonderful when she called him by his real name. For some reason, he didn't want her to call him Ole. He tried to think of some witty reply, but decided to go with the truth.

"You tell me," and then he told the short version of his story.

"I dreamed of living in Hawaii since I was kid in Iowa. I attended Drake University, post grad at Iowa State. I landed my first teaching job at University of Hawaii for one year then Stanford for nine years and finally was offered a dream job at University of Washington in Seattle. After too many decades in the shivering cold of the Northwest, I had to leave. I liked the rainy weather, but the every-day, all-purpose, forty-one-degree cold was torturing me with chronic neck pain. I needed a warm place to live. Maui seemed like a good choice. I spent four years planning the move with my wife and youngest daughter. When I quit my job in Washington, my wife of twenty-seven years, found a boyfriend and divorced me rather than move to Hawaii." He looked into her blue eyes, she was listening intently but not smiling anymore.

"I also have two grown daughters. I left a family of wonderful in-laws that I love. I left a large circle of musician friends, I bid, 'Aloha oe' to my friends at the Seattle Yacht Club. I left my Rotary Club friends, academic friends, patients at rest homes where I used to entertain. I left a lot of dear people behind. I miss them all very much, especially my daughters. But I could not endure another day of debilitating neck and shoulder pain in the Evergreen State. It's a beautiful place, but it's too close to the North Pole.

Tanya and I sold our home on a golf course, the lawn mower, the snow skis, the water skis, the ski boat. I sold my twenty-seven-foot Cal Sloop, almost all my books, my shop tools, framed art, my sculptures, my favorite Cadillac and the Apostles, my twelve very-old Bonsai trees."

Coco was quietly thinking or judging while she sipped her rum and Coke. Finally, she asked,

"You sold your sailboat?"

"Yep"

"Whoa brah, you really wanted to move to Hawaii. You're a musician? Tell me about that."

Her eyes were the cold color of blue glaciers with laser heat beaming out of them. Ole couldn't read that look. His heart was thumping in his throat. He couldn't stop his personal confession,

"I heard Bob Dylan sing when I was thirteen. I thought to myself, 'That guy can't sing and he's on the radio. I can do better than that,' so I bought a guitar from a pawn shop and taught myself to play. I wrote my own songs like Dylan did. He inspired a generation of song writers who knew they could sing better than him. But none of us can write like him. I played in a lot of bands for fun, but was never a working musician until I retired over here. Starting next week, I'll be playing Tuesday's and Friday's right here at the Pioneer Inn. So how crazy am I?"

Coco set her empty glass down with a loud 'clunk' on the

wood table.

"You win the prize, brah. You're crazier than anybody I've ever met."

Idiot, you blew your chance. You should have lied and tried for normal. His inner coach is pissed.

He struggled to gain some respectability,

"I love all those people, but I was in serious, every-day pain due to the cold back there. It's warm here, my bones are at 75 to 85 degrees every day. No more pain. I won't ever live in a cold climate again. I feel at home here on Maui and for some wonderful reason, with you Miss Coco, a perfect stranger."

Could you shut up and let the beautiful, perfect stranger talk?

But Coco remained thoughtful without saying a word, so, in-spite of what his inner coach thought, he felt confident. He wasn't ashamed of his life. Ole rattled on,

"I am who I am, as Popeye and Albert Camus both said. I am the sum of my choices. I'm a hopeful romantic and a dreamer. I am the captain of my life and I do not fear my own karma. So, do I win the crazy prize?" he asked with a laugh, but it wasn't very funny. "What do I get?"

Coco sat perfectly still and looked serious. Her perfect stranger lips began to smile.

"You get to come home with me."

18

Show me How

Ole felt a surge of nuclear energy shake through him. He was glowing radioactive gamma rays of surprise and happiness. He settled the bar tab with Gina. Holding hands, Ole and Coco walked under the Banyan Tree. He saw Setko still painting at her easel. Uncle saw Setko notice that he had a girlfriend with him. She waved her paint brush at him. Ole waved and held up his painting to show he still treasured it. Coco and Ole crossed Front Street and found their cars. By some weird coincidence she was parked right next to him in the three-hour-free lot. She had an older model open top Jeep with torn leather seats and missing doors, but it had seat belts and a roll bar. His car had a parking ticket for being there longer than three hours.

"Dang, I can't afford a ticket," growled Ole.

"Here, give me that." She took it and tore it up. He noticed she didn't litter. She put the ripped pieces in the pocket of her nicely too-tight shorts.

"I've had a dozen of these. Nobody arrests you if you don't send the forty-dollar fine to the address printed on the back. It's a private, not a city owned lot."

Local knowledge rules, brah. Pidgin coach is impressed with Coco.

She jumped in her Jeep and headed north. He followed in

his Caddy. She had a very heavy foot. Traffic was moving at its normal forty to forty-five mph, but she was pushing sixty and changing lanes so fast that Uncle wasn't keeping up with her.

Don't lose this one, his inner voice warns.

The homes, the ocean and golf courses went blurring by. They passed Ka'anapali, Kapalua, D.T. Fleming Beach, and Honolua Bay. They leaned into the hairpins out on the North Shore like race cars in a rally. Surf was up and the waves were too big. There were helicopters circling above, filming the professional surfers, who ride those fifty-foot monsters.

Uncle followed Coco for another ten minutes around the Pali coast. Then without any warning or turn-signal, Coco suddenly cut to the right and spun gravel up a one-lane road. She plunged deep into the rain forest. The rough path was red dirt with pot-holes full of water in wide red ruts. It was hard on his shocks but Uncle wasn't about to turn back now. Another half mile through the jungle and Coco bounced her jeep across a wide clearing and down into a ravine. She barely slowed as she actually jump-bounced that jeep over a dry stream bed about six-feet wide and up a steep slope on the other side.

There might as well have been a big sign saying, "No Cadillac's beyond this Point". Ole stopped and turned off the ignition key. He watched as Coco slid to a stop under some Banana trees next to a green, plantation-style bungalow. It was surrounded by a large mowed lawn with a dozen chickens in the yard. There were yellow Hibiscus all around and a washing machine sat quietly under a lean-to roof on one side of the house. Ole could see some clothes hanging on a line out back.

"E' komo mai," Coco called. (Come on in)

Ole walked across the dry stream bed. She took him by the hand and led him to the wrap-around covered lanai of the house. The afternoon was hot with no breeze this far back from the ocean.

"I made some sun tea this morning. I'll bring you a glass," and she disappeared through a screen door into the house. Ole sat down on a big wicker sofa covered with clean, comfortable cushions. The jungle pressed in with a humid hug. The hunched over trees appeared to be taking a nap in the sunshine. Uncle Ole searched the jungle branches. It looked like a perfect place for winged monkeys from Oz to hide. Every direction he looked, everything was green. The trees, the hanging jungle vines, the Jeep, the house, the cushions he sat on, everything was fifteen shades of green. Coco returned with a green plastic pitcher of tea and two tall green glasses filled with ice.

"What's your favorite color?" Ole asked.

"Red. Why?"

"Hah? Just curious, is this your place? It's so perfect."

She poured the tea. Her graceful hands almost hula dancing as she moved.

Wow, she's gorgeous, don't say anything stupid, enjoy the

moment, wise advice from his Guru.

This time, he listened to the wisdom. He sipped his tea and kept his mouth shut. She sat down on the sofa next to him, her leg touching his. She had changed out of her black shorts into green short-shorts. Her body heat was hotter than the weather. Ole's thrill-meter was running into the "red", Coco's favorite color.

"I lease this place from the owners in the next house up the valley."

She offered no more, she leaned forward and tasted her cold tea. Her tank top revealing the most beautiful smooth brown shoulders and shapely lower back. Ole wanted to take her in his arms, but he liked her so much he was willing to take it slow.

The afternoon was quiet, quiet and hot. Full sunshine broiled the green yard and forest like an oven. He liked it hot. His neck no longer hurt. When the tea in his glass was half gone, a soft rain began to mist down the valley with a sighing breeze. Even the rain had a living-green tint to it. As the veil swept past their shelter, it was almost like the island exhaled a long, slow breath. It brought with it a cool fragrance of rank jungle. The rain was drumming softly on the roof of the lanai. Nothing more needed to be said. Ole sipped his tea. Coco appraised him with her beautiful blues.

The wind and rain stopped suddenly. There was a long pause. The sun had briefly dimmed with the cool rain breath, but now it was brighter, pulling vapors of steam up into the sky. He shielded his eyes with one hand like a sea captain looking out over the green lawn. The glare was intense. Then somehow the wind came back up the valley from the sea. It was as if the valley began to inhale, pulling the brackish ocean air high into the mountains above.

There was another pause, no wind at all. The full sun continued baking the jungle. Then in less than a minute the misty rain exhaled down the valley, bringing cloud cover and relief from the heat once more. They drank their tea in silence, waiting. Soon the mountain breathed deeply in and they could smell the sea again. The powerful sun light so bright it hurt his eyes. *What's going on? This island breathes?* His inner chemist is as amazed as he is.

Ole finished his tea and leaned into Coco. He put one arm around her shoulders and said nothing. He could feel her relax in his arms. She held his hand, closed her eyes and cuddled into his chest. Ole felt so at home with her. His quest was to find a new girlfriend today; he hoped it could be Coco.

You don't know this woman but she's beautiful, likes you, trusts you and she's here snuggled up next to you. See, all you need to do is visualize and keep trying. Follow your dreams, stay the course and your dreams can come true. His inner guru was starting to sound like Jiminy Cricket in a Walt Disney movie. He found his voice,

"Am I imagining this? The way the valley inhales the sea air and exhales the mountain rain? This is the coolest thing I've ever seen, next to your blue eyes."

"Yes, it happens a lot. You like my eyes?"

93

"Oh, my stars, I sure do."

They held each other and were quiet for a while. She had a happy temperament, she wasn't stoned and her blue eyes ,were amazing in that beautiful Hawaiian face. He leaned in to kiss those pretty lips. She met him more than half way. The jungle disappeared. He could not remember his name. She kissed like she drove, reckless and wild. He heard birds singing merrily overhead. Maybe this was a Walt Disney movie.

"Will I be in your new book now?" Ole whispered.

"Of course, you will. You are handsome and prize-winning crazy. You may be the hero who finally rescues the girl from her many lonely nights, disappointed by those other crazy losers."

"How could I possibly rescue you? You have life by the tail. I have never met anyone, anywhere, who had their life so together. But you do need help with your kissing."

"Show me how." She panted softly.

They practiced for a long time there on the green cushions of the green sofa, in the green house in the green jungle.

"Am I doing any better?" Coco asked, coming up for air.

"Not really," he lied. "You're gonna need a lot of private lessons."

They laughed like two teenagers, free and relaxed and easy. Other than four roving hands, the reckless kissing did not progress to naughty sex. They both were content to take it slow. Coco made a late afternoon lunch of some veggies wrapped in soft pita bread. Uncle Ole ate with Zen awareness. It all felt real, but it was so perfect, it might be one of his dreams. He scanned the trees again for winged-monkeys.

This is real brah. His referee making the official call after viewing the replays of a day full of amazing events.

19

Lucky Come Maui

They decided to go watch the sunset. Coco wanted to drive but Ole wanted to live to see his first pension check, so they took both cars. He followed her jeep down the muddy access drive and along the Pali to a scenic lookout that had a few sunset worshipers already waiting.

The sun was still three fingers from the horizon. They parked and got out to walk up the rocks for a better view.

There was a man up on the cliff in the shade of some trees. He was standing all alone, playing a viola while he watched the sunset. He was deep into a jazz version of 'Fiddler on the Roof'. Ole and Coco held hands as they climbed closer and sat on the rocks nearby to listen. He sounded pretty good. The song ended and there was a pause, and then he played 'If I Were a Rich Man'. When there was just one horizontal finger until the ocean swallows the sun, he played 'Sunrise, Sunset' and then finished with 'Aloha oe'. It was Maui magic.

"The locals call this an *a'ha* moment." Coco said.

They kissed again, so busy with the honey of tongues they missed the green flash when the sun disappeared below the straight-edge horizon of the sea.

"You're getting better, but you have a long way to go." He coached her with a smile.

The fiddler put his violin in its case and walked near them as he climbed down the hill.

"Tanks for 'da music brah," Ole offered, trying out some pidgin for the first time in twenty-seven years.

"Mahalo," said Coco.

"My pleasure," said the fiddler.

He must have seen Coco's eyes because he stopped and smiled at them both.

"I'm Captain Billy Bones," and he bowed.

"I'm Oliver Gold and this is my friend, Coco." He thought that sounded rather possessive. He let it ride.

"Do you live here, Capt?"

"Ten woner'ful years now, how 'bout you?"

They smiled and said yes together.

"Lucky come Maui," Captain Billy said.

There was a long, peaceful silence. They all looked out to the horizon. The afterglow began to build. Beams of pink light stretched up into long red wheel spokes. The spokes met a curved cloud of orange and darker orange up over their head. It looked like the rim of a wheel arching above them for a brief shimmering moment of illusion. It was absolutely... amazing, one of those forever-making moments when time quickly slows down. Almost at the same time, the three old souls whispered the same thing... "The Dharma Wheel!"

The beautiful wheel turned as it must, but very, very slowly. Its colors seemed to evaporate with the roll of the earth into the night. Soon there were only rumors of pink left in the sky.

"Well that was something, yah?"

"No kiddin' Capt. I've never actually seen the Dharma Wheel except in books and in meditation.

"How long have you been here?" Capt. asked.

"Almost a week," said Uncle Ole.

"Stick around on Maui and with time, you will see your dreams shape your future. The night Lotus must open with the moonlight."

Is everybody on this island cosmic? His inner coach amazed by a whole day of amazement.

"Aloha you two," said Captain Bones.

"Goodnight Billy," Oliver said with a nod.

"Aloha 'oe," Coco whispered to Captain Billy, with a touch of softness.

It was the kind of Aloha 'oe, given to old friends, who may never meet again. Capt. turned for one more look into her blue eyes. Then he smiled and walked to his vintage BMW, put the top down and drove back toward Lahaina.

Uncle Ole held on to Coco and didn't want to let go. His thoughts were calm, but his heart was excited. She was a wish come true, the perfect answer to today's girlfriend quest.

This is special, don't rush it. Go home. Ole knew his conscience was right this time, but he couldn't say goodnight.

"Well I best be getting back Oliver." Coco decided for him. "Wanna stay at my place tonight? You won the 'most-crazy' prize remember?" She winked.

"Coco, I think I should go home. It's been wonderful meeting you and the kissing practice is improving. Let's have 'coffee' again tomorrow, shall we?"

"You really are the craziest person I've ever met." She looked a little sad.

"I do want to collect my prize Coco. Can I call you tomorrow?"

"I have a phone but there's no cell reception out this far. It's the way I like it. I can write without being disturbed."

"Will I disturb you, if I come visit you? I think I can find your place again."

She seemed distracted. She turned away and looked out over the darkening ocean.

"No you won't disturb me Oliver. Hasn't it been a perfect day?" Her voice sweet with soft melancholy.

Not sure what to say next, Uncle squeezed her hand and

she turned for a goodnight kiss. The kiss was warm but too short. She sped off in her green jeep. Ole looked back at the sky and took some deep breaths. The wheel had turned. His inner voice was quiet for a change. He got in the Cadillac and drove back to Yu'layne's house.

He began to wonder why he didn't stay the night with Coco. But he knew the answer. Kissing someone besides Tanya had been fun, but felt empty. He was still in love with her. For him, falling in love was a thirty-year emotional investment. But loving Tanya for a lifetime wasn't paying any dividends. He felt like he needed her, but that check would only bounce from now on. She seemed to be able to start over just fine. She had found a boyfriend at the church they occasionally attended. That was months ago; Ryan somebody. She suddenly became an every Sunday attendee. Tanya would get home Sunday evenings after a full day of brunch and shopping or 'something' with Ryan.

How does anyone fall 'out' of love? He really wanted to know. He had a whole lot of those stupid Cupid-arrows still stuck in his heart and they hurt like hell. For a grown man with several post-grad degrees in chemistry, he was clueless about women or how to start dating again at his age. He wanted a girlfriend, but had no idea how to pull out those arrows and patch up his heart. He had so many happy yesterdays with Tanya; all of them over now. Today he learned a big lesson about his tomorrows. His heart was ready to collect the 'prize' that Coco was offering.

Stupid love, his mind scolded him.

20

Dear Ole

That night Ole tossed and turned in his lonely bed. Coco was everything he could want in a woman. She was smart, creative, beautiful, and had a certain confidence about her. She was a Hawaiian Zen masterpiece with blue eyes. She was delicious to kiss. He kicked himself in his already black and blue heart over and over, and over again for not staying at her place.

The next morning, he woke early, but waited until noon, a reasonable hour to go calling on his new friend. His mind was hooking up jumper cables to his heart, trying to convince the old beater to start over. During the drive along the north coast road he didn't see the surfers or the ocean, just the road and Coco's face. Sometimes it was Tanya's face.

Stupid, stupid love, it's so dumb to stay in love with someone who has moved on. His coach knew, so why didn't he get it? *Remember what John Wayne used to say?* Coach lectured, *"Life is hard… but it's harder… if 'yer stupid."*

Ole parked the Caddy in the first clearing. Across the dry stream the cottage was right where he left it, but the Jeep was not there. He could see a manila envelope stuck in the screen door. "OLIVER" was written on it in large enough letters that he could read it from where he parked. The jungle was inhaling sunshine and a warm ocean breezes as he walked across the dry creek and up to the lanai. He emptied the envelope out on the green make-out couch.

One copy of "Budget Traveler's Guide to Northwest Washington State" fell on the green cushions. It was autographed by the author,

"To Ole, the craziest man I've ever met, with Aloha, Coco Lani Smith"

There was a handwritten-note stapled to the front cover.

"Dear Ole, you are a wonderful man and I wish you good luck on Maui. I fly back to Seattle tonight to revisit all these 'secret Northwest places' and prepare the next edition for publishing. My editor is pushing me to finish this in the next ninety days. My flight has been booked for weeks. I did not tell you yesterday because it was such a perfect day we had together. I wanted to give you this book last night. It's your 'prize' for being the craziest man I've ever met. Thanks for the kissing lessons. You are a good teacher. I'll include your story in my new book. Hopefully we will meet again. Aloha Oliver, Coco-Lani"

21

One Plate?

His first thought was to speed to the airport and catch Coco before she boarded her plane. Just like in the movies, she would be so happy to see him. Coco would rush into his arms, they would laugh and cry for joy, embrace tightly and kiss with wild abandon. But... then what? This isn't the movies, his re-play referee had made the call... said, *this is real.* She has her career as a writer with deadlines. He'd finally retired to Hawaii and wasn't about to fly back to cold Washington state. It was the worst kind of bad timing.

Ole was amazed to find an exciting, beautiful friend like Coco and lose her, all in twenty-four hours. The impermanence of life is always there giving and taking away. He had learned that the Dharma Wheel is the way of the universe, it must continually turn. Yesterday the sun and rain were nurturing a new friendship. Today the dharma was crushing him under a double tractor-size wheels of heart-ache of emptiness, Tanya and Coco, both out of his life.

Resilient as ever when faced with dharma drama, Uncle focused on his determination to be happy with or without Tanya or a girlfriend. He lengthened his daily meditation. He did his pre-dawn Tai- Chi at a nearby Pohaku Beach before surfing the four-foot waves at 'S' turns. Ole thanked himself for going slow with Coco. He thanked his inner-Zen coach for reminding him he was still married in his heart. He had to give it more time.

'Give' seemed like a good word to meditate on. He remembered his original plan for moving to Hawaii, to give more than he received. That evening he drove his Caddy to the Kahului side of Maui and found one of the two local nursing homes. Both are called Hale Makua. (House of Our Parents) He arrived at the rest home in time to play his flute for the elders while they ate supper. The smiles he received from the kupuna (elders) made him forget his own small troubles.

He cruised home in his big Cadillac, with his arm out the driver's side window. The warm, winter wind through his fingers and tonight's volunteering gave him an exciting euphoria. His Hawaiian retirement dream was almost perfect.

He went back the next night to the other Hale Makua in the town of Wailuku. Again, he entertained a dozen old folks in a modern cafeteria. The two hours of flute music kept him in practice. The soft notes echoed gently back from the pastel concrete walls. Uncle played with his eyes closed. The echoes reminded him of an old album by Jean-Pierre Rampal playing flute in the Taj Mahal. He thought it sounded almost that good. The old folks must have too. They clapped or banged their forks on their trays. He put his flute back in its case and stood up to leave. One of the nurse-aides came over to thank him.

"That ve'ly nice," she said. "I bring you one plate."

Uncle looked at the soft, colorless food on the trays of the kupuna near him. It was not appealing but the nurse was cute.

"Sure, thank you." He pulled his chair up to a table where two elderly Japanese ladies were sitting. They each looked

104

over a hundred years old, small and frail but smiling.

"May I join you ladies?"

One nodded her head again and again and laughed a lovely, toothless smile. She brought a broomstick arm up and covered her mouth with one boney hand. Her fingers were twisted with arthritis but her eyes were filled with love. Music is the thread that sews hearts together and Ole knew how to sew with a flute. The other old lady was just as animated and spoke broken English in a tiny, tiny voice.

"Domo arigato, Mr. Mrusician-san, ve'ly nice Mrusic," she went on, "Say, you know what? Today I diagnosed with Alzheimer's."

Yikes, what you gonna say to that, brah? His thoughts now full of caution.

"Oh?" seemed like a safe response.

"It's not so bad," she continued, "even a'lound my own fami'ry, I meet new peop'rle every day." She laughed and laughed.

Ole was not sure if she was telling him the truth or if this was some kind of nursing home joke. In either case, she thought she was the funniest thing since Carol Burnett so he laughed with her.

"Here's your dinner sir." The cute nurse set a roast-beef dinner down in front of him. It looked good and smelled delicious with lots of mashed potatoes and gravy. She gave him a cloth napkin, knife and fork, dinner roll, salt and pepper and a desert brownie topped with whip cream. The two Japanese kupuna looked shocked.

"Auwe! Where 'dat come from?" said the old comedian. The other Japanese tutu kept nodding her head up and down and from side to side. She looked like she was about to cry.

"Aunties, you no can chew 'dis kine," said the cute nurse.

Weary resolution formed stoically on their faces, the old ladies stopped staring at the young nurse and looked only at the plate of meat.

"Mahalo dear, what is your name?" Uncle asked.

"Bethany," she pointed to the name tag on her uniform blouse.

"My name is Oliver Gold," he stood up and bowed. He had noticed her before as she brought trays in and helped the elders eat. She was Japanese, slim, graceful and attractive, sort of. She did not radiate high energy or very much confidence. She returned the bow.

"A'roha, Mr. Gor'd-san."

"Please call me Ole," he smiled.

The two Japanese elders at his table also bowed and twittered little wrinkled smiles at him and at each other. Then they resumed gazing at the food on Ole's plate. Bethany noticed and asked if Ole-san would like to sit over by the nurse's station. He picked up his plate and desert and bowed goodbye to the two Japanese kupuna. Bethany got the rest and escorted him over to a private table with one chair. When he sat down he bowed his head and said a quiet grace his mother had taught him, followed by a meditation prayer of gratitude. Bethany watched. When he started to eat, she asked if would like coffee.

"Not unless you put some Bailey's in it." He smiled.

"So so'lly O're-san, I drank a'rrah whiskey, empty b'rott'le," she laughed. "I b'ling Coca-Co'ra."

"That would be great, domo arigato."

He ate his dinner slowly with deep appreciation. Looking around at the old folks he was realizing again that the impermanence of life had to be law. He tasted his food one bite at a time. When that bite was swallowed there was a space of renewed hunger followed by another bite of food. Music was the same, soft notes held carefully apart by empty silence yearning for the next note. Day and night, on and off, young and old, love and heart-ache, it's the law. It wasn't an epiphany. He'd known this for years. It was more of an assuring reminder that the wheel always must turn.

He also realized that nursing homes could be a good place to meet a girlfriend. Here were local women with jobs, not tourist girls who live or write travel books across the ocean.

"Give and you shall receive brah," his inner Jesus knows.

He watched Bethany return with a can of Coca-Cola and a

tall glass of ice. This simple moment made him happy again. The unflattering uniform she wore made her petite figure look pudgy. Her black nurse shoes made her look old, but she was probably in her mid-thirties. He liked her pretty face without make up and she was kind. Bethany left the Coke and went about her duties. When Ole finished his meal, he took his flute case and headed for the door. The two old Japanese ladies smiled at him. He bowed and waved goodnight. He felt grateful again, to be healthy enough to walk out of this place. Whatever joy he had given these kupuna tonight was half the satisfaction he felt from volunteering. He looked for Bethany as he left the cafeteria but did not see her. Once outside, there she was with two other workers, smoking cigarettes. She put hers out in an ashcan and came up to him with a piece of folded paper. He turned to thank her for dinner and she reached up and gave him a soft hug, slipping the note into his hand.

"Come again O're-san," closeup, her black hair and her breath stank like a tire on fire. She smiled very demurely with nicotine-stained, brown teeth and nodded her head up and down.

"Thank you for dinner, Bethany." Uncle Ole walked to his car and looked at the note; her phone number. He tore the note into small pieces and tossed them under his driver's seat.

"Stinkin' cigarettes," was all he said.

22

Shazam

Two weeks wandered by in a whimsical retired way. Uncle wrote a letter to Tanya and each of his daughters telling them of his progress so far. He told them he loved them, missed them and hoped they could all come visit him someday. He urged them to be kind, be determined, follow their dreams and leave the rest to karma. He gave them all his new address on Makahiki Street. Within a week he had replies from all three daughters each wanting to come to Maui as soon as Papa could send them the airfare. He planned to do this as soon as he could save up the money. He didn't get a reply from Tanya.

You need a girlfriend dude. Your wife has other plans.

On his ninety-nine cent Hawaiian calendar, the blank boxes of days eventually fell together in a heap all the way down to the bottom right-hand corner of the month. He went online to his Bank of Hawaii checking account.

"Shazam!" He hollered. The day his first 'pension ship came into port was a beautiful thing. It was almost divine, like Sanctifying Grace filling the empty milk bottle of his sinful soul back in Catholic grade school. It felt that good.

Ole flipped the calendar to the next month and counted the days. He did the math.

Okay, after you pay the rent, child support for Brita, and your credit card minimums, you have twenty-eight bucks a day to live or starve in Hawaii. Either be careful or find a job. His inner accountant is starvation-dead serious.

He'd go hungry before he took another 'job,' but he was certain he would work before he starved to death. Starving sounded really, bad. His music gig twice a week turned out to be too much fun to be called a job. It paid well and the tip jar filled up each night. Now with his pension kicking in he'd make it. He could save the music gig money for those airfares he wanted to buy for his daughters. Ole sat at his computer looking at the digital deposit and smiled. His daughters would love Hawaii. Almost everybody does. He thought of Tanya and his chest hurt again.

Let her go brah, he remembered the taxi driver's advice.

Uncle Ole had heard about online dating. He was sitting at his computer. Miss blue-eyed, adorable Coco had taught him that perhaps random chance was not the best way to find someone. He'd found his car and a place to live in newspaper ads. Why not shop online for a girlfriend / wife?

You gonna try marriage again? His mind wondered.

Uncle Ole had enjoyed being married. He figured he could be a good husband again if given the chance.

Ole searched and the first web results were Strike-a-Match.com and Asianeuro.com. He posted a brief profile on each, and mentioned he was seeking marriage. He added a rugged, selfie-photo taken out on the Kapalua shoreline. The results were startling. Within minutes of typing in his location as Maui, Hawaii, he had three friend requests.

"This'll be interesting," he mumbled to himself as he opened the new contacts.

The Online match-making fantasy was fun. It was actually, amazing. He discovered that if you are a man, with an address in Hawaii and you still have a pulse and are under the age of one-hundred and ten, you still have a chance. In fact he learned that there are thousands and thousands of beautiful young women in this world that want to be your wife and become an American citizen.

On Strike-a-match he received over twenty-nine hundred inquiries in the first twenty-four hours. On Asianwife.com he got three-thousand, two hundred and ten in the first week. Even though Uncle specified in his profile, that he was looking for someone forty-five to sixty years of age almost all the women that wrote to him were between eighteen and twenty-six. Every single one of them was flippin' gorgeous. He typed a 'cut and paste' reply that he used to answer almost every one of them:

"You are very pretty. I am flattered that you wrote to me. But it would be better for you, if you find someone closer to your own age. Have a wonderful life, good luck and goodbye."

It took a lot of hours on the computer but it was something to do. He had a lot of spare time these days. Most of the young women never wrote to him again. A few either could not read English or they were so stubborn they kept writing. There were five middle-age women attractive and interesting enough to chat with, which he did for that first month. But the most important thing he learned was that everyone was thousands of miles away from him.

Why can't you find someone searching for a boyfriend, right here on Maui?

A few nights a week, he would walk to the Sand's of Kahana Resort to add another happy hour to his already happy days. From his bar chair he could keep an eye on the hot tub and pool for the cute rich, local girlfriend he was wishing for.

One rather thirsty evening, he met a beautiful red-head in the bar named Peggy Sue. He had never met anyone who actually, had that name before, but he liked the song and he liked this tall slim doll. She was funny and quite the flirt with no rings on her fingers and enough vodka screw-drivers in her to build something from an erector set. They struck up a conversation about the Napili neighborhood. She lived there, just one mile away. She was an advertising salesperson for a new phone book company.

It was so unusual to meet a single woman at this family resort that he got his hopes up way too fast and before he had time to think it over, he was buying her drinks. They sat at a small private table for two and had more laughs and more drinks over expensive dinners. Her free electrons were all over the place and he was radiating his best intoxicated confidence.

He could see the empty spa tub from his table but with his back to the bar he did not see the angry looking young man walk in. Ole's conversation was out on the loose fringe of absurdity.

"Hey Peggy Sue, wanna go skinny-dip pin' in the hot tub?"

"Hah! You can't skinny dip in a resort hot tub Ole. You wanna go to jail? Maybe we could try it some night in the ocean," and she winked, "just you and me Ole. I'd like that. I'd like that very much."

She had suddenly changed from friendly to very friendly. She was looking over Ole's shoulder, watching the young man move her direction. She moved her chair closer to Ole. She took his hand and slipped her long leg up between his legs under the table. Thrills were racing circles around his solar-plexus, his seven chakras were a string of firecrackers popping up his spine and sending good vibrations down south of the border. Even his feet felt turned on.

Let's dance! Coach is lit up too. *This is just what you wished for this this morning dude, a cute girlfriend living on Maui. Ask her if she drives a Mercedes? Say something romantic.*

He was about to suggest taking a naked swim in the ocean after dinner when that angry young man slid a chair up to their table.

"Mind if I join you two love birds?" he sneered.

"Who're you cowboy?" Uncle tried not to slur.

"Me? Oh, I'm just Michael, Penny's fiancé. Don't bother introducing yourself. We're going home, right Penny?"

"I'm not goin' no place wiz'shoe buster, you called me a 'Wal-Mart-whore and I'm not like that, 'zoe get lost."

"Your name is Penny? You have a fiancé?" Uncle is a little slow on the uptake after a few drinks.

"Come on bitch, I'm taking you home and I'm gonna punish you good."

"Ooo Michael, I'd like that," she crooned, her pretty face snuggled into his shoulder. "I was naughty again yah? I'm zoe sorry, Michael. Are you gonna spank me? I'm gonna need a good hard… really 'ard spankin' 'tis time. I'm zuch a baaad girl my darling Mikey. Le'z go home, you can tie me up in the 'naughty-girl room'. She slumped over on his shoulder but winked at Uncle Ole.

"Zorry Ole, gotta go, I'm too naughty…ah? T'anks for dinner, les' go for a swim... s'umtime."

She let go of his hand and hugged Michael. He stood and pulled her up by the arm. He took a fist full of hair on the back of her head and pushed her toward the door.

She looked up at him with obvious lust.

"Are you mad Mikey? You know I'm gonna bee yer naughty girl tonight. I can't 'elp it. What chu gonna do 'bout it bad boy? Ooo I can't wait baby. You know yer' the only Mikey-bad-man for naughty lil' ol' me."

Ole was jaw-dropped amazed, listening to this crazy woman and her game master. What a marriage that was gonna be. He tried to think this through but it hurt to think. He went back to one of the comfortable bar stools, paid seventy-seven dollars for the two dinners and drinks and ordered another rum on the rocks. He should a been counting his drinks, but he forgot where he left off and had to start over. He'd read a lot of books about starting over in Hawaii. After the last few months, he felt he could write one. He was getting good at it.

Grumpy Dollar was smiling. Ole had never seen him smile.

Maybe he's seen this, "Peggy Sue" performance before. If so he sure didn't warn you brah. Maybe he get's his kicks this way.

The rest of the evening blurred slowly down to closing time.

"Go home Uncle," Dollar ordered. "I'm closing up."

"I y'am home,"

"Yah can't sleep here brah, go home." Ole looked a lot more inebriated than usual.

"You need a ride home?"

"N'yah brahba, I'm frine as sandpepper. I can do 'dis in my sleep with one eye tied behine' my back."

Ole knew the way home. It was only a thousand miles uphill to the Beverly Hills and then one turn into the Hollywood Maui district of fancy homes on Makahiki street. He got home eventually, but his knees hurt as bad as his heart when he got in bed. He might have crawled the last two-hundred miles.

23

Certified Mail

Around ten the next morning Uncle was taking a long hot shower and decided he felt so good he should be singing. It was another happy hangover. But for some reason he couldn't think of a single song. Maybe his inner juke box had gone broken.

During the second cold rinse of his hair he remembered last night and a record dropped onto the turntable of his forty-five-rpm mind.

"Peggy Sue, Doo Doo Doo, pretty, sexy, pretty, skanky Peggy Sue…" That was as far as he sang. In his mind, he broke that record over his knee. He'd been played like a chump. It was so bizarre it was kind a funny.

"Sure are some crazy, crazy women in Hawaii and I'm not so sure I wanna get me one". His juke box wasn't working quite right.

After a breakfast of six grapes and a package of soda crackers from his empty-looking shelf in Yu'layne's refrigerator, he was feeling absolutely… grand. His 'reality indicator' was reading a steady 60% sober.

To stay on his twenty-eight-dollar-a-day-budget, he wasn't going to be able to buy food for a few days. Last night cost over a hundred bucks. He didn't want to think about it. Ole found a clean Aloha shirt and managed to get it on right side out. He always wondered why Hawaiian print shirts are sewn together with the bright colors on the inside and the dull, faded looking colors on the right-side-outside?

He made sure all his music gear was in the Cadillac; he thought he had a gig at the Pioneer Inn tonight because he thought it was Friday. On a whim he checked the calendar in the kitchen. Yep it was Friday. He looked through the house mail that someone had tossed on the kitchen counter. He was half hoping there might be a letter from Tanya answering the one he sent last month. He was surprised to see a postcard addressed to him. It looked officially important. It was a bright green card from the Lahaina Postmaster. A notification of a certified letter he must sign for at the post office.

Ole drove his big car into town like a little old man, keeping it within the speed limit and even using his turn signals, a rare sight on Maui. When he got to the post office, he signed and dated his signature as best he could and opened the thick legal-size envelope from Washington's, King County Superior Court.

"KAAA---BOOM!" It might as well have been a letter bomb; the concussion he got was that tragic. His eyes were punched in and his ears were ringing. Tanya had filed for divorce.

Of course, he knew this day was coming. It's what she wanted. But that didn't help him feel less shocked. He had foolishly hoped she would miss him in his absence, like he missed her, and that somehow things would work out okay. Being a romantic optimist can feel really stupid sometimes.

Her request for dissolution included a court date for next Wednesday, just five days from right now. That was the moment... that Ole's heart began to harden toward her. His knees and elbows began to shake so bad he had to sit down right there on the curb in front of the post office. He expected to have more time to respond and reasonably discuss this. Five days was not much time for discussion and she didn't answer his nice letter. He thought about that another three seconds. Of course, she answered his letter. This was it.

Another document was attached. He read on. It was her 'Statement of Fact.' It burnt into his eyes like tear gas. She claimed that he had verbally abused her and willfully abandoned her. *Whaaa?* That he left her with all the family debt and not much else. She claimed he had been a terrible father to the children when he was around; but he was seldom around for them, so she raised all three kids by herself. That he ridiculed them and was not supportive when they were teenagers. That he was gone most of the time pursuing his own selfish career. *Incredible!* His eyes were stinging, but he read on. She petitioned that the court should assign all of his Washington State TERS 1 pension to her, due to her current indigent condition and her twenty-seven years of faithful support for him during their marriage.

Ole sat in front of the post office in apparent calm, just another old guy sitting on a curb to rest. No one passing by would know that all Hell and Purgatory were breaking chairs and furniture in his mind. Dream Shark fear and defensive anger raced adrenalin through his body. He wanted to jump up and run for twenty miles. He almost did, but realized he couldn't even stand up. All his energy was blowing out his eyes and ears. He sat there like a roaring sports car, full of jet fuel, yet grounded by four flat tires.

The wife he had loved for so long had turned into some Aztec witch, ripping his live, beating heart out of his chest. How could she write those terrible things about him? How could someone as sweet as Tanya, want to financially destroy him like this? They had been friends for a long time, married all those years. They never fought about anything. The only thing they ever disagreed on was moving to Hawaii. He had tried for years to convince her how much fun living in Hawaii would be. They would only have to work part-time; they would have his pension to spend together. They could raise their youngest daughter in warm Hawaii, where she could learn to surf. He would be free of the chronic pain in his neck and shoulders.

Four years ago, she told him she was not moving to Hawaii. Two-years ago she made it clear the physical chemistry between them was over. She wouldn't even hold his hand anymore. But he thought they would go their separate ways as friends, maybe even get back together someday after a few months of separation. Twenty-seven-years is a lot of forward momentum. But Tanya had grown colder the more he got warmer about the idea of moving to Maui.

She had her own career, her own retirement savings. He never thought she would try to steal his. How mean was this person? Maybe he never knew her at all, until today. She must figure she has to write such junk about him in court documents to win her case. With this one envelope full of painful, poisoned words, she had run up her true colors: white crossbones and a skull with a death grin, on a black flag.

Random cars stopped near him in the post office parking lot. He sat there on the curb like a statue dedicated to the broken-hearted dreamers who used to believe in love.

He didn't leave in the middle of the night and abandon her. They sold their home on the golf course, paid off their remaining mortgage and split what was left. She drove him to the airport the day he flew to Maui and kissed him goodbye. He asked her one last time to come with him. She had turned away and never looked back. He had watched her walk through the airport, treasuring every moment he could still see her, until she disappeared in the crowd. This was Hawaii's fault. These balmy islands had stolen his heart; he had to go back to them.

A couple of Myna birds landed at his feet. A small dove landed on his head. He sat still as a statue; couldn't move if he tried.

He helped Tanya move into the condo in Bellevue. She got all their furniture, and the Pontiac convertible. He bought new front tires for that car before he left, so she would be safer on the rainy winter roads. That's not abandonment. He was a supportive husband and loving dad. It deeply hurt to read that she called him a terrible father. This wasn't his sweet Tanya writing. This was some slime-ball attorney spicing it up, trying to piss him off and start a long court battle to produce high fees. The message they both sent was deadly clear.

She doesn't want 'you anymore, but she still wants your money. Worse, she knows that when she gets your pension she

*will have destroyed your happy, 'let's move to Hawaii dream.'
A dream you wanted to share with her. If she wins this and
gets your pension you're gonna be a homeless person over
here.* His inner crime-strategist is pasting the picture together.

He read on. In the scary small print that followed all those
pages of lies, there was an important instruction to the
Defendant (him).

*"If the Defendant or his counsel does not appear in court on
the appointed date, the court will rule in favor of the Plaintiff."*

*Yikes! By scheduling a court hearing with short notice, Tanya
and her merciless attorney are planning a 'shock and awe'
attack and will win all the marbles by default in five days! You
gotta think brah, you gotta do something!* This crime collage
was pasting together like a train robbery plot.

Ole, stood up so quickly the dove let go a load and flew
away. Uncle went dizzy and nearly fell over. It felt like Tanya
had kicked him in the stomach. He couldn't breathe. He sat
back down and tried to slowly inhale. It took longer than
usual, due to the fact, that he was only 61% sober. His yoga
training took over, he remembered to exhale completely, only
then could he pull in a full breath of air. By eventually taking
control of his breath, he gained some control of his emotions.
His vision and his thoughts cleared for a moment.

You need a good attorney brah. Betta' get one right now. His
mind was done pasting the picture together. It was worse than
a train-robbery. It was a photograph of trench warfare from
World War One.

24

His Good Ole Buddy, The Lawyer

Ole knew only one attorney in Seattle, an old sailing buddy, Ben Haller. They had crewed together on Ben's San Juan 28 in club regattas. He found Ben's number still in his cell phone. With one shaking finger he punched the speed dial key. Of course, Ben was out of the office, so Ole left a brief message on his voice mail,

"Ben, call me. It's Ole, Ole Gold. This is urgent. I'm on a starboard tack with a privateer on a port tack, it's a collision course. I need you law man, call me asap." And he left his number.

As Ole leafed through the pages of divorce palapala (legal documents) one more time, something snapped inside him like a dry stick. He was no longer married. It was over. His warm heart fire for Tanya blew out; all that remained was ice, cold, broken ice. He didn't want a war, but the first shots had been fired. Instead of simply drifting apart from Tanya he was going to have to fight her. She knows he can't afford a court battle. She's the strategist. All the mud she's slung on these pages paint him a villain. Any judge reading her statement would hate him. He had to be there in person to defend himself.

His next call was American Airlines, to book a flight to Seattle next week. He wasn't going to call Island Wings Airlines. He barely survived that turbulent landing, the free Mai-tais weren't that great, and his guitar case was crushed. A small injustice compared to this, but he wasn't going to fly with them ever again, unless there was no choice. Turned out American was all booked up, so was Alaska Air and United. Island Wings still had a few first-class seats available arriving at six a.m. Wednesday morning and only two-thousand-six hundred dollars, round trip.

That number brought him to the threshold of his sober senses and Ole knocked to see if anyone was home. When plain old, 'Common' answered the door, he realized he should not book anything until he talked to his attorney. He tried to keep breathing slowly, but his heart was in a panic. He'd never been sued; never been in a court room in his life. He rubbed some of the bird crap out of his hair. Uncle was trapped in a nightmare in broad daylight. What else could go wrong today?

He knew better than to ask that question. Within seconds of such stupidity, a black water-balloon of tropical rain rolled swiftly down the mountains and drenched him like a barrel of Gatorade after losing the Super Bowl. Ole ran for his car through the pouring rain.

Do you get wetter running in the rain or walking? Even at only 63% sober his inner coach still had a sense of humor.

Uncle wasn't laughing when he shook the locked handle of his car door.

Locked out? The voice isn't joking anymore, either.

He stood there in the shower for a few stupid seconds trying to find his keys in his pockets. No keys. Maybe he locked them in the car?

Well your hair is getting a good wash, look for the acceptance of it all, dumb ass. That Zen comedian in his head just won't shut up.

The last thing he remembers is getting his mail out of his post office box and then the divorce bomb went off. That's it!

You left your keys in the mail box again; you're showing your age, old man.

Ole ran back under the covered lanai of the post office. His three keys were dangling there in the ignition of his mail box door, which was hanging open. Uncle shook the water off his face and hands and locked the mailbox.

Now, get into some dry clothes and sober up so you can play your gig tonight at the PI. Coach sounds just like his mother sometimes.

Getting sober would be easy compared to escaping this legal grenade. Its five day 'pin' had been pulled.

Ben Haller didn't call back. Ole watched the Monsoon come down. The rain gave the sidewalks that steaming wet cement smell that used to make him happy. Today the rain smelled like the bird crap running down his face.

But there, rising over the Maui Mountains defying all sadness, was the most beautiful rainbow Uncle had ever seen. It shouted, 'Hope' just like the one Noah beheld right after he ran aground. But at 64% sober Ole's eyes were two burnt holes in a wool blanket. Stinging bird doo-doo was blearing out all the bright colors of Hope.

When the rain let up a little, he walked to his car and unlocked it. He got in slowly, stiff as a hundred-year-old statue, and getting stiffer by the minute. He leaned his marble head on the Cadillac's steering wheel and as the rain began to drum louder on the roof of the car he cried until he felt worse.

25

Voodoo Doll

Ole sobered enough to get into dry clothes and arrive at the PI on time. The Friday night crowd was a happy bunch. He tried to pump up his vibe to match their breezy vacation moods. It wasn't easy. He struggled to smile, he struggled to breathe. His guitar was in perfect tune, but to Ole's anger-addled brain, it sounded bad all evening. After he forgot some of the words to his own songs and missed some chords, he played flute instrumentals until eight o'clock, packed his gear and left in a hurry.

The next morning, he could not get out of bed. He wasn't hung over this time. He hadn't had a drink in well over twenty-three hours and fifteen minutes. This time he was paralyzed by his emotions. What a difference twenty-three hours could make. One day ago, he was just disappointed by pretty, blue-eyed Coco flying away, petite Bethany being a smoker and Peggy Sue using him for a free dinner and to make her fiancé jealous. Still Uncle had felt hopeful. Life in Hawaii was wonderful. His small disappointments with women, were nothing compared to this sinister divorce destruction spinning like a tornado, closer every hour.

Today, he was more than angry, he was sad and he was scared. It was an awful mix. It was like being in Edgar Allan Poe's fearsome story. He was strapped down in a pit of worry. The sharp fact that Tanya might win the fight was the swinging pendulum. It was a blade swinging lower with every passing

126

second. It was terribly 'Poe-etic.' He tried to sleep but that horrible pun was keeping him awake. He tried to get up and do some Tai Chi. He tried to get up and go pee. He was so under the mud he couldn't move his head or his cold feet.

This was no happy hangover. This was some deep, dark Voodoo. When he did breathe it hurt like hell. He could imagine Tanya pushing a long, thin hat pin into the chest of the stuffed doll she'd named Oliver. She had packed shave ice on the doll's feet and hands; he was shivering. It felt like there was a two-inch long ice pick stabbing him repeatedly in the back and a ten-inch long wine press screwing down on his wallet. She didn't want to kill him. That would stop the flow of cash she was counting on. But she did want him to suffer.

How could she torture him like this? He didn't want to think angry thoughts back at her. He knew what the Buddha taught,

"Taking revenge on someone is like drinking poison and expecting the other person to die."

He didn't want Tanya to die. He wanted her to be happy. How is it possible that a divorce fight over money could make her happier than moving to Hawaii and spending the money with him? It was so confusing and hurtful and just plain sad. His cell phone rang. One hand pulled free from the ice and found his phone.

"Umf?" He couldn't even talk.

"Ahoy Uncle Ole, you Okay? It's me, Big Ben getting' back to ya. I couldn't return your call yesterday. I was in court all day making a ton of money, ha, ha, hah." The same old Ben, only

127

his lawyer joke wasn't funny this time.

"Tanya is divorcing me Ben." Ole spit it out. The words tasted like dirt.

"She has fired a full broadside of cannon into me. I need you by my side in court next Wednesday at ten a.m."

"Damn sailor, that's awful news." Ben sounded sincere this time. "It's awful short notice too, in fact that's illegal short-notice since you now live out of state. I can get you a thirty to ninety-day extension and give us time to work on your defense. Fax me what she filed, every page. I'll take care of it. And I won't charge you my full fee. I'll knock it down to two-hundred an hour. That's the best I can do. The firm I'm with won't send me to a lunch briefing for less than that."

"Thanks Ben, what's your fax number?"

And so, with defensive action taken at last, Uncle was able to get out of bed and limp to the bathroom to pee. Instead of his normal fire hose pressure he peed a thin stream like a little old man, for the first time in his life.

26

Ms. Tracie

The first real date he had from someone he met online, was with Tracie from California. She was thirty-eight, and had been writing to Uncle on and off for about three weeks. Her photo was great, a lovely Asian woman, height and weight proportional. She seemed a good match, interested in music, fine art and literature. She looked sophisticated, a very classy dresser in all her pictures. She sent him a message saying she would be flying over to meet him in person in a week. He's thinking, *hey yah... maybe this online dating thing will work after all.*

Uncle typed some questions to Tracie on his desktop computer. He offered to pick her up at the airport... no, she wanted to rent her own car. Cautious is a good thing in online dating. *Okay... she's smart, good looking and cautious. Did she have somewhere to stay?* Yes, her friend owns a condo at the Royal Kahana so, has offered to let her stay there. *Whoa, that's only a half-mile from where I live.*

A week went by, Tracie called Uncle when she got settled in at the Royal. After some random small talk, she surprised him.

"Let me take you out to dinner Ole. How about tomorrow night. Pick you up at seven."

"Sounds fun, where we going?"

"You'll see when we get there."

"Oooo, a mysterious first date? I like it." Uncle was intrigued. "I'm really looking forward to meeting you in person, Tracie." He gave her his address. "See you then."

At exactly seven-o'clock, Tracie drove up to Yu'layne's house in a rental car, but not your average rental car. This was a black Thunderbird convertible, the new one that looks like the nineteen-fifty-five series, which had been Ole's dream car ever since he was a kid. He always wanted to drive or just ride in one of those old classics but never got the chance. He opened the door of this new retro-sports car and there's Tracie, a living doll. She is stunningly beautiful, like a model, wearing a sleek black mini-dress with a Asian-style high collar, slim, long legs, a little make-up, not too much, a little light perfume, not too much.

I'd like to test drive you too, he's thinking as he clips on the seat belt of the leather passenger seat. It never ceases to amaze him how life can be shaped by envisioning what you want. Sometimes you get everything you wish for and more, like a hot Asian date and ride in a Thunderbird convertible.

He tried to remember the last time a woman took him out to dinner, maybe never. Tracie eases down the quiet street, but turning on to Highway 30, she punches it up to seventy and heads for Lahaina eight miles away. More happy small talk, a few good laughs and moments of unsaid strong mutual attraction soon found them walking down Front Street, holding hands. Free electrons were at work all around them, spinning and connecting, heating up a catalyst in his heart and his pants. Ole's geek mind was trying to name this raging chemical feeling.

You could call it, 'Lust-helium' or 'Hydro-Asia-sexscilica' either way, you patent this and you win the Nobel prize for coolest first-date ever.

"Ok Tracie, where're we going?" Ole asked.

"Kimo's."

"Great choice, been there?" he was blustering a little, he'd never been there, way too expensive for his twenty-eight dollar a day budget.

"Ole, I've been to every restaurant in town over the years. Kimo's is always, my first choice."

The cute, skinny Filipina hostess at Kimo's seated them upstairs at a cozy candle-lit table overlooking the diners on the lower level and the ocean beyond. Along the railing there were tiki torches burning. It was way after sunset, but there was still a reddish romance blushing the sky. Ole was thrilled to be in this classy place with such a hot-looking date. They made small talk about the sunset and the magic of Hawaii. He watched her mannerisms. Her gestures were natural, not posed or over animated. Tracie was sophisticated, alright. Ole could see she was pleased with him as well. They both knew what they wanted. It wasn't dinner.

Tracie ordered a glass of California Chablis. Ole asked for Bacardi Gold and Coke. They each chose the same entree, Mahi-mahi, grilled. Everything was perfect. While they waited

131

they ate each other's smiles with their hungry eyes.

Tracie held Uncle's hand. His thrill meter revved all the way up into the red zone.

This is more like it brah. His inner Romeo wants to burst into a love song right there in the restaurant he's so turned on by this Asian doll. He keeps his cool, maybe he'll sing under her balcony later tonight.

Tracie began to tell him her story. She lived in Los Angeles near Ventura. She came to Maui every six months or so, whenever she got mad at her husband. Uncle removed his hand from Tracie's lovely long fingers.

"You're married?" He hadn't been this shocked since Coco left and Peggy Sue changed her name and became engaged.

"You've been chatting with me online as a single for three weeks and you forgot to mention *that* little detail?"

"You know, it's a very unhappy situation for me," she replied in a matter of simple facts sort of way.

"What's wrong with you? If your marriage means so little to you, just state in your profile, that you are married, seeking an affair. I am certain you would attract the kind of men you are looking for."

Uncle was pissed. Not that his moral ground was much higher than Tracie's. He was still legally married, but he was guiltless about starting over. His divorce was inevitable. With a deceiver like Tracie, any kind of relationship would be a waste of time.

Ole realized he was being used again. He felt so much anger that he was afraid to touch the table. His built up sexual frustration might cause the whole place to burst into flames. He shut up and started deep breathing. Yoga is practicing deliberate self-control. He tried to smile, couldn't do it.

Don't judge her brah, you don't know her pain. Maybe her divorce is about to be filed and she too feels unwanted. His Buddha mind reminding him that other people's truth is unknowable. *She owns her drama, you own yours. What're you gonna do now?*

There was no confusion in his thoughts. Maybe other men would take this kind of easy opportunity. He ate his free, grilled fish dinner, tasting every bite. Tracie went on to explain that she loved her husband, she just got mad at him sometimes and had to get away to their condo at the Royal here on Maui. She tried to explain how she needed the excitement of an occasional tryst to keep her sane. Ole wondered how crazy you have to be to claim you're 'sane.' They finished eating in silence. He was over his anger, but this date was over too.

"Let's go," he said softly. It was still a beautiful night. It was a good dinner with a sexy, rich woman. He tried to adjust his attitude to accept it as it is.

Every moment is a treasure brah. Occupy the present.

She drove him home. It was a very quiet ride but he found the fun in it. He's in a beautiful sports car with the top down on a warm winter night in Hawaii. He tried to convince himself he was happy enough for one evening. He couldn't do it. The truth was too powerful. He was horny as a bull-elk in Yellowstone Park during a rut concert. He'd met Michelle, Setko, Coco, Bethany, Peggy-Sue / Penny, and now Tracie... still no magic. Well Coco was wonderful magic, the kissing kine. But single life on this romantic island, was making him crazy. If he'd planned on being celibate the rest of his life, he would have retired to a monastery, not Maui.

When Tracie drove up in front of Yu'layne's house, Ole thanked her for dinner and said good night. He was careful not to touch her as he got out of the car. Kissing her good night would have lit a California wildfire. Beautiful, almost perfect Tracie drove away in that black Thunderbird convertible. He wanted her. She would be willing and thrilling tonight, but he couldn't do it. His luck finding a girlfriend was a jinxed roller coaster; lots of anticipation on the first slow climb, a fast curve thrown at the top and then a screaming drop into a wake-up splash of soaking disappointment.

He needed to think. He needed a drink. Ole walked to the Sand's of Kahana beach bar to soak his head in a bucket of rum. The one drink at Kimo's was just a tease. He needed a few more. He needed to think. But as he sipped his Bacardi-sugar-cane on the rocks, once again, it hurt to think.

27

The two Maui Rules

At least life in Hawaii was warm. His neck and shoulder pains went away or maybe they were insignificant compared to the knife wounds of evil divorce words. *Stupid love, stupid, stupid love. Life is harder if y'er stupid.* John Wayne was right. Meeting and dating women in Hawaii were teaching him stuff. Sometimes it was stuff he'd rather not learn. Tracie was fishing online for a local boy-toy when she started writing to him. What a marriage those two must have. It made his marriage seem even more valuable, at least to him.

He swirled the ice on the empty bottom of his third, 'think'. He'd heard people here on Maui, occasionally mention the 'Two Rules'. He didn't know about these rules before he arrived. When he did hear them, he remembered the two simple rules Jesus taught a couple thousand years ago. His Dad and Mom had passed the wisdom on to him. Anything that's handed down over one-hundred generations of parents is an heirloom worth holding close to your heart and passing on to your kids. The Hawaiian version was interesting:

Rule One: Be kind to people. Be compassionate, be patient, be helpful, be open to happiness, embrace opportunities. He wanted to embrace Tracie, but he did not want a girlfriend or heaven forbid, a wife like that. Uncle ordered another rum drink, this time without the Coca-Cola. Dollar the bartender frowned at him. Dollar was another mystery. But he could wait.

Rule Two: Try to give more than you take. Hawaii is populated by givers, volunteers, lovers and friends of all races, willing to learn from each other and share what they have. Don't hold back, pass on a random kindness and expect nothing in return. He finished the rum and left a five-dollar tip on the bar. His emotions were messing up his logic. He couldn't afford to leave a five-dollar tip. He left it anyway. He wanted another drink but Dollar was ignoring him, watching some football re-runs and frowning. Ole picked up the five-dollar bill and stuffed it back in his shirt pocket.

Uncle thought about the, 'rules'. They say that if you move to Maui with a bad attitude and break these rules, the island will chew you up and spit you back to the mainland. Obey the two rules and doors open, blessing you with new friends and new opportunities. Your days become filled with happy moments one after another. Social chemistry kicks in and you meet the people you are supposed to meet.

Ignore the rules, and your path will be blocked with 'pilikia' (trouble). Your own bad karma will start kicking you around so hard your numbered days on Maui might go something like this:

You'll get a speeding ticket, because you think it's cool to break the rules. The officer's slow ticket writing makes you late for work so you lose one of your jobs. You can't find another job but you need two jobs to pay your rent. The rent goes up. Never mind, you don't have to pay increased rent because your landlord just sold your condo to someone else. You must move out. You can't find a nice, affordable place.

You find an expensive place with barking dogs and roosters crowing next door. You don't know anyone with a pickup truck that can help you move because you haven't bothered to be nice to anybody, so you have no friends. You rent a moving truck for one day. You hurt your back lifting your sofa / hide-a-bed by yourself. Your rental truck is too small for all your stuff. It takes two days of truck rental instead of one. You lose the truck keys. The replacement set costs a hundred bucks. Someone steals your bike. Your old car breaks down. It costs a thousand dollars to fix it, so you nearly max-out a credit card, paying more to repair the car than it's worth. You have a flat tire the next day. It costs sixty dollars to repair the tire. A week later, you have two flat tires. You totally Leo your credit card buying two new tires for the front of your junk car and on and on.

That is the kind of pilikia (trouble) you get for breaking the rules. Uncle had met several drifters here in Lahaina, who were selfish, mean people. They moved here to stay, but couldn't live by rules and had to return to the mainland.

Their lives back home didn't get any better: They returned to their hometowns in Chicago or Detroit, back to jobs they hate. Only now their seniority is gone forever. The co-workers they stepped on as they climbed the company ladder years ago, are now their supervisors. They find themselves shoveling snow for hours to get their car out of the driveway to go to the job they no longer want. They slip on the ice and sprain an ankle, hurt their backs and slide their cars off the road.

Another ice storm the next day and they slide into the back of police car. Their car insurance has lapsed. Big fine.

Expensive damage. During the summer they swelter in the insufferable one-hundred-degree humidity and get bit by a thousand and five mosquitoes, They struggle to breathe, they sneeze and cough all the time due to some allergic reaction to all the pollen in the air and eventually die, still mean, selfish and unhappy.

Uncle thought about pretty Tracie and all this pilikia stuff. He still had her number in his cell phone. He finally got Dollar's attention away from the world of flat-screen football. He told the moody old bartender about Tracie.

"Hah? You want me to feel sorry for you? That's funny." But he wasn't smiling. "Maybe you're not young anymore, but you're rich and single. I wish I had your problems and you had mine."

"Careful what you wish for," laughed Uncle, not feeling rich or single. But, Dollar was right. Dollar was so right. Life was good. He finally got to Hawaii. He lived in a million-dollar home, and was starting his life over, dating interesting, 100% crazy, beautiful women.

"How about enough sympathy fo' bring one rum ova hea," he tried some pidgin on Dollar.

"Okay Uncle, but if you ever whine at me again about anything, I'm gonna charge you double to drink in here."

"I been looking for another bar anyway. Some place with a beautiful, happy girl for a barkeep instead of a grumpy old man."

They both had a good, insincere laugh and Uncle Ole got his rum.

Dollar went back to watching football. Ole pretty much forgot what Tracie looked like. He deleted her number from his phone. He didn't see any of his local drinking buddies or Peggy Sue. It was a tourist bar, so there were new faces here every week. He drank alone and didn't bother to count his drinks. Some nights like this one, he went over his twenty-eight-dollar a day survival budget. When the bar closed at midnight, he left the five-spot on the bar for Dollar. He couldn't afford to leave it, but as soon as he did, instead of feeling poor and on a thin budget, he felt rich and generous. He waited by the resort's grand portico for a while, but his limousine driver didn't pick him up so he wasn't as rich as he felt and had to walk and crawl home again.

28

Friday's Dream / Lao Tzu

A chilling rain shower was falling through Uncle's lanai window. He shivered himself awake, shook his wet face and rolled over a couple of turns out of the cool rain.

Sweet, sweet blessing, smells so fine, I love dis' place, his inner voice chuckles and he's back to snoring again.

Uncle smacks his lips. He's a dream child back in Iowa at Grandma Edna's house. She's making Spam sandwiches for lunch. She slices the white Wonder Bread diagonally, the way he likes it. There are Bread and Butter pickles on the side of the plate.

The plates are Tutu's antique China. Some have been broken and glued, proof of their history and value. Grandma chose one without cracks or chips for her Ole. It's one of her few remaining undamaged plates, a gesture of love and trust. She knows he likes her fine China. Blue landscapes are glazed onto each one. This one has distant blue mountain tops and blue trees painted on blue hillsides. There are hunched-over Chinese men carrying blue umbrellas and lanterns through the white plate's blue village.

Ole walks the path by the river, it's always snowing here. Snow falls all around him and on his face. The snow feels so real, he shivers. The path leads across China to mysterious, future places far up in the mountains. His feet are warm, even though he's barefoot. His feet look bigger now; he's a grown man again. His robes are white as the snow on his shoulders.

He meets someone, an older man, walking the same path with measured easy movement. Of course, it's Lao Tzu. Master Tzu wears a richly embroidered robe and hood that hides his face and eyes but not his long white beard. There is snow on his shoulders also. They walk side by side and quietly climb the wide steps of a bridge that arches over a blue and white river. Master Tzu stops on the bridge and turns. Now Uncle can see into his calm, brown eyes.

"Your path is long my son."

"What do you see master?"

Lao Tzu stares far away over Uncle's shoulder. His eyes glazed over in a trance. Then he speaks with awe in his voice,

"I see rainbows in your life. Like blessings, they lead you by day. Their ghosts inspire you by night."

Uncle has dream questions. They rise up like word balloons, over his sleeping head, each one filled with Chinese writing and shaped like big question marks, red? yellow? green? The balloons float out over the snowy hills and then,

"Pop! Bang! Boom!" The balloons are popping, and Uncle wakes up.

Chapter 29

Red Cardinals

The popping and banging turned into the loudest trumpeting this side of New Orleans. It was crazy loud. Ole opened his good eye. There was no trumpet player in his room. There was just one bright red Cardinal outside his window singing like a rock star.

"Why trumpet in my window, bird brain? All these homes and windows and you pick *my* window?"

Yer talkin' to a bird, dude. You think he's gonna talk back to you? You're the bird brain.

The Cardinal kept yelling louder, right there, two short branches up from where the three love doves were doing the "Wooly Bully" again with wild abandon. Old King Cardinal can't stop calling out to the whole world,

"Ker cheep-cheep- cheep- cheep- cheep- cheep- cheep..." Repeat, "pete- pete- pete- pete- pete- pete- pete," again and again and again.

Uncle pulls two pillows over his head. He surrenders to bad thoughts. *Note to self: Buy a bee-bee gun. How much bad karma could that possibly be? One little bee-bee shot to the bird butt, not a real bullet. Not much pilikia, shoot red bird in the rear, scare him away, small bad karma, maybe get red lights all the way to Lahaina some morning, small punishment yah? So worth it.*

Ole yells at the red bird,

"Gwywan na way!" he threatens in his best gruff voice.

And so the Cardinal stays where he is, and keeps on repeating his song even louder. Oliver doesn't hate birds, but this one won't quit bragging his stuff. Reaching around his bed now, looking for something to throw, Ole finds his water bottle. Ah, so thirsty. But he can't get his fingers to work off the plastic cap.

So, Jim, your mission, should you choose to accept it, is to disguise yourself as James Bond 007, disarm the locked water bottle, quench your thirst and save the world from the evil, red agent, 'Octo-Cardinal'. His coach is such a comedian. *This tape will self-destruct in five seconds.*

It takes a little over two whole minutes for Ole 007 to get the bottle cap unscrewed. He slakes his throat with cleansing waterfalls of Hydrogen^2 and Oxygen. All his shriveled chakras revive and bloom into seven big yellow Hibiscus. His solar plexus now filled with happy Hydrogen becomes a sea of Chi. He stops drinking before he finishes the last slosh in the bottle. *Need ballast to throw.*

He rolls to one side and is about to pitch a fast bottle-ball at that red bird up the side of his beak when he hears a female Cardinal's song. It's sweeter, lighter and more beautiful. Her clear notes go skipping across the morning air like a child skipping over a bridge. The male bird drops an octave, husky and low, no longer a trumpet, more like a soft baritone. The female's call goes fluting high above with perfect counterpoint. Their beautiful love song, sung for generations down through time, maybe millions of years. How could he think of shooting them? They're musicians. *'And ne'er was piping so sad, and ne'er was piping so gay.'* Ole remembers a line from one of his favorite Yeats poems as he drifts backwards into sleep.

30

Same Friday at 32,000 Feet

Desiree Lee Scarlioni stretched her sexy legs as far as the economy class United Airlines seat would allow... never quite far enough. The two young Marines that sat on either side of her enjoyed the view. Her skirt traveled north as her long bare legs went south. Perfect thighs, smooth skin, nice tan, pretty, little bare feet with each toenail painted a classy light purple with some kind of white design on it. Too far to see and they didn't care about her toes anyway.

The boldest marine brushed the back of his hand along her knee,

"First time to Maui?" he asked.

She pressed her knee against his hand, or maybe that was another stretch.

"Yes," she lied, "where should I start?"

The shy Marine found his voice first and answered,

"Great snorkeling,"

Desiree ignored him. She turned to the one with the adventurous hand.

"What do you think?"

"Lunch first. Mama's Fish House, you and me."

He placed his hand right on her beautiful bare knee and gave a squeeze. For the last six hours of the flight from San Fran' he had been inhaling her shampooed scent. He had memorized glimpses of her lovely face in that black forest of hair. Just sitting next to her, his brain was addled by the effect she had on him. She seemed interested during all the nonsense small talk they had shared on the flight. Now she leaned into him, her lips almost touching his ear.

"Can you handle it?"

"With both hands," he whispered back, his lips kissing her ear.

The Boeing 769's tires smacked the short runway with three tremendous slams followed by the scream of its jet engines thrown into reverse under severe protest. Once the pilot got her stopped, the telescoping walkway extended out and poked itself into the jet's passenger entry. The big Boeing aircraft gave a happy shudder. The long awaited, "Ping" announced the seat belt light was turned off. All the aisle passengers tried to rise and unbend. You could almost hear their backs popping as they stood up for the first time in hours.

Leo, the Marine with the roaming hands stood and backed up for Desiree to stand in the aisle along-side of him. Male and female passengers alike stared at the big Marine and the Italian fashion model with the purple mini-skirt. She had that kind of celebrity pose that demands attention. As she reached up to the overhead compartment, her mini-skirt rose up higher revealing her round butt cheeks and purple panties. She struggled to free her jammed travel valise. The bold Marine put his right hand on the middle of her back. With his left he pulled down her heavy bag, as effortlessly as if it were a paper-back book. With her purple jacket and big purple purse on top of her wheeled purple carry-on, she was the most glamorous woman the Marines had ever seen. She was pin-up magazine perfect. Everyone near her was content to sit still and watch.

"What's your name soldier?" granting him a pout of a smile.

"Leo Mam' and I am not a soldier. I'm a Marine. And yours?"

"Desiree Lee, and I'm not a Mam."

Standing so close together gave them both a thrill, she put one arm around his trim middle and gave him a light hug. His blood began to pump in his ears and lower.

"And I'm Frankie." The shy marine hesitating, but determined to meet this doll. She ignored him again and was already moving down the aisle ahead of bold Leo.

Not much later, Leo looked like Desiree's personal sentry as he pulled her five matching purple suit cases from the slowly turning luggage wheel. He stacked them on her push cart.

"Staying long on Maui?" He asked.

"A whole week," she lied again.

Wisely, Sergeant Leo held his tongue and the luggage remark he was thinking. Instead he said,

147

"Too bad your toenail polish doesn't *quite* match your suitcases."

"Ha hoot ha hah," she laughed a little too loud. .

"Oh, and I so hoped no one would notice. I'm usually more careful." She apologized and he-hawed another laugh.

"I'd bet you're hungry. How about lunch?"

Always the heart-breaker, Desiree made that 'ooo' shape with her mouth that women do, before they say, no. She leaned closer, gave Leo a sisterly kiss on his one-day beard and turned for the rental cars.

"Sorry, meeting someone, Ta tah."

Leo's shoulders slumped like a kicked puppy and even Frankie, ever in his shadow, frowned with shy pain.

31

Same Friday / One Slippa

Awake, if not yet coherent, Oliver is searching his room for some landmarks to steer by. He finds the clock on his desk, one-thirty pm. *What? It's afternoon?* Last night must have been amazing. He vaguely remembers singing,

"One tequila, two tequila, tree tequila... floor! Ha, ha, hah."

OooKaaay... so much for getting an early start, Coach sounds confused. *What's on Friday? Something on Friday, what was it?* Even smarty-pants inner voice has no clue this time. There's still some tequila burping out his nostrils.

"I don't' even remember drinking tequila last night." He whispers too loud.

You gotta get up and get going. You need some breakfast, need lunch. Nah, you missed breakfast and lunch, brah. Gotta get going, or yer gonna miss supper, ha ha hah. Gotta get going, you sing at the PI tonight. Gotta be sharp, not B flat, ha ha hah. Gotta sober up, gotta drive to town. Whoa tiger, first you gotta pee. The bossy 'gotta-voice' in his head just won't shut up.

Uncle is coming around. His face is moving around anyway. The sweet Cardinals are still singing like stars in a Walt Disney video. Macho Dove is done shakin' his two girlfriends in the bushes. It's' a beautiful Maui day, what's left of it. He pushes off the edge of the bed. The two explosions that burst painfully into his ears are his big feet hitting the floor. His knees, hips and all the rest follow him up with a stagger and he blunders out his slider door onto the lanai. The Cardinals and Doves all fly away.

"Ex-scuse me, little bird buddies." He laughs out loud and hears his own deep voice. Ole feels so good he could sing. He tries... "Runnzzwhudda bozza nova," no can.

Brilliant sunlight is making a big loud splash all over his lanai like too much white paint. The wood deck is really painted red and it's red hot. It's burning his bare feet.

"Hoo'yah! Where's my rubba-slippas?" He yells.

Focusing one eye like a binocular, Uncle hops back into his room. He sees one slippa by the bed. The other one's gone missing. Uncle swings his head looking around for the lost sandal. He swings a little too fast. Whoops! The lanai, the bushes and the ceiling go spinning with the momentum. Gravity wins, champion of all hangovers, it pulls supreme. Ole goes down like a tree falling on its back on the rolling hills of his bed. Clouds of bed dust pouf into the sunlight and drift in little motes that grow wings like tiny flying monkeys and flap away out his window. Nobody can enjoy a hangover the way Uncle Ole can.

32

Un-Busy Bees

All the tiny, flying monkeys were gone. The fallen trunk of Uncle Ole is enjoying the planetary embrace of gravity. He laid there so long that mosses and lichens were starting to grow on him, welcoming him home to restful compost. It was an earthy feeling. Gravity held him tight, like his own mother giving him a welcome hug.

You should call y'er mother brah, that mysterious voice still in his head.

Since moving around too much seemed hilariously impossible, he decided to give Newton's law of potential energy a test. He held his breath and waited. Nothing moved. Success, he was 100% potential. It was a great feeling. *Now, how do I start the kinetic engine?* He wondered. He had no clue, no starter button, no spark plugs, he rested there like an abandoned car almost rusted completely into the hillside.

At least his eyes could still move without making him dizzy. He watched a few honey bees flying around some yellow Be-Still Flowers outside his window. They were happy little bees, turning in lazy circles like the nothing thoughts in his sleepy head. Maybe they were retired bees like him with 'Mead'-ium size hangovers. Un-busy bees, pidgin-slangin' each other,

"Why hurry buzzin cousin'? We got all day, yah? Let's cruise ova and check out the cute chick bees. We get da flower juice

later brah, ha hah."

The wind blows, the bees buzz. Ole's so content, lying in bed on a Friday morning, 'er rather, afternoon, no job, no hurry, no painful hangover, no worry, no place to go until tonight.

Moments of contentment like this never seem to last long enough. Since he was feeling so peaceful, of course a distant alarm began to ring for attention far away under the stairs in a broom closet in the basement of his mind. There was something important he was supposed to do today. In another three seconds the alarm quit ringing.

Hey- hey- hey, how about those Seattle Sea Hawks? Ha ha hah. I wonder how much gold's left in Fort Knox? Where's my otha rubba slippa? His mind is hanging looser eva'day.

33

Same Friday / This Mash-Up

Ms. Desiree Lee and all her purple luggage were helped into the Hertz shuttle van by a handsome twenty-something Filipino driver. As he pulled away from the curb, instead of looking to clear for traffic, he was staring in his rearview mirror at the gorgeous Italian model. She was sitting in the center of the back seat with her long legs stretched out in front of her. He could see a small purple color spot under her mini-skirt that in high school, boys called a beaver shot.

There was a sudden loud crash like busted glass and the shuttle bus shook like a bomb went off. The driver had hit the side of a passing Alamo shuttle van. His driver's mirror burst into flying pieces of shrapnel and its metal support dug a long nasty gouge into the side of the other shuttle. Everything came to a stop.

The doors of both vans opened automatically and all the passengers got out. Confusion took over with lots of angry shouting, some nervous laughter and lots of heads shaking.

Desiree Lee strode right up to the two angry shuttle drivers and as she approached they stopped yelling at each other and stood staring at "Her Royal Purpleness".

"Gentlemen, could you be so kind as to discuss this little mash-up later? I have a very important meeting at one-o'clock and I'm sure these other people have places to go as well."

Then she smiled her beautiful Hollywood smile. Those drivers would have run and jumped into a shark tank if she had asked them to. They both apologized to the lovely doll and called for all passengers to get back in the vans. That was it. The shuttles rolled the half mile to the rental lots and the passengers applauded Miss Desiree's classy diplomacy.

The car she had reserved was a Hyundai Sonata. But the clerk behind the counter was the same driver who had seen the beaver so without hesitation, he upgraded her to a Mustang convertible. She thanked him with a kiss on the cheek and drove away, laying a patch of Mustang hoof marks all over the parking lot.

34

Same Friday / Yu'layne's Long Hallway

Mother Gravity finally eased up on Ole's fallen tree of a body. He could move his arms and legs. His awareness meter was reading a steady 21% sober again. He swung his feet over the side of the bed and covered his ears with his hands this time. The two dull thuds he heard and felt as his feet slammed the floor were bearable cannon shots. Standing up firm but hang loose this time, he turned his feet for balance. He became a Tai Chi master breathing in perfect rhythm, pushing clouds of confusion out with every deliberate exhale.

"Om mani pad mi hum," he whispered the six-syllable mantra.

Uncle was making progress. He didn't fall down this time. His extremely full bladder was pushing him toward the door. He found both slippas.

You amaze me, brah. Even his inner voice sounded more confident.

He gets his feet moving in kinetic energy patterns called walking and crosses the lanai into the shared kitchen. His need to pee pushes him right past the refrigerator where he usually stops and on into the long hallway. The hall has a kind of 'Alice in Wonderland' look going on this afternoon. The hall's walls were a chess board of sunlight squares and black empty boxes of shadow. The carpet had become a path of rose petals. He thought he saw playing cards painting the rose carpet red as it ran down the hall to a miniature bathroom door impossibly far away. He slowly moved his feet in the right direction.

Easy does it, Grasshopper, he hears his inner Tai Chi voice of caution. *One foot at a time like on that old Kung Fu show.* He's a Shaolin monk walking on red, rose-petal rice paper.

Uncle Ole was having a little trouble with Newton's laws of motion. He made it to the first door on the right and had to rest. Leaning against the wall he thinks kind thoughts about the two beautiful Chinese women that rent that small bedroom. Ling was the talkie-talk one. She told him her long Chinese name several times, but he could never pronounce it. So, he called her Ling. Ole has studied her beauty as if she were a living treasure. She reminds him of a porcelain China doll with a pretty, round face. She has beautiful black hair cut to shoulder length. Ling wears no make-up. doesn't need any to be beautiful. She likes to lounge around the house in sweat pants and a t-shirt with one bare shoulder showing. Her skin is a pretty shade of pale yellow-white. She has small dainty feet with no toenail polish. Ole leans on the wall. He's mesmerized by the image of her, not with sexual desire he tries to convince himself, more like appreciation for a work of very fine, Chinese art. Uh huh, it's a little confusing, especially this morning.

Liang, her roommate is the quiet one. But she's a walking sex bomb. Tall, slim and poised, she seems to be always posing. Maybe in her mind she's a model in a magazine photo shoot every minute of every day. She always wears the hottest fashions. She also wears too much make-up, so that gives her that hungry-model look. Thin, graceful Liang has the most

156

mysterious slant to her eyes. Somehow even her pointy elbows are sexy. Liang's lips are a tremendous temptation for Ole. They are those puffy, kiss-me looking lips. Several times when she was close in the kitchen, he almost leaned in for that kiss. He has not built up his courage yet, but thinks about this a lot. Liang's body heat adds ten degrees to any room with unspoken sexual innuendo.

The Chinese girls have come to Ole's gig at the Pioneer Inn twice this first month. They like his music. He likes them. They sleep 30 feet from his room every night. Some nights it's hard to fall asleep. Now, Ole listens through their door not stalking, just curious. There's no sound, no infrared heat coming through the walls. They probably left for work hours ago. The girls both graduated from some university in Scotland. They earned BA degrees in hotel management.

Yah, mega-rich mainland Chinese parents now send their girl children to Scotland colleges brah. Coach is not surprised.

Ling and Liang both speak English well enough to understand, once your ears dig through the Scottish-Chinese accents to what they are trying to say. All that education and they work the day shift, front desk at the Ritz Carlton for a few dollars over minimum wage. Go figure. But then he used to teach at Stanford and University of Washington but now he plays music in a bar for a hundred bucks a night and tips.

Don't judge people brah, and forget go figure, try go pee. That wise voice may be coming from his bladder.

He Tai Chi dances his feet further down the hall. On his left is the closed door to the master bedroom, the most expensive rental in the whole house. Antonio and Maria, an Italian couple live there. Cool, friendly, professional artists. He paints in acrylics, very beautiful paintings. She designs and sews together beautiful clothes. They seem to love each other. Ole likes them. Sometimes they cook gourmet meals and serve them out on the lanai to everyone on this level of the house.

The Chinese girls have also cooked for Uncle. But the attraction he feels when he's near them is so distracting he can hardly eat. They confuse him in a wonderful way.

Uncle turns around and stares back down the crazy hall; measuring the distance he's come so far. He focuses his eyes and figures it's a little under a half-mile back to the kitchen. Up at that end is one special door that's almost always closed. Once upon a time there was no door. The hallway opened into the living room of the house. Now it's walled up with the mystery door of closure. The landlady, Yu'layne rents every available room in her house and lives in her living room. No one goes in there.

Yu'layne also cooks for everyone from time to time. Ole learned she is fifty-one-years-old and looks like she is only thirty-five. Yu'layne goes to Yoga classes 4 times a week and can stand on her head out on the lanai for a long time. He never timed this, but she looks great upside down in a white bikini with her long legs stretched up into the air. Ole's head feels funny thinking about it this morning. It's that full bladder feeling. He's got piss for brains.

Why can't you walk down the hall and go pee?

The door of vast-relief appears almost full size now; he may have to duck his head to get inside if he gets there in time. It still seems a long way off.

I think maybe you should lighten up on the tequila shots, suggests his yoga coach.

He mans-up and walks with determination past the last hall door on the right. The young couple in that bedroom, almost never come out. As far as Uncle could tell they have no jobs and no friends. He saw them once in the kitchen and wondered who they were.

The door to the bathroom is unlocked. Victory! Soon, Uncle has showered, shaved and is hovering around 55% sober, he wraps up in a clean towel and almost runs back to his room.

35

Same Friday / Lunch Date

Miss Desiree Lee parked her Mustang convertible in the Foodland Grocery store's twenty-minute zone and hit the auto top button to raise the bonnet. She walked her breezy, runway-model walk as she cut across to the sidewalk. When she reached Starbucks on the corner, she slowed down. Starbucks is a place where you go to be seen. She liked to be seen. The old men chatting at the outdoor tables there could not stop staring; paper coffee cups burning their hands. The tourist crowds parted on the sidewalk like Moses had raised his staff. Her body heat added another ten degrees to Lahaina's eighty-six-degree streets. Lamp posts leaned like wax candles as she slowly burned by.

Her arrival at the entrance to Kimo's made a similar melt down. The skinny hostess who greeted her blushed deeply with jealousy because Desiree looked so amazing. When the waiter's saw her, they froze in the heat, trays like flying saucers over their heads, aprons blowing in circles around their waists, sweat running under their shirts. The bartender dropped the stack of white plates he'd just dried. Twelve China treasures hit the tile all at once. The explosive sound murdered the ambiance of the Friday lunch crowd. Everyone's eyes went to the bar and then to the tall Italian Sirocco posing there in the open double doorway. What an entrance. Lady Ga Ga couldn't have done it better.

There in the lobby of the restaurant an ocean breeze blew

Desiree's black hair around her face like a photo-shoot wind-machine. The fan set on soft breeze, loose and sexy. That single frame moment in time when beauty is stolen by a camera and survives for a month on some fashion magazine's page. This sort of celebrity entrance is not all that uncommon on Maui. Restaurant employees see this type of schmooze every week. But this woman was the "Celeb 'de Jour".

The slim hostess, recovering her normal tan, skin color, hesitated for a moment, then she led Desiree through the restaurant. She looked like a scared goat stumbling along a few feet in front of a magnificent Bengal Tiger. Anyone could see that terrible carnage was about to happen. The hostess led Miss Desiree to a small table for two near the bar. With a dramatic hand gesture toward a table set for four closest to the ocean, Desiree Lee whispered, but it sounded like a roar in the hushed restaurant,

"Over there."

The Hostess smiled meekly and on little goat feet, escorted "Her Majestic Purpleness" to her desired table, the one with the best ocean view and where everyone could see her. It was where you'd expect to see a movie star. The wait staff would re-tell the legend for many years of how the Tiki lamps by her table mysteriously lit themselves into flames and burned the entire time the hot Italian model sat there.

"Are you expecting someone to join you miss?" asked the red-faced hostess.

"No," she lied and then added, "thank you," with her brightest, insincere smile. *Where is he?* She looked around at

161

the other tables.

While seeming to study the tall menu and without being too obvious she stole a glance at her Lady Rolex Oyster knock-off. It was one-twenty-five. She was intentionally, breezily late for her one-o'clock date. She had planned to be care-free about it, a little apologetic but not too much. That's the only way to start a first date. She poker-faced her considerable disappointment, that her online chat mate from 'Strike-a-Match.com' was not already here, waiting anxiously to meet her in person. She expected to see him at a back table stewing impatiently in his own sex juices getting warmer by the minute. The kind of man juice she liked. She was very upset that he had missed her grand, late-arrival scene with the clashing cymbals of broken china plates. What a waste.

Where is he? Some nerve this guy. Her thoughts smashing into each other like atoms at Hanford. *He's late for a lunch date with me? Dressed like this? The drop-dishes-gorgeous, mini-skirted, four-inch high-heeled answer to every man's prayer. Me? Who flew all the way from California to meet this loser? Me? Who turned down a lunch date with two handsome Marines, seriously?*

Her skin was beginning to redden like a Minnesota tourist after one day in Hawaii. Desiree kept smiling on the outside, but she was a road flare burning red-shooting flames on the inside. White-hot coils of barbwire were turning painfully near the tips of her hard nipples. There was a vinegar taste on her lips. Her facial angst was bruising her perfect complexion. Her eye shadow was leaking down both cheeks. *Those weren't tears,* she told herself. *No way, just a sweaty awkward moment.*

She ordered her lunch and ate quickly there at the table with three empty chairs. She did not taste her food, never looked at the ocean or heard it. An hour passed. No show. She would have words with Mr. Oliver Gold of Maui. Maybe more than words, maybe she'd kill him.

36

Semper Fi

U.S. Marine Sergeant Leo De Vino and his quiet pal, U.S. Marine Corporal Frankie Scarpino followed their dream girl's convertible around the shoreline of West Maui to the Lahaina Foodland parking lot. They waited until she put the top up on her Mustang. The back and front seats were filled with purple suitcases. Hanging back a good two-hundred feet they followed along; two handsome Marines on leave, seeing the sights of the town. They need not worry about being spotted. Desiree Lee never looked back, but she seemed in no hurry to meet her special date. They watched her sway down the sidewalk. She stopped to look at her purple reflection in store windows and eased her way along in a sizzling slow burn over to Front Street.

She paused at the entrance to Kimo's Restaurant and stood there posing for the crowd. The Marines watched from the art gallery across the street. They heard a lot of dishes hit the floor and figured she was the distraction. Leo was sure distracted. He had barely said a word to Frankie on the ride from the airport. Frankie did not mind. He was content with silence. After five full minutes Leo figured she must be seated with her friend by now. They walked into Kimo's and turned toward the last two barstools way in the back where they were out of line of sight. They saw her at a table with three empty chairs right in the middle of the place along the ocean railing. There were two Tiki lamps burning in broad daylight on either side of her table. She was facing away from the bar. Even from behind she was beautiful, with long thick black hair that spilled down over her bare shoulders and her long legs crossed sexily and sticking out into the aisle under one side of her chair. Leo and Frankie were in the right spot to watch.

"Semper fi Marines. What'll it be?" Nick the Greek bartender pushed a couple of coasters in their direction. This was quite unusual behavior on Nick's part. When someone new sits down at a bar on Maui, the barkeep makes like he doesn't see them. They know he does. But he will pretend to be the busiest guy in the place even if there is no one else seated at the bar. The reason for this is a secret sort of bartender wisdom passed down from his mentor or gleaned from years of experience. If he ignores customers for awhile the mean ones will go away grumbling and find a different bar. The easy-going, happy people will meet their barstool neighbors, tell a few stories and have plenty of time to decide what they wish to order. Sooner or later the bartender will greet them warmly take their orders and mix their drinks. It's the best way to keep the bar filled with good people. Nick's quick personal attention to them said a lot about Nick's respect for American servicemen.

"Two Budweiser's please, bottles if you got 'em?" Leo did the ordering for them both. Shy Frankie is fine with this. In mere seconds the two long neck beers were standing at attention on their coasters.

"First one's on the house for our U.S. Marines," said Nick.

"Mahalo brah," Leo thanked him. He knew that much

Hawaiian. Frankie smiled his thanks, took a long deep pull and stared at Desiree's black hair. The big Greek went back to sweeping up hundreds of busted porcelain shards.

"So, where's the guy?" Frankie putting four words together in a complete sentence was sort of a record. Sergeant Leo stared at him like he'd never seen him before.

"Hell, if I know." Said Leo. "Here's to all the mysterious women in the world." They knocked their bottles together and drank deep.

"Drinking to all the mysterious women in the world may keep us drunk for years." Frankie quipped.

"Whoa Frankie, y'er becoming a regular statesman. Maybe you should run 'fer congress or the senate. You know... since 'yer finally learning how to talk in whole sentences."

"Screw the damn politicians," Frankie cursed. He tried to sneer but it ended up in a smile.

"What? Frankie! I never heard you swear, ever. What's the matter with you? Besides, y'er not even old enough to swear. How 'ld'er you anyway, m'be seventeen, m'be eighteen-years-old? I don't think you're even old enough to drink in here."

"Screw you too. You know I'm twenty-three and I could rip you in half anytime I want to. You and your mad-hat chase after that purple piece of tail." He waved his beer bottle in the direction of Desiree's table.

"Hah! That's more words 'outta you than you've said since

we left Pendleton. So, she's got your blood up too. What is it with that doll?"

They both stared at the back of her beautiful head of hair. Leo ordered two more beers. They watched the yachts out in front of the restaurant turn slowly at anchor, with a push from the in-coming tide. Nick brought them a bowl of nuts and chips. The dozen flat screens were showing re-runs of some golf tournament. Fortunately, the sound was off. If you tried, you could hear some kind of twangy, country-western song falling softly out of the overhead speakers.

The two Marines checked every face for the out-of-place dangerous men or suspicious women. They were Marine Military Police, MMP's. Their instincts were good, trained to observe the small details that could lead to trouble. Leo's instincts were on edge along with his patience. No one arrived to meet Miss Desiree Lee. It had been a half an hour now.

"What's with that? She lied to me Frankie. She wasn't meeting anybody or they didn't show up. Who in their right mind would stand-up a babe like that? She had to be lying." Frankie went back to saying nothing.

Leo was not used to being put down by a woman. He was twenty-six, handsome as they make 'em, especially in uniform. Women like marines in uniform. They preferred officers over sergeants, but he met girlfriends where ever he went, sometimes, much more than friends. He wanted this one. Desiree was not just mysterious, she pissed him off.

Why is that such an attractive way to start a relationship? He wondered.

167

Shy Frankie ordered the last round of beers. They both knew that three was their limit. Four could bring on fist-fights even among friends. Frankie watched golf. Leo watched Desiree. She sat still as a statue until her food came. Leo tried to see what she ordered but he was too far away. Once the food was in front of her she ate like a famished banshee. Elbows and napkins were flying in all directions. In under two minutes she was all done. Desiree pushed her China plate to the edge of her empty table.

Amazing, Leo's thinking it over. *Even I don't eat that fast, unless I'm mad. Whoa, that's it. She's mad as hell, she was stood up. Some jerk blew off her important lunch date. What an idiot. I'll bet she wishes she was at Mama's Fish House with me right now.*

He breathed a sigh of deep relief. His self respect was back to normal. *She had seemed so friendly at the airport, like she was interested in him. She certainly would have gone to lunch with him if she had not made other plans. Miss Desiree really did have a commitment. There may be a happy ending to this after all.* He finished his beer. Left a tip for Nick and grabbed Frankie by the arm.

"Come on kid, I have a plan."

"Wha'z 'yer rush Romeo? Let me finish my beer."

"Now Corporal," he lifted Frankie off his bar stool with one arm and set him walking toward the door.

"We're 'outta here."

Frankie grabbed his bottle and finished it by the time he was hauled passed the reservations desk. He smiled at the skinny hostess and set the empty by her cash register.

Desiree never saw them enter or leave. Leo headed them both back across the street to the art gallery.

"Make like y'er an art collector Frankie, and keep one eye on Kimo's door. I'll do the same."

It was a good idea to use all four eyes. The place was not slowing down after the lunch hour. Kimo's patrons squeezed their way in and out of the restaurant through the crowd of cigarette smokers out on the sidewalk.

"When you see her come out of there, I want you to cough or somethin'."

She came out that second. Frankie coughed. Miss Desiree looked both ways, undecided about where to turn next.

Yep, she's been stood-up and she's open to new ideas. Leo's thinking up a plan. *If she looks this way, I'll make like I don't recognize her.*

She looked straight at him. His glance was down, studying some watercolor painting of a banana tree. He was good with seeing from his peripheral vision. And he had his Maui Jim shades on so his eyes were hidden. He saw her start across the street right for him. He emptied his mind of all but the lovely banana painting in his hands.

"Hey soldier!" She chirped merrily.

169

He looked up, his face a wonder of non-recognition turning quickly into a sly smile.

"I told you girl, I'm a Marine not a soldier. What chance is this? I thought you were meeting someone named, Ta Tah."

"Oh, it was just an old girl friend from high school. She lives here. We had a quick lunch and she went back to work. We hadn't seen each other in years so we had a lot of fun catching up. You know, girl stuff. She's a captain on one of the dive boats. Sooo anyway, it's very nice to run into you again, 'aah?... Leo, right?"

"Very good, and this is Frankie." Leo said, insisting that she recognize his friend this time with a civil introduction.

"Hi Frankie," she smiled at him realizing for the first time that he was better looking than the handsome Leo with the roving hands.

"Sorry Frankie, I was totally rude at the airport. Flying makes me so up-tight, I take it out on everyone. My friends tell me I'm a real bitch when I travel, hah?"

Nobody agreed or disputed her own self opinion. This seemed like a totally different person. Normal, funny, down to earth and apologetic about her vices. She was still lying like a foreign diplomat, but nicer lying.

"What was your name again?" Frankie asked.

"Ha hah very funny, nobody ever forgets me."

Frankie was beaming. He held his chest out, his blue eyes confidently returning Desiree's direct gaze.

"We're on our way upstairs to Mooses," Frankie said. "Why don't you make it up to me and buy us all a drink?"

Leo looked at shy Frankie with new respect. Miss Desiree laughed out loud, too loud, so they all laughed too loud together. They skipped up the stairs for a cold one.

37

Beer Number Five

Moose McGillycuddy's was crowded. The U-shaped bar right in the middle of the place had tourists and local sports fans, mini-skirted business girls and homeless-looking bums clinging like oysters to both pontoons. Every one of them watched the beautiful Italian model and the two US Marines enter and settle on three bar stools at the far end of the loop. None had ever seen a three-some like this at their bar. A few of them probably thought they were hallucinating.

"Maybe she's a movie star. I think I saw her in a movie once," whispered Doc, who wasn't really a doc, more like a waterfront pharmaceutical salesman.

"And there's a uniformed Marine on either side of her tight as two bookends? Talk about protection. No guy in here would dare make a move on that doll." Doc had considered and reconsidered that move ever since she walked in.

"Maybe she's some kind of Italian diplomat here on government business," returned his pal Larry, another salty dog with a full face of tobacco-stained whiskers.

"Maybe she's one of those new high-class hookers moved into town," said Happy Jack, rumored to be a millionaire retired Alaskan fisherman who was always bumming a smoke. Everyone hoped Happy Jack was right.

Leo and Frankie were so proud to be seen with this doll that they sort of forgot to scan the place for dangerous faces. They were having so much fun neither wanted to admit that beneath all the camaraderie they were in a fierce competition for Desiree's attention.

Shy, quiet, unassuming Frankie was suddenly the chatting, buzz-haircut version of a CNN talk-show host. His smooth ceaseless stream of clever remarks made him sound like an expert on everything. Miss Desiree's attention was all his. She laughed and nodded her beautiful face his way too often for Leo's mood. He wanted to impress this girl. But Frankie was pitching all the curves. Man, this doll had some curves.

It looked like Frankie was throwing a no-hitter against Leo. Desiree seemed enchanted. Leo wanted this girl. This game was about to go into extra innings.

He tried to push a few words into the game whenever Frankie shut up long enough to sip his beer. Miss Desiree would turn and smile at him with that big-eyed interested look, then turn back to Frankie. She had tried to buy the soldiers a beer, but due to the towns respect for the US military, three cold Buds we're set up in front of them 'on the house.' Miss Desiree got a free beer just because she was with the Marines and because she was so gorgeous. Bartenders know that good-looking women in-house are good for business. Desiree got a kick out of the free beer.

"So that's why soldiers wear their uniforms when they come to town."

Leo almost corrected her again, but didn't bother this time. Danielle the tall, red-head bartender knew most every face in the place. But these three were new in town. She wondered what their story was. She figured she had heard every story, truth or fiction, more times than she wanted to count. Her own story was more amazing than anyone else's. Years ago, she too had been a Marine. Back then, her name was 'Dan.' She was happier now, out of the Marines and living a new life as a wahine bartender. Due to her muscled physique, nobody ever gave her any trouble. Danielle could only wonder about these three. She also wondered if she should serve them. She was trained to read a customer's behavior and these two marines looked a little buzzed already. She served them the free beers anyway; maybe because she wanted to hear their story. The beers she gave them, did put the two Marines over their limit and into their 'Danger-Zone.'

The afternoon crowd at Moose's was kind a loud. Some college football games were on the flat screens hung on every wall. Leo's attention wandered from Desiree when Alabama threw a fifty-yard touchdown pass and the sports crowd went wild. Leo didn't follow football much. It was okay but baseball was his game. He'd played two years for the Baby M's, a farm team for the Seattle Mariners. His star burned bright for a while but after an injury to his shoulder, pitching ninety-mile an hour fast balls was no longer possible. He was still good at batting so without any other work skills, found a job twirling a baton with the Marine Military Police.

The football fans started moaning and booing when the pass was called back due to a holding call on the offense.

Leo was focused on Desiree again. She was thin and yet built like a brick house. He was six foot-four, barrel-chested and powerful. He could bench press three-hundred pounds.

MP's had to be tough. He was a perfect match for Miss Desiree Lee. Surely, she must realize this. The heat he felt coming from her on the plane this morning had lit his coals. He was ready to bar-b-cue something. He had an inch on his pal Frankie, who was six foot-three but Frankie had studied Martial arts since grade school. He was a fifth degree Black Belt. Leo had never considered fighting Frankie until today. Now the 4th beer and the thing with Frankie and Desiree getting so cozy, were making him lay odds that if push came to push, he could knock Frankie off that barstool in a heartbeat.

Desiree Lee was over-animated, laughing too loudly at all of Frankie's jokes. She told him again, she felt really, bad about being so rude to him at the airport; so, she ordered the next round of beer. Danielle hesitated for a moment but couldn't say no to the beautiful Italian fashionista, or her handsome escorts. That was beer number five for each of the two Marines.

Now, Frankie was expounding loudly about his last tour in Afghanistan.

"The worst of it was spot checking the local vendors coming on base." It sounded like he was bragging.

"I expected to be blown up any minute by some Jihad nut job in a dented Mercedes. That and the damn heat and dust."

Leo steamed and watched how Desiree hung on almost everything Frankie said. But she kept checking her smart phone which she held in front of her next to her beer. This meant she wasn't focused on Frankie either but on some mysterious idiot who had stood her up at lunch. Even so, she was turned in Frankie's direction most of the time.

Leo's coals were sparking blue flames. He knew for a fact that bastard buddy of his had never been to Afghanistan. He was making it all up. Leo was offended that a Marine would ever lie about his life like that to impress some girl. But then again this was not just some girl. This was Miss Desiree Lee, looking like one of the top ten fashion models in the world. Here she was in a short purple mini-skirt, sitting right next to him, ignoring him.

The big screen football game was in the last few minutes so the crowd was beginning to cheer louder. Even other people's fun was beginning to annoy Leo. His ears were flaming red. He looked down at his hands. At the end of each of his pressed uniform sleeves there were fist's the size of concrete blocks. He had enough military training to keep it professional. He had enough beer in him to punch somebody, somebody named Frankie.

Big hero Frankie was showing Desiree his bronze marksmanship medal. He always wore it pinned in the right spot above his shirt pocket. He thrust his chest out a little too far, almost touching her beautiful face. Frankie was bragging on and on about how hard it was to earn such a prestigious award. Leo's coal fire had ignited a welding torch of anger. The two-hundred-forty pounds on the hoof, bull of a Marine sergeant was about to cut a weld into Frankie's jaw.

That beginner's rifle-shooting medal Frankie was bragging about was so easy to get, eight-year-old kids got past it and on to the Sharpshooter medal in shooting clubs all-across

176

America. Desiree leaned closer to have a look at his wonderful medal. Frankie put his arm around her bare shoulder and leaned in like he was about to kiss her. Leo stood up, the fifth beer muscling up his envious fury. His fists were sledge hammers. Leo started his back-swing.

"Fuck the Marines!" The shout came straight at them like a Tomahawk Missile. The bar noise dropped to a silence so thick you could chew it. Miss Desiree choked on her beer, coughing and sputtering foam across the bar and all over her smart phone. Leo and Frankie and everyone else searched the far end of the room to see who could be so stupid.

"I am Sergeant Leo De Vino of the United States Marines. Who the hell in here iz 'sat bone-head dumb?"

From out of the shadows, in a far corner of the bar, a US Navy Sailor got up from a table. He was a giant of a man, big as a farm mule with bulging arms and a butch haircut.

"Sez me." He shot back and stepped out into the sunshine of an open window. He glared his challenge, flexing his muscles which almost burst the seams of his extra-extra-large shore-leave whites.

Time stood still. Dust floated in the slanting light around his broad face like in a western movie. Behind him another sailor slid his wooden chair back with a loud scrape, and stood to face the Marines. This one was bigger than a mule, more like a farm house.

Suddenly, Leo and Frankie were brothers on the same team. There was no parley, no hesitating, the Marines rushed the two sailors. To the tipsy afternoon sports crowd at Moose's, the room seemed to slide heavily downhill in the direction of the four big men. The biggest sailor, the House, stepped out in front to meet the Marine's attack. Leo had time to think how easy this was gonna be. Divide and conquer.

Instead of barreling right into the House, he went to the floor wisely missing the terrible force of the sailor's first swing. He kicked the big boy in one knee and stuck his own leg behind the swabee's other knee. Frankie was right there with a tag-team push that sent the big guy tumbling over backwards and into his loud mouth buddy. Neither went all the way down, a surprise to everyone. But the Marines training was so precise that Leo sprung up from the floor punching hard, while Frankie moved in closer to his now off-balance foe. Both Marines went to page two in the MP training manual to end a fight quickly. Three quick gut crunching blows right-left-right. Then two hard direct hits to the nose of each sailor, left-right. It was amazing to watch. The drunks in the bar cheered! It was so quick it should be over.

Somehow, the big sailors were still standing. The House picked up a heavy chair and swung it into Leo's ribs. He went sideways, staggering across the dance floor. It looked like he was doing a Vaudeville side-step with his arms swinging loosely around his knees. Frankie saw an opening and landed a fast karate blow on the neck of the House and a spin kick to the chest of the Mule. The crowd went bananas, adding wild shouts to every punch. What could be more fun than a live fight in a sports bar?

Even after his lightening karate attack both sailors were still

178

on their feet. Frankie stepped in closer to Mule and shot rapid fire slam fists into his belly. Leo went to page three of his training and rushed straight at the House. This time with a whole table held in front of him like a big flat battering ram. It worked. Frankie leaped out of the way just in time and the two sailors went ass over backwards and smashed into the table where they'd been drinking. A dozen empty bottles went flying against the wall and shattered all over the floor. The huge moose head hanging in that corner heeled to port and the weight of its five-foot antlers almost pulled it off the wall. Old moose looked as drunk as everyone else as he stared over his big nose sideways to watch the fight. Frankie moved in fast while the sailors were down. He rolled Mule over on his front and twisted a beefy arm painfully around his back. Frankie held him down with a knee dug deep in his spleen. The sailor roared in pain as his arm neared bone busting limits.

House pushed up against the heavy oak table that Leo wielded and with a shove that looked easy, sent him across the dance floor again. This time, Leo the Marine, went down for the first time. House stomped over quickly and gave him a heavy kick in the same ribs the chair had damaged. With a reluctant wail Leo rolled on his good side and jumped up to defend himself from another kick.

Danielle, the ex-Marine, wanted to jump in and get a fist into each of those sailors. She looked for Bubba, the bar's big bouncer, but then remembered he doesn't come in 'til eight. The professional and feminine side of her picked up the bar phone and dialed 911. Miss Desiree giggled like a monkey. She took big swigs of her beer and wiped off the froth with the back of her delicate, beautiful hand like a red-neck housewife.

Frankie turned his head when he heard Leo wince in pain. His attention on his pinned victim wavered. The Mule took advantage of the opening and rolled free. He got up on his feet and sent powerful blows into Frankie's face with both fists. Frankie backed away, ducked to the right and stepped in closer. The surprise Tai-Chi move distracted his opponent. Frankie grabbed him by the wrist and pushing hard forcing his elbow further in, setting his stance right, he threw the big Mule over his shoulder like a duffle bag. The Mule flew through the air and with a tremendous "whomp" almost broke the floor. He lay there like a huge, overturned sea turtle, flat on his back with a very surprised look on his big face. The Judo flip looked so staged it was funny. The crowd laughed as one, cheering the Marine on.

House pushed Leo up to the bar. Desiree grabbed her cell phone and her beer and fled toward the railing that overlooked the street. Leo was surprised that these stupid sailors were still in the game. His ribs were knifing a message to his brain that he may have only one more inning left to play. It was time to end it. But his self-confidence went bye-bye when the House punched him so hard in the head that he literally flew off his feet and found himself sitting on the bar. Another fist was coming at him so he fell on his undamaged side, flat on the counter and swung his feet up with a heavy kick to the sailor's chest and then stood up as fast as his tortured ribs would allow. His jaw hurt real... bad, his head was ringing from the last punch and he thought he heard sirens. Leo's powerful kick sent the House bent over and back-stepping across the room. The sailor had the wind kicked out of him but he did not go down. House caught some breath, shook his big shoulders and came rushing at Leo, roaring like a

Viking berserker.

Standing on the bar, in a bar, was a new experience for Leo. He had two seconds to think. Over his right shoulder he saw something long and sleek. He reached for it, gave a powerful yank and pulled the eight-foot, mounted Tiger Shark off the wires that held it to the ceiling. With both arms around its head he swung it in a tremendous arc like a giant baseball bat. Doc, Jack and Larry on that side of the bar dove off their bar stools to dodge the mighty arc of that fish's deadly tail. With a less than a perfect back swing, Leo's follow through was major league all the way.

"Outta the park!" He yelled and swung as hard as he could. The fish's three-foot wide, sixty-pound tail clobbered the amazed sailor right up the side of his head. He hit the fence way out in left field and landed on his broken face. House tried to get back up but his lights went out. He sagged back down on the floor like a fat sea lion. Leo thought he heard him snoring there in the wide entrance of the bar. Nope, the snoring sound was the blood and the pain roaring in his ears. The sirens were getting louder too.

During all of this, Frankie walked calmly around the Mule on the floor. He took a few deep breaths after the strain of throwing him over his shoulder. The guy must weigh four hundred pounds. The big sailor shook it off and suddenly came up fast with a huge fist that Tai Chi only partially blocked. The momentum sent Frankie up hard against the corner wall. The moose head fell to the floor with a thunderous crash that shook the whole building. Mule stepped in quickly and sent punch after punch into the cornered Marine. Most swings

181

were deflected left and right by Frankie's martial arts training. But some got through and were doing damage. Frankie's nose was bleeding all over his uniform.

Still standing on the bar like King Kong in his own bloody uniform, Sergeant Leo watched with considerable satisfaction at seeing Frankie take a few hits.

Frankie's calm while under attack was fascinating to watch. It seemed like his thoughts were far away drinking tea in a rose garden on a quiet summer afternoon. All the while his hands moved in a blur, defending then striking. Leo wondered if he really could beat Frankie in a fight someday.

Frankie may have looked calm on the outside but he was tiring. His face hurt like hell. He had seen Leo swing the shark home run. He had a similar idea cooking in his well-battered head. When the Mule stopped his attack for one short breath, Frankie grabbed the Moose head off the floor like it was a folding chair and swung the ninety-five-pound head into the face of the Mule. He heard skull bone crunch or antlers breaking and the big sailor went down and out.

When Danielle heard the Maui cops running up the stairs she winked at Desiree and nodded toward the back door over by the restrooms. Miss Desiree took the hint and ran, slipping out and away. The first policeman up the stairs blew a whistle and in the stuffy afternoon heat, yelled as loud as he could,

"FREEZE!"

38

Marines Meet Maui PD

The two marines got a quick squad car ride to the Maui Police Station complete with flashing blue lights but no sirens. Once there, they were greeted with gentle hands, clean bandages, coffee, muffins, and magazines in the officer's lounge. No charges were filed. Marine Military Police and local PD's speak an unwritten code.

Not so for the two big sailors. They were dumped roughly into the holding cell for drunks, washed down with a garden hose and left to dry. Tomorrow they'd face charges for damages to the bar and be released to Navy MPs from their ship anchored out in front of Lahaina. An AWOL on these two had already been received at the Maui police station.

The day shift police officers who brought the Marines in that afternoon got off at six-thirty. As officer Mel Sims punched the time clock he turned to the two MP's.

"You boys need a ride somewhere?"

"A ride back to town would be appreciated." Leo answered.

Frankie found it painful to talk so he didn't. There was considerable damage to his once handsome nose.

"Sure thing, let's go."

Mel drove a shiny new Dodge Dakota four-door pick-up

with four reclining leather seats, air conditioning and a powered-up stereo.

"Maybe we should get civilian jobs." Leo joked. "You know like Maui cops have, jobs with real paychecks and sick leave and such." He laughed but not too loud. His ribs hurt somethin' terrible.

Mel laughed loud enough for all of them.

"My wife's got a good job. It's her truck." He dropped them off at Moose's.

"You two might want to finish your evening somewhere other than back up there," pointing to the upstairs bar they had recently busted up. That was all he said. He drove off, muffler's rumbling with local power from his wife's shiny new truck.

39

Dumb as a wood Floor

It was Tuesday night, another, 'Ole Gold' music gig at the Pioneer Inn. The hotel was 104 years old, soaked to the bone with booze and history. The music Uncle wrote and performed, fit the old place like a Marlin spike in a sailor's grip. His songs were ballads of whaling days, tar-jack sailors, wandering ghosts, pretty women and rum. He sang his songs and played a half dozen accompanying instruments: guitar, ukulele, silver flute, fiddle, Irish penny whistle and Bamboo flutes. The most unusual was his hundred and thirty-five-year-old English Concertina. He was back in his groove this evening, no more fear or anger. The divorce was grinding away in the callused hands of his competent attorney, Captain Ben.

The historic old bar was nearly full. His first set was just underway when he saw her come swinging in like one of those runway models. Everyone stared. She had that kind of show-off Hollywood, 'somebody' in her style and a professional confidence in her walk.

Gina, the number one waitress and hostess for the night, seated Desiree Lee at the only available table about half way to the back along the white railing. Only then did she look at Uncle Oliver. Her look could have burned down the city of Rome. She was the most stunning woman he had ever seen in his life, some kind, of Italian-Sicilian, Puerto Rican beauty queen.

Oh, my stars! That voice in his head was back. *Wow, Wow, Wow!*

His temperature rose five degrees. Uncle sang his next song with his whole body. He sang like a red Cardinal to his mate. He knew his songs were just flat pieces of paper until he pulled one out and sang it with all his might. The performance of each song took him back to the very day he wrote it. He could see blue sky over white sails stretched by the wind. He saw the gulls circling and tasted the joy and the rush and the rum of it all. Often as he sang he imagined a pirate dancing drunken circles right there in front of his boom mic. Tonight, he was that pirate and his good eye was on Desiree.

Sure, he recognized her the minute she walked in. She was one of the five women that had chatted with him on Strike-a-Match.com and the one he was supposed to meet for lunch last Friday. Too bad he didn't remember that date until later that afternoon. It was that crazy hangover Friday.

Why would you miss a date with her? You're an idiot. His coach is utterly confused.

He made eye contact with her all evening, not sure what she must be thinking. She must be mad as hell at him yet here she is, listening close to every song.

When his show was over he knew what he had to do. It had been a good night. The tip jar was fuller than usual. He took off his guitar, wiped it down with a clean cloth and carefully placed it in its new hard case. Then he walked straight to her table and sat down across from her.

"Aloha Desiree, I owe you…"

She did not let him finish.

186

"Oh! Now, you remember me?"

"Ah, of course I do," he was beginning to melt there in the headlights of her sniper kill-gaze.

"Do you know what day it is?" She growled.

"Tuesday," he held his ground with hard data like that.

"Why didn't you call me and let me know you couldn't meet me for lunch?"

"It's complicated," Women understood complicated.

"I don't know why I'm even here tonight?" She was sexy even when she was pouting.

"Why are you here? I know I should have called or something. I am sorry, if that helps at all. "

"I came to see what kind of jerk stands up someone LIKE ME, who flies all the way from California to meet him. Do you have any idea how rude that is?"

"I don't know what I can say to make it right Desiree. There was this emergency I had to deal with and it overwhelmed me. That's the truth."

"What was so damn important?" Was the surf up? Did you over sleep? Were you writing a new song?" She was bubbling lava steam like a volcano about to blow.

"Why didn't you pick up the phone and call me? It's been four days since then. I thought we were friends? "

"I owe you more much more than an apology... can I buy you dinner, right now?"

He expected her to rag at him some more, get loud, cuss and storm out making a big scene. But instead she leaned back in her chair, pulled off her light purple, cardigan sweater, exposing her lovely brown shoulders and plunging V-neck blouse that revealed a seductive amount of her pushed up orbs. He tried not to stare but he had to; she was perfect. He tried to stay alert, ready to fend off a swinging fist. She looked so classy and exotic it made Uncle ache deep down there. Her smoldering Italian eyes burnt across him like a brush fire, two flaming brush fires. He could feel the heat clear across the table. After a real long, sixty-second minute, she said,

"I'll have the Prime Rib."

Ole excused himself from her table,

"Think I'll sing a few more songs for you, Desiree."

As he put his guitar strap back over his shoulder the crowd cheered for a Hana hou. He was back in his comfort zone and he thought he was out of range from her anger. He didn't want to be scolded or stink-eyed any more tonight. But he couldn't take his eyes off the beautiful Italian woman.

After Gina brought dinner to Desiree's table, Ole sang and watched her eat. She sent him a scowl along with a double-barreled blast of stink eyes.

He smiled back with Aloha. *She owns her anger brah. Occupy your own life.*

Ole had never seen anyone eat like she could. She gorged herself on that Prime Rib with wild abandon, like a cheetah tearing at the meat-throat of a gazelle. She was nearly in the throes of ecstasy. It was kind of sexy in a twisted sort of way. Uncle was mesmerized by her. He set the guitar in its stand and setting caution aside, joined her again at her table.

Great wild dogs of Africa, he thought to himself. *What were you thinking? How could you have messed this chance up so bad? She's a smokin' hot Mediterranean pin-up doll cut from the pages of your wildest dreams. Why, Why? You know Ole sometimes you're as dumb as a wood floor.*

Desiree leaned back, still chewing her last bite of food. Some buttery steak juice was running down her chin. Ole had never seen anything so lovely. He couldn't speak.

"If you'll excuse me?" She stood up, picked up her Louis Vuitton purse and her sweater and walked toward the washrooms. Ole groaned with admiration as he watched that long-legged doll walk away on those four inch heels. He ate up her every move. Gina, the waitress gave him a knowing wink that he figured was supposed to mean,

"Wow! You really scored this time, Ole."

If Gina only knew how he had stood Desiree up she would slap him. While he waited for Desiree's return he figured he'd get a start on putting his music gear in his car.

Mark the manager always let him park his vintage Cadillac right in front on Wharf Street. Uncle Ole had detailed it until it looked brand new. It was a classic and added a kind of dated ambiance to the historic old hotel. Plus, it was easy to unload and load his music stuff from there to the stage.

It was taking Desiree a long time in the washroom. Ole finished loading his gear in the DeVille's trunk. Ten minutes had gone by; far too long. He walked past the front desk and knocked on the wahine restroom door.

"Desiree? Desiree are you in there? Anybody?" No answer.

"I'm coming in." He pushed open the door. There was no one at the sinks, no one in the stalls, Desiree was gone.

40

Zen / Pretty Please

Later that week Ole received some more mail. It was a bill from his attorney for one-thousand dollars as a retainer to 'get the ball rolling.' With the bill was a statement for services rendered so far, six-hundred-dollars. Ben had included a letter explaining that he had gotten the divorce hearing postponed for ninety days. He added that now that he was Ole's legal counsel, Ole would not have to appear in court in person. But, he would have to fax a defendant's statement, including any proof of his involvement with raising and caring for the children. Ben would also need a list of his complete assets along with his current earnings, W-2's of recent employment, pension payments he was receiving and copies of his last three years tax returns. With the typed letter there was a hand-written note clipped to the bottom of the page.

"Don't worry buddy, Capt'n Ben."

Ole's immediate worry was how to pay this bill? He called Ben's law firm and fortunately they accepted credit cards over the phone. He used his Bank of America card to pay the thousand bucks. He was not sure how he was going pay off his credit card for the music gear and this one for the attorney, the child support for his daughter still in school and still have $28 a day to live on. But, he was relieved to have ninety-days to 'Get the ball rolling' as Ben put it. Tanya would not win by default.

Relief and worry are a weird mix to swallow, so Uncle went back to bed and tried to sleep it all away. He figured this would be healthier than more drinking. He tried to sleep. Then he didn't try to sleep. He couldn't sleep. His internal calculator reduced his daily survival budget down to fifteen dollars a day. He gave up trying to sleep and not trying to think, rolled his yoga mat out on the floor and turned to his old friend, meditation. In a few breaths he felt a little calmer. He tried to find his memory pond of inner peace. It took another twenty deep breaths and then he was there; the reflection pond at Greenwood Park in Des Moines, Iowa. He was a freshman at Drake University. He had read about Transcendental Meditation in 'Life Magazine.' He laid out a wool blanket on the grass at the edge of Greenwood Lake. It was a warm spring morning and he had a couple of free hours between classes. Three months earlier he'd been ice-skating here on ice so thick city employees pulled the skater's warming hut out on the lake with a dump truck. So much can change winter to spring. He could hardly believe this was the same place.

In that same article in 'Life,' he'd read about the Dharma Wheel; the meditation symbolism for the Universal law of perpetual change. It fascinated him that a twenty-five-century-old Buddhist explanation, could fit perfectly with the modern chemistry classes he was taking. Energy can never be destroyed. It can only change forms.

On that first day's meditation attempt Ole began by drawing a pencil sketch of the woods and the pond. Maybe this is why he still remembers it so well. A little, house fly landed on his sketch. Its wings and head were reflecting car wax rainbows of color. He watched the small live creature warm itself in the sunshine and then 'fly' away in no, particular hurry. He drew the fly life-size on that corner of his sketch paper right where it had landed. He still has that drawing among the few bits of personal treasures he brought with him to Hawaii.

After the fly left him there by the pond, the sun's reflection coming off the water, bent light into his eyes. His eyes became a prism coloring the world inside his mind and made his spirit shine like car wax. As if that wasn't amazing enough, the moment he would never forget, gently happened. His mind became the Sun itself and his eyes became a pair of two-way lenses. The incredible force of sunlight inside his head was unstoppable, shining out through his eyes and projecting the lake, the trees and the colors of the world. It calmed him to see and be what he saw, all at the same time. He wondered if the world was some powerful force dreaming him, or if he, himself was dreaming the world? Within and without, here and there all became the same thing.

He suddenly had the answer to that big question. *'Is there Outer Space in life?'* Of course, there is. He could feel Outer Space moving within him. He was never more alive. The Dharma Wheel we all share, turns in spiral galaxies at the sub-atomic level in all living things. The other big question came to mind. *'Who am I?'*

For years he'd been taught to pray church prayers to have a 'spiritual experience.' That morning, he realized he was a 'spirit' having an 'experience' called life. It was his first Zen moment. It changed him forever. Forty years later, Uncle the Spirit, could find that peaceful pond within seconds of taking one meditative breath.

On his path of life and change, Uncle Ole met a meditation teacher named Soho Machida. Soho was raised a Christian, then as a teenager he entered a Buddhist monastery in Japan and was a monk for twenty years. Feeling bored he applied and was accepted into Harvard College where he studied Christian Theology. He went on to write thirty-four books on meditation. He has travelled the world teaching the healthy advantages of his style of 'Arigato (Grateful) Meditation'.

"It's like learning to fly a small plane," he told Uncle. "When you first practice take-offs, you use the whole runway before you get up in the air. After many flights you can pull up sooner and be soaring farther and stay up there longer."

After a lifetime of practice, Ole could sometimes make a whole day, one long meditation of stereo sound and extra-sensory touch, taste and sight; a totally human experience. Then like flipping a coin from right to left brain he could weigh nothing and almost evaporate back into the spirit world of formlessness.

Today, the mix of rolling ocean of relief and the terrifying Dream Shark of worry, kept him from getting off the runway. Maybe he was trying too hard. He did an hour's worth of slow yoga and that took the kinks out of the twisted rope muscles in his neck.

Toward evening he turned to his other solace, music. He took his guitar and walked down to Kahana beach. The setting sun was toasting clouds like marshmallows. He didn't take a rum drink with him this time; didn't stop at the beach bar; the yoga had done its magic. Relief temporarily won out over worry. In fact, he felt great. His normal confidence had returned. It was a beautiful night to be alive, a radiant night and he felt joyfulness projecting out of his eyes instead of tears for a change.

There was a large revival meeting of 'sun-downers' on the beach in front of the Valley Isle Resort. Ole headed their way. As he approached they waved him over, maybe because he was carrying a guitar, maybe because he was projecting love in all directions and they felt it. A tall older man set down his beer can and went up on the lawn by the palms and got a beach chair for him.

"Welcome, I'm Jack, this is my wife Marlene. This is Bill and Bonnie, that's Chubby Checker and Tom Hanks, Dwayne and Zina, Michael Jordan, Jim and Sue, Captain Kangaroo, Mike and Linda, Captain Billy Bones and Lorena, Paul and Patti, Dr. Seuss, Steve and Lee Ann, Herman Hess, Al and Diane. The Big guy there is my golf buddy Al, his wife Kathy, that's Steve Miller, Bruddha T and Ligia and John, Dan and Marla, Michelle Wei and Sergio, more golf buddies. That's Denny and Karen, Tom Selleck, Judy and Tim, Ray and Diane, Tim and Ella, Billy's Dad Floyd and Tom the submariner both Veterans of WWII. That's Billy's mom Pat, There's Judy, Jan and Paul, over there, fighting again are Grumpy and Lady Smurf, Suzie, Melinge, Famous Mike, Famous Amos, Carl Sagan, AJ and Annie, Jeff and Judy. This is Bob Marley Jr., there's Andrea, Jack and Sally, Cliff and Callie, Maui Jim, Barry and Lindy and Tommy Bahama... "

"Whoa Jack," said Uncle Ole. "I'm getting a nose bleed trying to remember all those names. Alohaaa everybody, my name is Oliver Gold and this is my guitar 'Coco-Lani." He just made that up to be funny but when he thought about it, that was a great name for his guitar.

Everyone smiled and nodded and smiled and nodded again, happy sunset worshipers accepting him into their congregation. A few even had drink holders stuck in the sand next to their chairs; experienced, professional sunset missionaries.

"It's time," someone said.

There was a bit of digging as nearly everyone reached down into beach bags and pulled out conch shells. It was almost time; Mother Earth was dancing her slow pirouette, turning away from the sun. The West Maui Mountains were giants in the sunset's stage lights. They bowed low in front of the black curtain call of night.

"Ahhh," a dozen voices sighed in awe at the incredible blueness of the sky. Perfect blue became bluer if that's possible as one half of the sun disappeared below the ocean's mirror edge. The marshmallow clouds were toasted fully red, about to ignite. Some of the sun-downers started pounding on their shells to knock the sand and geckos out. A few had their conch pressed to their lips, already warming them up with soft hums.

"Watch for the green flash," somebody else said.

The sun slipped away and at the same instant there was a brilliant green spark the size of a pencil tip to officially announce the start of tonight. It was the cue for the sun-downer shell band to play. With perfect timing twenty conch shells moaned their ancient call together. It was a cacophony of moose rut yearning and Polynesian magic. Old Bill, Denny and Bruddha Tom blew for over a minute. Their faces puffed out to purple before they ran out of air. Their last wailing note faded down the beach, jumped into the ocean and was swallowed by the deep rumble of the surf. There were a few moments of quiet as the surf hushed up the beach. Then everyone cheered and clapped for the three conch-blowing champions.

"Wow," whispered Oliver. *Maui is such a cool place to live. Folks back in Seattle don't do this at sunset.*

Ligia, Captain Billy and his pretty wife Lorena began to play their ukuleles,

"Somewhere, ova 'da rainbow..." they sang.

Ole sat down with 'Coco Lani' and joined in. When the song ended Ole asked.

"Hey Capt, didn't I meet you out on the Pali one sunset? You were playing the violin, yah?"

"That was me. I recognized you too Ole. I play my viola out there on the cliffs soz' I don't bother the neighbors here at the condos." Captain Billy was wondering where the brown wahine with the ice-blue eyes was this evening but he didn't ask. Instead he said, "If I've learned anything on Maui, I've learned you meet the people you are supposed to meet here."

"Ah hah," said Uncle.

"You sing one," said Capt.

Uncle checked the tuning on Coco and sang as sweet a song as any of them had ever heard. He sang in both Hawaiian and English, a happy song with a sad melody.

"Hana hou," (play one more) said Ligia.

"Okay one more but then I want to hear you three sing again." He sang with his full passion, a song as sweet as the first.

"Wow," said Billy, "do you play professionally?

"Yah, I actually have some songs on i-tunes and I just got a gig at the Pioneer Inn on Tuesdays and Fridays, come and sit in with me some night, you guys are great."

"You make a living as a musician? Billy wanted to know.

Ole didn't want to talk about his pension from teaching, he may soon lose it in court; so he just said.

"I get by. Hey, I'm living here on Maui with all you millionaires."

Everyone cheered. Most of them were millionaires, and tonight they'd been drinking like millionaires.

In the tropics on most nights, right after sundown there's an afterglow of color that lingers for a while in a dull way and the bedazzle-paints the sky. It's typically five to ten minutes of lovely yellow and red twilight that's always worth waiting for. Tonight, the yellow paint stayed on the clouds longer than usual and turned into polished brass, as shiny as Aladdin's lamp. It was spectacular brass, like flashing cymbals in a marching band. Somehow the magic lamp wished itself even brighter and lit the sky with flames of fourteen-carat gold. Then amazingly, everything changed into purple. Perhaps conjured up from legend and ocean kingdoms far away, dabs of royal-purple ink began to blotter softly down from the top of the sky, tainting the once-perfect, golden clouds. The sky became darker and deeper lavender and it spread like a 'Mood Indigo,' until all the golden clouds were tie-dyed purple. Within seconds the mirror of the ocean captured the color of the sky to ink the entire horizon all the way to the beach and painted the breaking surf a light purple. The fantastic contagion spread, purpling the sand and palm trees. The painting was complete when the people on the beach were glowing purple also: as if everyone had turned into aliens from planet Purple-Upitor.

"Ah…"

"Ah…"

"Ah…"

Twenty nearly speechless purple sun worshipers stood still with purple drinks forgotten in their purple hands.

"This only happens once or twice a year," said Captain Billy. "It's so strange that highway traffic slows to a stop. Little kids drop their bicycles and stare."

"It looks 'photo-shopped,' like something on the internet," whispered Ole. Only this crazy picture felt real. Uncle Ole stared like a winged monkey that had been magically 'purpled' back to Oz. He thought he was in one of his dreams. But not even his dreams, were this purple. It 'broke 'da eyes,' a slang pidgin he made up for really spectacular moments. There were just not enough superlative adjectives in English or pidgin to describe the beautiful sunsets and women here in Hawaii.

Too soon, the Nemesis of Day, the Black Knight, tipped back his dark cup and drank all the wine out of the sky. From far away and 13 billion years ago, starlight became visible again and gave the night even more magic. Ole started to hum a tune that just came to him from the starlight,

Star light has sound? Asks coach.

"Of course, it does," and Uncle finds some words to match the melody that's downloading into his soul from 'out' there:

"The stars come out one at a time, one-at-a-time... the stars come out one at-a-time... I wish on a star... wish you were mine... oh... I wish you were mine... I wish on a star, wish you were mine."

He told himself it wasn't about Tanya this time. It was about some future lover, who was driving her Mercedes with the top down and looking up at the stars tonight and wishing for him.

The evening sunset service was over. The purple-baptized, believers had witnessed their solar Jehovah at His best. The crowd began to thin. Lorena took Billy's hand and they said goodnight to Ole. Lorena gave him a friendly Hawaiian hug. So did Ligia. Bruddha Tom shook his hand. Captain Billy's eyes caught his with mutual understanding; there would be other nights like this.

"See you later, neighbor-gators," said Ole feeling extra witty and confident.

"Neighbors?" asked Capt.

"Yah, I live over on Makahiki Street."

More cheering; professional drinkers celebrate anything. The captain smiled at Oliver.

"Come again, Ole."

"Mahalo music brah." Ole pidgin'd back. But Ole didn't go home. He walked down the beach to his favorite sand dune and sat down for some more music on this delicious night. He could stay up 'til dawn if he wanted to. No wife would complain, no alarm clock would ring and no boss would miss him. No boss, no- boss, no- boss, he liked the sound of that so much he might write a new song, a no-boss-a-nova.

Ha hah, you're funny even when you haven't been drinking. His mind coach sounds proud of himself.

Uncle was thinking he might play guitar all night. It was a night of new friendships and new songs. He worked on the song about the stars coming out one at a time. Ole sang with quiet passion. His songs were his life story. He was a living poet and a fifteen dollar-a-day millionaire, with no boss.

He said a prayer of gratefulness for this chance to live in Hawaii and find a home, nice friends, a music gig and purple sunsets. It was all treasure to him.

Even though it was kind a late, occasional tourists were still walking the beach in front of his small sand dune. They passed twenty feet in front of him along the surf's ever-changing edge. There was enough starlight and ambient resort light to see everyone as passing silhouettes. Romantic couples, parents with kids, seniors with dogs, just plain weird looking people with one or two parrots on their shoulders all wandered by in a shadow parade.

Plato would like this, observed his philosopher coach.

He loved them all. Uncle sent helpful vibes and blessings along with each one of them as he sang. The beachcombers waded in the surf or left barefoot prints along the wet sand. No one was in a hurry. Some of them stopped to listen and then walked on. Some kept walking but smiled at him. Some ignored the lone guitar player on the sand dune. He watched a tall slender woman walk slowly by. She stopped to listen to him sing for a while and then continue on down the beach. He could not see her face, just the shadow of her pleasing figure.

When she came back by again she walked up the slope and sat down on the sand next to him. She didn't say anything. He smiled and studied her as he finished singing 'Ghost Memories' his favorite sad song about lost ships and lost love. The woman next to him was very, very cute.

"Hello beautiful," he said.

"Hi handsome," she said.

"What's a pretty thing like you doing in cheap dive like this?"

"Hah! You need to learn some new pick-up lines, beach boy. Maui is not cheap."

"The beach is free."

They both started laughing. She looked fresh and gorgeous. She was barefoot but not in a swimsuit. She wore black short-shorts showing lovely long legs and a white t-shirt with no bra under it, another liberated woman. This one smelled good, like suntan lotion. Ole noticed perfect full bumps pushing from under her shirt right where they should be. She was young, maybe twenty-three or so. She was blonde, a messy hair blonde. *Maybe she just woke up or maybe she pays to have her mop styled all messed up like that.* He doesn't know much about women's hair fashions. He didn't much care for blondes anymore. Tanya was a blonde. After so many years with her he was now dreaming of a brunette or an Asian with black hair.

Hey... go with the flow brah, coach whispered.

"Play another song for me beach boy."

"Sorry, I don't play on demand."

"Please," she whined.

"Oh, is that a request this time?"

"Uh huh," She nodded. "Pretty please,"

"Ok, Pretty Please. That's what I'll call you tonight."

He smiled and played 'Sweet Leilani,' while he sang she snuggled closer so that her bare leg was touching his. His response below his waist didn't surprise him. She was warming him up like a vintage tube amp. He sang the sweet song with passion. She hung on every word.

"Okay, Pretty Please, now you sing one for me."

"Is that a demand?" She smiled.

"Yes."

"Well too bad for you, I can't sing."

"Nonsense, everyone can sing; are you too shy?"

"I'm not shy, am I?"

He had to agree she had come over and sat down close to him, she wasn't shy.

"I can't sing."

Ole was trying to look her in the eyes not at her t-shirt. She was a living doll. He was no longer married in his heart. That was so over. Except on legal paper he was still married.

Legal schmeagal, don't blow this. You can forget Tanya. Coach knows.

"Ok Pretty Please, sing 'You are my Sunshine' and I'll sing along with you, if that 'll help?"

He played a little guitar intro and nodded for her to start. Her voice was horrible. It curdled the soft night air like moldy sour cream in a cup of black coffee. She was absolutely the worst singer he had ever heard. She was worse than Bob Dylan. But Ole played one whole verse and let her finish the chorus,

"Please don't ta-ache my sunshieeenie awaiiaaeeiiee-yal."

"You were right dear, you can't sing."

"Told you,"

"What can you do?" He was curious. She was lovely. It was exciting to have a sexy young woman take an interest in him.

"They tell me I'm a good kisser," and she gave a shy smile, wetting her lips with her tongue. Something suspicious was blipping on his chick radar.

"How old are you Pretty Please?"

"I'm sixteen, almost seventeen next month."

"Yikez girl!" Ole stood up, "Find a beach boy your own age not a senior citizen." Uncle walked away shaking his head, waving his guitar around in fuming frustration.

This island full of crazies brah, you can't always go with the flow, reprimands coach.

"You told me to go with the flow. I could go with the flow all the way to jail listening to you!" Now Uncle's arguing with his own mind.

You should see a psychiatrist buddy.

　"I can't afford psych-therapy dumb ass, remember, fifteen-dollars a day?"

You're the dumb ass.

　"No, you are."

Then at least we agree on something.

41

You Don't Have a Dime

To avoid worrying about divorce court, Ole went snorkeling a lot. One of his favorite places to swim with the fish was at Kapalua Bay. There were rich Asian women there. He enjoyed looking at them. He kept projecting free, 'also rich,' electrons around himself, hoping to connect with one of them someday. There never was a more orthodox optimist than Oliver Gold.

After snorkeling he'd shower off at the beach shower and air dry while he practiced his balance and Tai-Chi out on the grassy ridge west of the Kapalua Hotel. This was the most incredible piece of real estate he had ever seen. Standing out on the point on one leg, he felt rooted to Maui like a young palm. Okay, an old palm. The sea power slammed into the cliff below and burst straight up with huge mist that would lightly salt down his face. His mind would drift away, far out to sea with the mist and the white clouds rushing out of the Maui Mountains. Once over the ocean the clouds and his troubles would evaporate into the sky. Then he would feel formless. How he could be formless and still feel, was a mysterious part of the 'human' experience. Anyway, It was a wonderful place to be. There was some kind of spiritual power in this ridge of land. The old Hawaiians felt it also. Ole had read that when Hawaiians die, their spirits jump off the western cliffs of the islands and into the next world. He liked that story. It fit with his mind-evaporating-cloud meditation.

Since he was not a Kapalua Hotel guest he was technically

'crashing' the property. Fortunately, the occasional security guard he saw didn't hassle him. He looked like any other tourist. When he was around the pool area it was easy to pick a fluffy hotel towel off the back of some empty pool chair and carry it around like he was one of the resort's millionaire guests.

Today, Ole lay back on a padded lounge chair by the pool and considered the four-letter word, 'work.' He hated to admit it but this retirement thing was making him a little stir-crazy. He was used to getting up and going to work. Repeating choices forms your habits. Habit is a wonderful / terrible thing. He always tried to choose work that was fun or at least interesting. Teaching was fun; he kinda-sorta missed it. But when he retired, his past career defined who he used to be. Who was he now? Was he a professional pool crasher?

Uncle was determined to re-invent himself... sure, being a Maui musician was fun. Rest home volunteer felt great, but how about his original plan to be a professional beach bum? The Trillion-dollar question was how could he make hanging out at the beach bring in a paycheck? He had a lawyer to feed now. How could he visualize this need, into cash-flow reality? He was a chemist not an alchemist. He went back out on the cliff and did some more Tai Chi. He surrounded himself with energy that projected free electrons that seek a beach job.

Uncle had very few credentials; he did have some California surf experience. Hawaii waves were 'mo' betta', warm water, long ride, easy surf. But, he could not see himself teaching surf lessons. That was for twenty-year-olds. There must be some kind of part-time, local-scene, beach-gig that would make his dream come true.

So now you wanna be part of the local 'scene'? You sound like a Hippie. Coach is still upset about the 'dumb ass' agreement.

Later that same afternoon, Ole was leaning on the counter where he exchanged his wet, pilfered towel for a clean one. This was a small cabana building convenient to the pool with a tremendous view of the ocean. He knew Kathy, the pretty blonde gal that worked there on a first name basis. Uncle asked for a fresh towel and was helping himself to a paper cup of water from the cooler with sliced lemons in it, and making small talk.

"Nice office you got here Kathy."

"Wanna work here? They're hiring."

Uncle almost choked on his cup of lemon water. *Another answer from heaven so soon?*

"Maybe. What's it pay?"

"Nothing," she laughed. "Well no hourly wage. But you make good commissions on what you sell."

Uncle had never seen her sell anything.

"What you selling, kisses? I can see you making a fortune." They both laughed and Kathy blushed.

"See this big display of Maui Jim sun glasses you're always leaning on, getting your finger prints all over?"

Nope, he had never noticed. He wasn't much of a shopper. He looked down at the display there in the counter top for the first time. The prices started at about two-hundred dollars. He bought his sunglasses at ABC stores for five bucks. Kathy went on,

"See these plastic bottles all lined up on the counter? Supremo, All-Natural Sun Block?"

He had never seen these either. When you don't have a lot of money to spend, you tend to ignore retail stimuli of all kinds. He picked up a small bottle of 'Supremo' and looked at the price tag on the back, 'thirty-two-dollars.

"So how come you never try to sell me this stuff?"

"You're a local. You don't have a dime. You crash the pool every other day, make like a yogi out on the ridge and drink our ice water. Why waste my breath on you?" She smiled.

"It's that obvious?" He wondered if his cover would now be blown.

"Don't worry, I won't tell security. I figure you are probably divorced, broke and hoping to score with some rich old widow or some senseless young trust babe you can fleece."

"Whoa Kathy, are you some kind a private detective or what?"

He was putting on his best, 'who-me?' face, trying not to be anything like the person she had just described. But she knew and he knew, that was him to a 'T.'

"Just observant," she answered. "I could write a book about guys like you."

"So how much do you make selling this stuff?"

"I usually make over a hundred bucks a day, unless it's raining, like it does too often here in the winter. I put in long days, six a.m. to six p.m. Oh and I gotta' push that cart full of dirty towels back to the hotel and bring fresh ones out for the Lords and Ladies of Leisure."

Uncle thought about it, *a legitimate reason to hang out at this beautiful place, meet chicks or rich widows. Sell some stuff, make a paycheck. You could do this. It's the 'beach boy job' you were wishin' for this morning! Plus, you gonna stay in shape pushing that towel cart around.*

"I'm in." He smiled his most professional, salesman smile. He'd never sold anything in his academic life. She probably figured that by now also.

"Here's a job application. Fill it out and go see Tony at the office in Lahaina. His card's stapled at the top."

"T'anks Kathy. You 'da kine." Sometimes he would try out some Pidgin on a white person. He would never attempt this with a native Hawaiian. He had too much respect for their ability to switch from perfect King's English to thick island slang.

Ole had a lead on a beach job. He laid the application on a pool chair with his rubba slippas to hold it down. The warm trades had picked up a little, pushing the heat of the land and more clouds out over the sea to disappear. If you keep trying to live Aloha here in the islands, you never cease being amazed at how one wonderful event follows another.

He smiled again at Kathy, and walked barefoot to the Kapalua Hotel's hot tub. It looked like a natural rock grotto of stone that was of course, man-made. The clean bubbling hot water was always one-hundred and four degrees.

The view from where he and the Lords and Ladies simmered in the Kapalua spa was 'broke da eyes' perfect. He could hear the surf bash into the cliffs down below and he saw the white spray that flew high up above the ridge and into the air. It was like some Hawaiian tourism movie titled, 'Trespassing Deluxe Hawaii Resort Hot Tubs on a Budget.'

Uncle could see the island of Molokai a few miles away. It bulked its ancient green shoulders up out of the sea and turned away from the black rain showers sweeping in from the east. It was one more amazing Hawaii postcard for his collection.

He kept losing his mind in the clouds and the sky and then the soothing hot tub bubbles would bring him back to his poached body again. After the sun set and the afterglow faded with mediocre magnificence, the hotel guests said goodnight and headed up to the resort restaurants for their ninety-dollar, five-plate dinners.

Uncle dried off with his fluffy towel and walked to the poolside snack bar for a fifteen-dollar Reuben sandwich. He wanted to do his part to keep the economy of this place going. It eased the guilt he felt for 'crashing' the place.

Sadly, within two years the understated elegance of the old Kapalua Hotel would be completely bulldozed and a gaggle of ugly looking timeshare towers would be built, go unsold and fall into bankruptcy. It would become the islands best example of 'progress' karma coming around and kicking greedy developers off the island.

42

KAM / Kool Activities Maui

Uncle Ole followed up on the job application and soon had two blue polo shirts with the 'KAM' insignia on the shirt pocket and a three-hour training session with four other new hires. When he got his name badge, he was officially on the KAM Team, Kool Activities Maui. It sounded like a fun company. It was. But he did not get the position at Kapalua. Pretty Kathy had that sweet spot sewn up for herself six days a week. His assignment was at the Embassy Suites Hotel, a pink pyramid-shaped building in an area called Honokowai.

His first day on the job was Maui magic. He drove his Cadillac into the under-ground parking garage. The cement floor of this place looked like it had been waxed. It was so slick that tires squeaked when car wheels turned on it. He walked from the cement underworld through an artificial lava tube and out into a Hawaiian Shangri-La. Aloha! It was a heavenly circus of tourists. Happy children jumped into the pools with colorful, inflated beach balls. Pretty women stretched out in bikini row, like oily, white fish drying on racks in the hot sun. People were laughing loudly and splashing water at each other. There was a big pool where teenagers and adults played water volleyball. A water slide for kids curved down from a high rock mountain that was probably man-made, but looked real. Kids cheered and screamed with delight. It was like stepping into a home movie, 'Our Very Expensive Family Vacation in Hawaii.' Once again It broke 'da eyes. Ole opened the towel cabana with his new key. There were now four in his pocket, Cadillac, Lanai gate, his small room and his beach office here at the Embassy. Life in Hawaii was getting more complicated.

Tony, his manger arrived while Uncle was setting out the Maui Jim display cases. Tony would be training Ole this week.

"Everyone staying at this resort comes to you to get their towels," said Tony. "You greet them with a cheery 'Aloha', not 'Hi' or 'Whaz up?' They flew all this way to Hawaii to hear someone say, 'Aloha' to them. That someone is you."

"Okay, got it," replied Uncle.

"Then you ask them how many towels would you like today?" And while you gather a stack of clean towels for them you say something like, 'I see you have sunglasses on. Here, try the new sport model Maui Jims'. Everybody likes to think of themselves as sporty. You may have to suggest this, two or three times. 'Go ahead try them on,' you say. 'Look out at the ocean and then compare them to your old sunglasses.' 'Amazing,' they usually say, because they truly are incredible glasses. They kind of sell themselves. It's easy." Tony finished his lesson and smiled confidently.

People were lining up already to get some towels, so Tony and Ole went into their roles. Friendly, harmless, good-looking towel guys about to get hundreds of dollars out of those room key charge cards all the guests carry. It was easy.

Kathy was right. He made over a hundred bucks that first day selling expensive sun glasses and sun block. He would walk around the pool and see people turning red from solar burn. Maui is the same latitude as the Virgin Islands in the Caribbean. It's like tanning under a broiler.

"Careful," he'd remind the beautiful women lying around on lounge chairs by the pool.

"That sun block you're using on your skin is not protecting you like it should. Read the ingredients in that stuff. See all those chemicals you are putting on your skin, really not good for you." Then he'd smile his most handsome, concerned smile. "Here, try a little sample of this Supremo natural sunscreen on your shoulders. Come see me in the towel palace over there. Buy a bottle of our natural sun block and I'll toss in a fresh towel and my phone number." He never got a date this way, but he sold a lot of sun block.

43

Table for One

Time flew like a Frisbee, smoothly across the week and landed on Friday, his next gig at the PI. Ole was pretty sure he would never see Desiree again. He was wrong. He had just begun to sing one of his best-selling i-tunes songs, when she walked into the bar all smiles, fresh as a tourist off a dinner boat. She seemed tipsy as one too. Desiree was a little shaky on those four-inch heels tonight. Gina seated her at a table before she fell over, this time a little closer to the stage. Ole couldn't take his eyes off her. His voice found its full range with a vibrato that could ring ship's bells far out at sea. If there had been any window panes in the place he would of broke 'em for sure. He smiled at Desiree. She smiled shark teeth in return. After that one song, he set his guitar in its stand and went to her table.

"Come back for some more great music?"

"Just bored," she quipped, ice cold again.

"Can I buy you a drink?"

"Dark rum on ice."

"Hey, that's what I drink."

"So?" An ice-cold question... *a foot thick.*

"A coincidence that's all, pretty funny yah?"

217

"Absolutely hilarious," she smirked. *Her icy remark, two-feet thick.*

Uncle waved Gina over.

"Gina, I'd like you to meet Miss Desiree Lee, Scarlioni. Desiree, this is Gina, the best waitress in Lahaina. Desiree is a friend of mine so, please bring her a dark rum and Coke and whatever else she likes and put it all on my tab."

Gina winked and said, "Of course, Mr. Gold."

Gina had never called Uncle Oliver 'Mr. Gold.' She kicked in with the formal status maybe due to the celebrity glow that surrounded the beautiful Italian woman. Gina was reluctant to serve her any drinks, due to her fuzzy condition. When she explained her concern to the bartender, he took one more look at that long-legged doll and mixed her drink. Good looking women in the bar are good for business.

"Okay Desiree, I'll sing you some songs to make up for everything," Ole said with an apologetic face. He knew he was trying too hard. But she looked and smelled so sexy tonight.

"Good Luck with that," she replied with a shrug. Her tumbling, gorgeous black hair had a perfume heavily sprayed into it, sending him a fragrance, maybe called 'Naked Praying Mantis.' It was an overpowering turn-on scent, laced with danger.

What is it with this doll? It's been a long time since you made love with Tanya. You're living on 'romance island' for months now, meeting gorgeous women, and no 'sex' so far, none.

218

Here's this delicious doll, hot as a jalapeño pizza, but cold-shoulder at the same time. Yah, that's confusing but she's here again to hear you sing. That must mean something. You better make it happen tonight brah.

He was thinking, but not too clearly, because he was horny as a Werewolf on caffeine, on a full moon night in Transylvania. Over her lovely, bare shoulder, he could see the full moon over Hawaii beginning to leer down at him from its current hideout up there in the west Maui mountains.

While Ole sang, Desiree seemed to hang on every phrase and it looked to him, like she ate every word; chewing each one into little pieces before swallowing. He had never noticed anyone ever listening so intently to his music. It's good verse but this was a restaurant not a concert. People laugh with their friends and drink and tap their feet to his 'dinner music.' They aren't listening. Occasionally someone will glance up at him and smile while they chew, catching part of the story of one of his heart-felt ballads. For most of them he could be singing nonsense,

"Baltta latta splotta hitch a zoom bah," no one would even notice.

Ah you know that's not true, his inner coach has forgiven the 'dumb-ass' agreement. *You're popular here. People listen, they buy your Cd's; they fill up your tip jar.*

He met Desiree's eyes in every story of every song that night. What was it with this one? Her beauty gave him the shakes. Her blazing model eyes sent flirting glances of affection mixed with angry stink-eye. The attraction he felt

219

was a super-conductive magnetism and yet repelling all at the same time. It was wonderful and scary.

Desiree ordered another rum and coke with her Coconut Shrimp. Then she asked for a Mahi-Mahi dinner with another rum drink and Hula Pie for desert. He watched her and counted drinks. It's not that he couldn't afford it, he could but it would empty his tip jar that's for sure. Uncle was fascinated by her voracious appetite and her stamina for booze. When his set ended at eight-o-clock, he joined her at her table.

"Hi doll, come here often?" Cheery as he could be.

"Get original, Mr. Gold-finger-singer-songwriter-wise guy, hiccup, hic-ip." *Was that a slight thaw in her voice?*

"So why are you here, Desiree? I thought you were mad at me."

"Y'am. Yer a baad man Ollie' Bloliver, bad to the bone... Mr. Ole Oop."

Uncle got up from the table, he didn't want her to get too smashed, just loose and willing. Ole nodded to Gina,

"Check please. She's had enough."

"Whaaa the f...?" Was the last thing she almost said before her beautiful face fell into the Hula Pie and she passed out. Ole turned her head to one side, so she wouldn't suffocate on chocolate and ice cream. What a waste. If every dog has his day, he was a Werewolves'-monkey's-uncle 'cause this was not his day.

Sober as a guitar player who's been horny for Italian Pasta all night and pumped up on Coca-Cola, it was Uncle's turn to leave early. He packed his gear to the Cadillac and sped away. Ole pushed the electric buttons of the windows all down and howled up at the moon,

"Oooooooooooooooooohuuuuuu'oooooooooo!" He growled like a timber wolf and drove too fast, howling all the way back to Yu'layne's house.

Gina didn't move Desiree, she was safe there. One side of her beautiful face and one ear, still deep in-the-pie; just another tourist wasting away in Lahaina-ville.

44

Chinese Fireworks

Uncle Ole was in a state of pacing, wolf-man, frustration when he padded up the stairs and unlocked the gate on Yu'layne's upper lanai. With the click of the opening lock, Chinese Ling and Liang turned to see who had arrived. They were just sitting down to a late-night, outdoor dinner. The two women looked so lovely there by candle light that it calmed him and he was able to greet them with a silent respectful bow. Both women returned the bow in their cutest way. Ling got up and without speaking a word she waved her hand offering to share their simple repast.

Uncle had not eaten dinner at the PI tonight after Desiree did a face-plant in the Hula Pie. He was so hungry in many ways. He accepted their offer with another bow.

While Ling went to the kitchen, sexy, smoldering Liang moved another chair up to the round glass table. She stood there and posed, holding the chair for him to be seated. She looked like an Asian model from some fashion magazine. Standing a little too close as he sat down, she let her hair brush over his shoulders, and along the side of his face. Her clean shampoo scent, a mix of cooked rice, peppermint tea and raw sex almost made him howl again.

Uncle took the bait and gently touched her arm with one of his wolf paws. She must have felt his need. She wrapped her long fingers around his hand and squeezed it tightly. Her touch was hot, an unspoken signal of passion.

Ling returned with a simple one bowl dinner of steamed rice and veggies. Before she sat down she started talking. Of course, she would. He was used to this. It never bothered him. He liked her. He liked them both. Ling's Scottish accent and broken Chinese made every sentence hard to understand, so he didn't even try. Ole focused on Liang. She posed with every tempting move she made. While Ling rarely made eye contact, demurely keeping her eyes down at her food, Liang boldly met his every gaze with an intensity that was feeding the fire in his forest.

He had always treated them with a brotherly respect. After all he was fifty-something, *who's counting?* He felt like a very trim, rugged fifty-something. Yu'layne had guessed him at forty-something, and he was a musician. Women like musicians. At least that's what he had always heard. He had been on Maui too long without a girlfriend. The Chinese girls were at most twenty-eight maybe twenty-five? But they had both come to his gig at the PI, twice, so they must like his music at least. Maybe they feel the same attraction he feels for them.

Forget it brah. Coach was not being helpful.

Uncle looked Liang over from head to waist. The dim candle light and the glass table blurred the view of her short-shorts and her lovely legs.

She probably feels your horny old man eyes brah, stop it.

He looked back into her eyes, brown and burning.

223

Intense is a mild word for those eyes. His coach was warming up to her. He wondered if he could win a stare down with sexy Liang. Nah, his mind would wander to her perfect body and he'd blink fo' sure. He blinked now.

Liang winked one eye back at him and smiling sweetly, she licked her lips.

That's an invitation brah! Say something cleva' quick.

Ole's so surprised he can't talk. But he's thinking, thinking. All he could think of was to wink back and smile. Then he had to laugh, maybe a little too loud.

"What so funny?" Ling had been talking of course. He'd missed the last few hundred paragraphs. She was looking directly at him. No more demure shyness. She was sensitive about her accent; she figured he was laughing at her.

"Nothing Ling, please go on," he said warmly.

She smiled and droned on with some story from her day at the Ritz-Carlton front desk.

"A guest pulled up for valet parking. When the valet, who looks too young to drive, asked for the keys to the Stingray, the owner would not hand them over to the boy. You remember that boy, the one I told you about that has that pink streak of color dye in his hair, the 'cute one.'

During all this, Ling stared at Ole for a full ten seconds before lowering her eyes and continuing with her never ending story. Uncle was radiating frustrated sexual energy in every direction. He had hoped to make it all up to that Italian hottie after his gig. With any luck he might have been 'making out' with Desiree on some romantic beach by this time. But kissing a drunken woman, even a gorgeous drunk woman is like kissing a pig. He wouldn't know about that, having never kissed a pig. It was an expression he'd heard back in Iowa. He tried to focus on his bowl of rice and veggies.

"Delicious Ling and Liang," he finally said something. His thought's running right on to, *I'll bet you're delicious too.*

It was a full moon Maui night. The Trade winds had slowed to almost nothing. The three candles on the table felt like a campfire. Was all this heat coming from the candles? No, the heat was coming from Liang. Ole didn't know it, but she had been simmering for Uncle for three months now; ever since she and Ling had moved into that room down the hall.

Under the table she rubbed her little bare foot on Uncle's hairy leg. His manhood went from hang loose zero, to sixty hard drive in less than four seconds. He hears that voice in his head whisper, *Ho 'kay brah. This one is chummin' the waters. Let's do some fishin'.*

Ole nods his approval at her and rubs his leg against her smooth thigh. It feels like striking a flint cap to a road flare. Ole looks through the glass table top expecting to see red flames shooting out of his shorts. Her willing thigh felt so good it almost burnt his skin, a wonderful aching flame to burn by. After a few minutes of this searing pleasure, Liang stood and gathered the empty bowls.

"I'm tired," she said.

"I wash dishes, goodnight Ole, Goodnight Ling."

She bowed, gathered the bowls and went into the kitchen.

Uncle's hopes fell through the floor. Was she just teasing? His frustration left him with a hard hunka, hunka burning love. He listened to Ling for a while, this time she made full eye contact, very unusual for her. Was there a hint of interest in her eyes too? He couldn't tell. Her look was much more sophisticated and impossible for Uncle to read. He liked her happy Scottish-Chinese chatter. He practiced patience, but he was anxious, almost trembling, wondering if Liang had really turned in for the night.

After a polite amount of time he said goodnight to Ling, bowed and went to his room. It took him a few moments to gather his towel and toothbrush and walk down the hall. This time the hall looked normal. There was fine Asian art lit softly in small alcoves built into the walls on each side of the hallway. It truly was a beautiful place to live. He stopped by Liang's door and tapped softly, once. It flew open like she was waiting for his knock. She posed. She had changed out of her high fashion, and into a simple Hawaiian sarong wrapped tightly around her tall figure. She held a pose, the wanton stance of a hooker waiting in the doorway of a Shanghai hotel. Uncle could smell too much fresh lipstick and makeup on her pretty face. There was the naughtiest pout on her lips. Her body heat flooded into the cool hallway like a desert wind.

"A hui hou Liang, see you later?"

She reached up on her toes and kissed him on the mouth. It wasn't a gentle kiss. Uncle can read a kiss. This one said "*I*

226

want you." Ole smiled.

"Come to my room, ten-thirty," he commanded.

She kissed him again, a little sweeter this time. He put both arms around her slender waist. Touching her like this, made him catch fire again. She felt its length pressed up hard against her and she laughed a naughty laugh as she covered her mouth with her hand.

Why do they always do that? He wondered. *It's not to hide bad teeth. Her teeth are perfect.*

He let go and continued down the hall to shower. Her door closed without a sound.

The lights throughout Yu'layne's house had turned down to a few reading lamps in various bedrooms. Uncle's lanai room was lit by moon light sneaking in the windows next to the bed. He turned his desk lamp up toward the ceiling for a little more soft, indirect light. His room had many advantages. Even on a hot night like this one, a little cool air tunneled through the side windows. He had thick curtains inside the sliding glass door for privacy. It was a great bachelor pad but one that had not seen an 'overnight' guest since he had moved in. It had been a crazy long time since he had enjoyed a woman. Ole's wolfish need was growing wilder with every minute he waited.

He laid there on his bed and wondered if Liang would show. It was now ten minutes past ten. He put some music on his Cd player. Rod Stewart's "Downtown Train" began to softly rock the room with its irrepressible beat. He turned the volume down low.

227

Ole opened a small bottle of Perrier water and tried to be patient. The Chinese girls told him they never drink liquor. He laughed out loud. His wolf mind repeating his thought.

You should lick her anyway, brah ha hah. The main dial on his passion meter was jammed all the way over to 'Dangerous' With that full moon tonight, someone should lock the wolf in his room.

Oh… yeah, lock me in with Liang! His coach is growling like a mad dog.

At ten-fifteen, there came two quick knocks on the door, a pause then, one more. He smiled, counted to ten slowly then he slid open the door.

"Why you make me wait? You bad man, you have such a long walk to your front door?" She looked around his small room, filled up with one full size bed. She had never been in here before.

"I was putting on my pants," he laughed.

"Foolish American, I take them off you right now," and she did.

Their fast and scorching first kiss took them both tumbling down onto the bed. Ole was kissing her madly while pulling her sarong off her shoulders when they were interrupted by another knock on his door.

"Liang?" Ling's timid voice was a whisper from outside the closed glass door and thick curtain.

"Liang?" She spoke a little louder this time.

"Aye," Liang returned softly.

Then Ling let loose with a fire-cracker string of strong Chinese words, overtones that sounded to Uncle like a mother's angry disapproval. Maybe Canton cussing?

Uh oh, he thought, *this evening is over before it begins.*

Liang made a soft Chinese word sound, a gentle reply to all the exploding fireworks of Ling's reprimand. The Chinese fire-cracker in his bed still had her fuse burning. Ling was silent. Then, Liang said something else, something warm and soft with a question mark hanging like a carrot-bait on a string. *Was that an invitation?*

The door slid open and Ling stepped inside. She slipped off her shirt and sweat-pants and stood there almost naked, looking at them with a hurt look on her China-doll face.

"Why you not ask me?" She pouted softly, then smiled.

Without her sweats, she wore only tiny black panties and no bra. Her pretty, round boobs had perky nipples popped out like those tiny tasty marshmallows. She crawled onto the bed and kissed Liang sweetly on the mouth. Then she put her arms around Uncle and kissed him just as kind, but with a desperation that crazed the wolf wild.

"Ooooooooooooooooooohuuuuuu'ooooooooo!" He howled.

Whoa is this for real? When it finally rains on Maui it down pours! Coach is genuinely surprised.

His teacher brain started computing the scientific odds of something like this happening. Both girls were kissing him now. He stopped calculating. From his inner juke box, came the rockin' sounds of 'Surf City.' Something about, *'goin' ta' Surf City and having fun, oh somethin' somethin' Surf City fun fun, fun… two ta' one, two girls for every joy, oh boy … a oooooo ah ah a oooooo."* He always liked that Brian Wilson song.

The two Chinese dolls taught him things that he'd never dreamed of, very sweet things. He responded with gentleness and then wolfish greed that quickly led to Mr. Macho Dove wild abandon shaking his branch with two chicks. When all their fuses were shooting white-hot sparks, they twirled in ecstatic explosions all over the bed like a string of firecrackers on a Chinese New Year. It was a wonder the house didn't catch fire. Uncle Ole, Ling and Liang growled and laughed together softly, hoping they were not waking up their neighbors.

Yu'layne heard the three wolves from the other side of her adjoining wall. She smiled like a Buddha, her thoughts, her own.

45

I Love him and I wanna Kill Him.

Fortunately for Desiree, she hit the chocolate desert, in the restaurant of the hotel where she was staying. So, when the Pioneer Inn closed at ten, the front desk manager recognized her and called two Filipino kitchen helpers to carry that dipped in chocolate, unconscious sleeping-beauty up one flight of stairs to her room.

She wasn't very heavy, maybe a hundred- and five- pounds soaking drunk. The boys talked about undressing her before putting her into bed. But their Catholic upbringing would not allow such a thing. Embedded catechism guilt lasts a lifetime. So, they wiped the pie off her lovely face, carefully laid her fully clothed, slender body on the bed and covered her with a blanket. They turned the air-conditioner on low. Before they left the room, they each kissed her on her beautiful forehead. True gentlemen, were these teenage boys.

The next day, when Desiree finally woke up, everything hurt. She had no clue where she was. This was not unusual. She was no stranger to hangovers so she didn't panic. She looked at her Rolex copy and realized she had slept past noon. Way past, it was four pm. She sat up slowly and stretched. That hurt some more and she retaliated by mumbling a thirty second mantra of filthy cussing. She needed a shower and a stiff Bloody Mary.

She kept on swearing until she had soaped all the chocolate

ice-cream out of her hair. A half hour of TV soap opera, volume cranked up so she could hear the show over her hair dryer on high, twenty minutes of expert make up and three changes of clothes, and she was dressed to kill. Desiree found her way back downstairs to the restaurant. This time she sat at the bar. When her Bloody Mary arrived, she stirred it with the celery stick and tried to sort out her emotions. She was not used to feeling confused. *Damn, why'd you get so wasted last night?* She talks to herself as much as Ole does. *Okay, you want him, wanted him for a long time now. He could not possibly remember you.* Three months ago, she had vacationed on Maui and heard him sing here at Pioneer Inn. He had shanghaied her heart with his haunting melodies and his words. *How'd that ever happen?* She wasn't brave enough to even speak to him that night, unusual for her. She pined away out of his line of sight, at the far end of the bar. She had sat right on this same bar stool that evening. She went ga-ga for Ole, like that old song from the radio that kept playing in her pretty head,

"Killing me somehow with his singing, killing me sweetly with his words." Something like that, it was hard to think.

She'd been simmering on low heat for Oliver ever since. She took a bite of her celery and spit it out. A Bloody Mary tastes better before noon.

When she found his profile on Strike-a-Match.com, she contacted him and over a few weeks and several cozy chats, she thought she had a friendship going. That is until she flew here and got stood up at Kimo's. She had never hated anyone as much as she hated Ole Gold. But her anger wasn't enough to cool her flaming passion. It was making her crazy. Crazier than usual anyway, and that's a scary kind of crazy. She felt obsessed by the thought of him. She was used to men being obsessed over her. *What can come of this?*

"I love him and I wanna kill him," now, she was thinking out loud.

"What's that?" Gina was just walking by with a tray of clean beer mugs.

"Nothing, dear, sort of arguing with myself."

Gina smiled, "I do that a lot," They both had a girl to girl laugh.

46

Unsatisfied?

Uncle awoke alone in his room with no hangover, no Ling, no Liang, but wearing a guilty smile on his face that just might last a lifetime. His inner psychiatrist was giving himself a lecture in pidgin,

Every guy gotta have one night da kine, brah. You t'ink it was so fun it mus' be so wrong? Hah! You were married a long time, 'das why. But Tanya all pau, brah. Yah, you still married palapala. Legal scissors gonna cut that pap'a. Not your fault brah. No blame, no shame. Life make crazy sometimes. Jus' be in da right place, right time. Like Maui, last night, full moon. You deserve good stuff brah. So, lover boy, you should be so choke-satisfied. How come you still t'inking about d'at crazy Italian chick? What'er you, nutz? Let her go brah. Be thankful. Count 'yer blessings, one, two, tree fool, Ling Liang and you.

Oliver yawns and roars as he stretches across the empty bed. The sheets smell sweet, like Liang. Ole's the new king of the girls 'Made in China' jungle. But, he's a melancholy old king. It was wonderful, sweet and kinky sex, the first in two long years, but without love.

You so pathetic brah. You need love to be happy? How much 'love' in the bank after thirty years loving 'What's-Her-Divorce'? What's love got to do with it? Remember 'dat song? Enjoy what comes. Accept compassion unto yer'self". His inner-Buddha is the host of his inner Self-Discovery-Channel.

Chapter 47

Who You Looking for Brah?

The following Tuesday night it was another packed house at the Pioneer Inn. As he plugged in his amp and tower speakers he looked out over the crowd but she wasn't there.

Who you looking for, brah? His coach knew the answer.

He would sing his best anyway with or without her. This crowd had come to hear his songs. He had local fans. Music was his drug. He didn't need to smoke grass to see colors in music. Smoking grass had messed up his sinuses for several years in college. Worse, it made him lazy. He quit smoking it over twenty-five-years-ago, didn't miss it a bit.

The Pioneer Inn gave him his drug for free now. All the Coca-Cola he could drink while he played his music. He took another deep drink and enjoyed the taste and the sparkling champagne-like rush down his throat. This was his one, long-lasting drug addiction. Ole did not consider the 'occasional' splash of rum in the Coke to be an addiction. He was such a disciplined character he could stop drinking either one or both any time he wanted to.

Isn't that the first indicator of Alcoholism? His inner counselor was concerned.

And when he did drink he never had painful hangovers.

Isn't that the second indicator that there is trouble ahead?

He had decided long ago that Coca-Cola was his worst vice and his best study buddy. The sugar and the caffeine gave him that edgy feeling that kept him at the top of his game. The occasional rum was the catalyst that pushed him to the outer limits of his absurd dreams. It would be hard to find anyone who could out-dream Uncle Ole after a night of rum and Coke. He was a professional.

48

Until Y'er Dead

Ole was done setting up and tuning his guitar and ukulele. He finished adjusting his guitar strap; he was ready. It was six-o'clock. He took a few deep breaths, stepped up to the microphone and began his set softly with his favorite sea-ballad,

"I'll take the chance, I'll take the stars… I'll take wind and sea. Cast away line, cast away doubts… cast away life for me."

Mysterious Desiree wasn't there in the crowd. He figured if she were still on the island she would wait awhile, and make another grand entrance. He had just thought the thought and she swept in like a movie star. Everyone in the place watched her walk across the room like she was floating down a modeling runway in Hollywood. Uncle Ole almost forgot the words to the song he was singing. She was wearing a short black number pulled tight over her tall, perfect figure. The mini-skirt showed graceful legs; her calves pumped up by her four-inch high heels. She made walking into a room an art form. He could tell she had not been drinking this time. Maybe *this* was his lucky night?

Oooo, she could probably dance in those shoes, brah. They look so natural on her. You should bed her as soon as possible with her shoes on. Coach can't wait.

That's exactly what men think about when women wear

heels like that. He kept on singing as his wound-up thinker kept on dreaming.

Then, there are women, brah. Aren't they a drug also? They should be classified as dangerous; certainly, they're highly addictive. His eyes rolled like two ball bearings as he and coach watched Desiree's sexy walk.

While Desiree made her grand entrance, Gina looked over at Uncle Ole. He shook his head... *no. No repeat of last week. Let her buy her own booze and supper tonight. We'll see what happens.* He can usually think and sing his songs at the same time. But, tonight it was hard to sing, all he could think about was Desiree. He watched her watching him, their eyes meeting only every three or four seconds. Once again she ate up every song, always listening, brushing off the occasional guy who wandered over to chat her up.

At eight o-clock, when his gig ended. The crowd was yelling "Hana huo," but not tonight. Ole put his guitar away and headed straight for Desiree. The crowd watched and understood. She didn't start with the cold shoulder this time. There was even a little apology in her voice.

"Sorry about last week." She sounded sober and sincere.

"I guess that makes us even, yah?"

"Not even close," but she was smiling mysteriously, kinda like a bank robber.

Uncle sat down. "How long you gonna be mad at me?" He really wanted to know. His wolfish needs were still surging from the pull of that wicked moon.

"Until yer dead." Then, "Ha, ha, hah." She laughed like it was just a joke. Her crazy laugh sounded too loud and artificial. Uncle grinned, so she went on. "Ok, maybe a hundred years."

Was that a little warmth in her voice? Uncle's curiosity was making his brain itch. He was spending too much of his life thinking about this hot and cold amazingly attractive woman.

"What's your story, Miss Desiree?" He had to know.

Guys know that when you ask a woman one question it can take weeks to get the whole answer. Desiree's dam burst and so did her cool façade. She started to cry. Not the 'po-po-pitiful me' kind, but real sobbing; the kind of crying that guys get uncomfortable with. All women know this and use it to their advantage. Desiree said she was mixed up inside. She must be, she couldn't stop the tears.

"When you stood me up last week, it felt like a rock was thrown through the glass of my bare soul," she sobbed.

Uncle was more interested in her bare body than her bare soul, but he liked the poetic imagery.

Desiree admitted that she'd heard him sing three months ago, right here at the Pioneer Inn and never forgot about him and his songs. Then she found his profile online and started chatting with him. "I thought we were friends?" She pouted so cute.

"Even friends make mistakes," he countered warmly. He was about done apologizing. His leg was touching hers. They were both getting an A+ in body chemistry. He was a retired chemistry teacher. He knew an A+ from a B. It was such an intense thrill to be touching an A+, he forgot the biggest lesson he had learned in college. *The prettier they are, the crazier they are.* Ole was so turned on by her body and her scent he almost didn't hear her start crying again. This time about her father dying a few months ago and leaving her a very large inheritance. That and the fact that she was pretty sure she had sold her house in California for nine-hundred and seventy-five thousand. She told him that when her house does close, she's coming back to Maui to buy a home here. Ok, now he's listening. She's rich and good looking and will soon own a home on Maui. Ole hadn't met a woman like that yet in Hawaii. His father had always told him it was just as easy to fall in love with a rich girl as a poor girl. He was feeling lucky. The night with the Chinese girls last Friday was proof of that. This could be another good fortune cookie for Oliver Gold. In the last few days, Ole had seen Ling and Liang in the kitchen a few times, bowed to them and received warm smiles. That's it.

Oops, he thought to himself. He wasn't listening again.

Her dog had died a week ago, 'Bubba' had been her pal for thirteen years. She started sobbing harder. Ole was feeling more sympathy than he could remember ever giving to any rich person. He offered her a drink of water and moved over to her side of the table. Uncle put his arm around her in a fatherly way. She sipped a little from the glass. It seemed to help. Her bare shoulder held close to his chest helped too. She was the broken-hearted world class model. He was the horny guitar player who had stood her up for lunch. He owed her some sympathy. *A bad way to start a relationship brah,* says his inner advice columnist.

"Where 're you staying Miss Desiree?"

"I thought you knew. I have a room here at the PI."

Uncle reached for the check on the table, but Desiree got it first.

"My turn," she surprised him. She paid with a credit card and made a big show of leaving a ten-dollar tip on the table. Ole didn't see her pick it up again as he got up to leave. She stuffed it back in her purse.

Uncle finished packing all his music gear in his Caddy and suggested a walk. They crossed the street to courthouse square where the hundred-year-old Banyan Tree was secretly making plans to overtake the whole town. It was a December night, about eighty-six degrees and no wind. It was so warm, his neck and shoulders never hurt anymore. He was walking hand in hand with the most beautiful rich woman he'd ever met.

Old fashioned Christmas lights were hanging in strings of mixed blues, whites, reds and greens from the lowest branches of the magnificent tree. Ole and Desiree sat down on a bench far from the street, in the shadow of one of its large trunks. Some teenagers sitting a block away were strumming ukuleles and singing, 'Jingle Bells.' The Myna birds had all settled down and quit their fighting chatter. It was sticky hot. Desiree had finally run out of words.

One car drove slowly by. It looked like an old rent-a-wreck. Ole thought he saw a couple of US Marines in the front seat. After a full five minutes of Desiree quietly scenting the night air with her sinister, sexual innuendo, Ole said, "I'd best get home." He wondered if she would agree or try to talk him out of such a stupid idea. It must have been the right thing to say. She slid closer to him and put one of her gorgeous long legs over his knee effectively pinning him in place where he sat. He didn't want to move. So he didn't. Desiree put her arm around his shoulder. For some eerie reason he felt like a fly stuck in a web. He didn't struggle. He wanted to kiss her, but because of that scary fly-feeling, he didn't. Ole had a vision of a male Praying Mantis about to be thrilled and then killed by his mate.

"Wanna see my room? It's air-conditioned."

What was happening? After months of no action on Maui, how did the stars all line up with the planets and Chinese and Italian women this week? Go, Go, Uncle Mojo!

"Sure," Uncle replied, trying not to sound excited or scared. He was both.

49

Ectoplasm

Uncle followed Desiree Lee up the stairs at the Pioneer Inn. She absolutely... oozed sex as she walked lightly in those dangerous heels. Her perfect butt was doing the Samba with every step she took. It was putting a sexy, eerie spell on him. Was he walking into another night of debauchery or some kind, of trap? Why was his horny anticipation slipping into worry?

Exactly half way up the stairs Ole felt a solid force field, something very tangible in the air. Whatever it was, it stopped his forward motion. It felt sticky like ectoplasm from those early twentieth century black and white séance films.

In his inner mind's movie theater, he saw a dusty cowboy, hands tied, blind folded and thirsty, walking up the steps of a gallows. There was a hangman up there wearing a cheap Halloween costume that looked like a Black Widow spider. He could almost feel the rope around his neck.

Next, he envisioned a falling guillotine blade and it wasn't slicing a cabbage. His nose soured with an acrid electric-chair smell, sizzling meat, like roast pork.

Is that smell 'Kuala you' brah? Coach is starting to panic. *Some kind a bad gumbo is cooking up these stairs.*

He could not take one more step. The Chinese girls had

been so sweet. Their silky-smooth free-electrons met all his pent-up wolf electrons with hungry pleasure. This drama queen had free electrons spinning around too, but they felt like baited fish hooks.

She's some fine bait brah, but I'm feeling it too, run! Run now, time to go! Coach has never sounded this terrified.

"Desiree, I'm feeling like I should call it a night. Think I'll head on home." He expected an argument or maybe disappointment at least. She didn't hesitate for a moment.

"Ta, tah, singer-boy, your loss." Confident, arrogant, that was her style.

She didn't even turn around, just gave one of those little backhand waves that girls do when they say, "whateva."

From behind her, Ole couldn't see how Desiree's angst was frying her face into an omelet. He didn't know her fingernails were cutting bloody slits in her palms as she clenched her fists. All he could think about was getting down those stairs and far, far away from this woman. Desiree opened her room door and all she saw was scarlet curtains of angry desire. She walked out on her ornate balcony and watched until her current obsession drove away in his big Cadillac.

Desiree went back into her air conditioning and slammed the lanai door. "So, that's how it is, eh? I turn up the heat and you take off? Why can't I have you my marvelous, guitar poet? Why do I even need you? I hate you! I hate you!" She ranted and cussed like a sailor as she unzipped and pulled her mini-dress over her head. Her flight home to the mainland was tomorrow. She was so angry that her love trap had not sprung tonight. She unstrapped her porn shoes and threw them at the wall mirror across the room. It didn't break like she wanted it to. She stared at her fried-egg face and yelled at her reflection,

"Mirror, Mirror, on the wall, who's the horniest whore of all?"

No answer from the mirror. She dropped her pretty clothes on the floor and crawled into bed. The A/C was on full cold but Desiree tossed in her own hot juices with her fingers inside her purple panties until her passion fruit was purpled, but not satisfied.

50

Late Night Snacks

The two U.S. Marines drove their old rental car around the Banyan tree square, made a left on Front Street and rolled slowly past all the stores. If you had asked them where they were going, Leo would say,

"Cruising for chicks."

Shy Frankie might not say anything. The truth was, they were both looking for that beautiful and so unforgettable Miss Desiree. The town sidewalks were empty. It was ten-fifteen, the town was famous for closing promptly at ten. On some nights a band would play at Mooses' bar until two in the morning. But they were 'persona non grata' up there.

They drove to Baker street and turned around in a church parking lot.

"One more lap around the track." Leo sighed.

Frankie did not reply. His nose was not bandaged any more, but it hurt when he talked. He did not want to talk anyway. He wanted to get laid. If he could not find this missing Desiree, then he would be happy with a Rosalie, Angelie, or a Corina-Corina. Leo felt the same way, he'd be happy to swing with any chick that was even half cute or half drunk, but he wanted

Desiree.

They rolled past Bubba Gump's and Longhi's, both closed. Kimo's was closing. The Lahaina yacht Club (members only) was still open. Their uniforms would get them in if they wanted to. They didn't. A few nights ago, they had tried the yacht club. The employees greeted them warmly and bought them their first beer. The place was okay, a full house. But there were no young single gals in there. A couple of nice-looking cougar-type women at the bar eyed them up and down. It was kind of intriguing but they left after the free beer.

The Marines drove on down the sleepy street. All the t-shirt shops and art galleries were shut tight. There was a dog sleeping on the sidewalk.

"What a swinging town you picked, Frankie."

"Hey big mouth, you're the one who chased 'Miss What's Her Purple' over to this side of the island."

That was a long speech for Frankie. He had not said much to his pal since the fight with the two sailors.

"Speaking of big-mouths, brag to me about your amazing rifle award, 'Marksman First-Class' hah? And tell me some more lies about your dangerous tour of duty in Afghanistan?"

"Shut-up Leo."

"You shut-up."

Leo turned the corner by the Pioneer Inn to circle the court house one last time and there, coming out of an ABC Store was long-legs herself, Miss Desiree 'What's-Her-Purple," the sassy Italian model.

"Whoa!" they said in precision drill unison.

Leo pulled over to the curb. Frankie leaned out his window and whistled his best wild wolf at her. It hurt his nose and face somethin' awful but it sounded like a police siren telling her to pull over and put her hands against the wall.

She had been sleepless since Uncle left her all wet. The restaurant had closed and she decided to go down and find some snacks. They found her. She invited them both up to 'see her room'. The Marines didn't have to fight over Desiree tonight. She showed them all her "rooms" and taught them how to work as a team and how to share, all at the same time.

51

Certified Mail #2

Life in Hawaii was just as wonderful as Ole dreamed it would be. Weeks went by. He played music in the rest homes, sold sun block at the resort and counted rainbows. Some days he saw three, the record was nine. Desiree Lee never returned to mess with his heart again. He figured she flew back to California to count her money. Ole tried to forget her but it was like forgetting his hands. They were always there waving around in front of him looking empty. He immersed himself in fun. He surfed 'S' turns reef by day and watched sunsets with Captain Billy and the Valley Isle sun downers.

He kept to his morning yoga and meditations raising his energy level to create sexy, free electrons all around himself. But there were no more fireworks.

Soon, whole months had torn themselves off the calendar forever. Uncle Ole got a lot of online messages from other women, but didn't bother to respond. He was sorta convinced that long-distance, internet dating was an emotional waste of time.

He nearly turned to stone one morning as he picked through Yu'layne's house mail. His paralysis came from another official looking green postcard from the Lahaina Postmaster. His fingers thawed enough to pick up the poison and read it. A new certified letter was waiting like a land mine down at the post office.

You gonna step on it brah?

Uncle made his body move toward the car, get in and like a mindless robot he drive to the post office. His hands looked metallic as he signed his name for the manila envelope from King County, Superior Court. It was a notice of his divorce trial date set for seven days from today. Tanya had filed her financial statement with the court and filed one for Oliver too. She claimed that he was making over eighty-four thousand a year, living like a king in Hawaii, while she was barely getting by on her measly fifty-eight-thousand-a-year job. That she was carrying all the family debt by herself and struggling to make ends meet every month. Again the last page spelled it out clearly: "If the Defendant or his legal counsel do not respond to this petition, or fail to appear in court on the date of said hearing, the marriage will be dissolved in favor of the Plaintiff."

"What?" Uncle had faxed all his financial stuff to Ben Haller's law firm almost three months ago. Ole opened his phone and called his attorney.

"Haller, Jones, Thorndike and Richie Rich, may I help you?" a woman answered.

"Ben Haller, please."

"I am sorry sir. Mr. Haller is out of the office. Can I be of assistance?

"Is that you Amy?" He recognized her voice.

"Yes it is, who's calling?"

"It's me, Oliver Gold."

"Hey Ole, how's the weather over there in Hawaii?"

They had crewed together on Ben's sailboat. Amy was some relation to Ben, but Uncle didn't know she was working for him.

"Where's Ben?"

"He's on vacation, Ole. He and Sue, Cliff and Pam and Cal and Denise are enjoying the life of the rich and anonymous down in the Caribbean on a new Beneteau 51, the lucky stiffs."

"He's supposed to be in his office working on my behalf. Did he receive the stack of financial docs I faxed him?"

"I have no idea Ole. Let me connect you with his personal assistant, please hold. Bye... "

Uncle began to shake. He wasn't sure if it was from worry or anger. After a very long thirty-five seconds, a man's voice answered.

"Hello Mr. Gold, this is Bernie Sheldon, assistant to Ben Haller. Amy asked me to check your file. Yes, your faxed documents are here, looks like twelve pages. How can I help you?"

"Have they been entered into court on my divorce case?

"No sir. There is no court stamp on them. They have not. There is only one stamped court document entered by our firm on your behalf. It looks like a request for postponement for ninety days due to your living out of state. There is a 'Request Granted' Stamp on the document. The ninety day extension ended last Friday. That is all that's in your file sir."

"Ben went sailing in the Caribbean without entering my response to my wife's divorce petition? I faxed all that stuff to him three months ago. He told me not to worry." Ole has never been so worried.

"Then he flies away on a vacation? Unbelievable! Your firm sent me a bill for one-thousand dollars to get the ball rolling. I paid it right away. What happened? The ball is rolling all right. In a few days, my wife is going to screw me out of my future next week. You, Sheldon, or whatever your name is, you're his assistant? He must have left this up to you. You didn't file these papers either?"

"I am not an attorney, Mr. Gold. I don't know what to say."

Oliver closed his cell phone. He was so angry he couldn't breathe for a full minute. Finally turning purple without oxygen, he gasped a deep cleansing breath and went to his room. He found his Seattle phone book that he brought with him to Maui. Back then, he was thinking he would surprise Tanya with flowers on Valentine's Day and would need to find a local florist. How stupid love can be. Today he paged to attorneys and poked a finger at the first column, Michael Burns, Family Divorce Specialist, law firm of Anderson, Burns and Kellar. Ole called Mr. Burns, explained his emergency, got the firm's fax number, gave him a credit card payment for one-thousand dollars as a retainer and crossed his fingers.

"I will be happy to represent you in court, Mr. Gold. Once

you have faxed me the pending trial documents and all your personal documents, I will take care of it right away."

"I want you to return fax to me, copies of my response and financial statement entered, dated and court stamped, today." requested Ole.

"It is noon here Mr. Gold. Fax me your documents today and I assure you I will enter them in court no later than tomorrow morning. I will fax stamped copies to you as soon as possible. That will be sometime tomorrow afternoon. Don't worry about a thing."

"Thank you, Mr. Burns. Goodbye."

Uncle wanted to go lay on the beach, he was feeling terrible. But his next call was to the bank that issued his credit card. He asked for a 'Stop Payment' on the one-thousand-dollar payment he had made to Ben Haller's firm. He had to explain it all again. The credit manager asked him to send a stop payment request by letter with all the details. It would all take time, but it would be done.

Ole needed a drink but this was serious, he stayed on task. It took about an hour to fax all his documents from Yu'layne's fax machine. When he was through, his stomach hurt so bad he wanted to heave. He went to the beach instead. He laid face down, flat on the sand until the healing energy of Maui made his stomach feel warm and calm again. If he had looked up he would have seen a double rainbow arching its majestic colors over all the happy and even the troubled people on Maui. He didn't look up.

52

Illegal Beach Fires

The next morning, Ole was still hurting. That's the price of loving someone. It hurts like hell to let go. He thought of his mother. Moms' are experts at letting go. He needed her advice. He opened his cell and called her. She was real, real quiet on the Iowa side of the phone call as he told her about the divorce. She did mention that as far back as anyone could remember, no one in their family had ever divorced. Ole remained quiet. Then her advice was simple,

"Be strong Oliver, be kind, be generous." Mom knew the two rules of living. She had been raised by good people in Iowa. Ole told her he loved her and asked how dad was doing? Mom said he was out fishing on the lake today. Ole thanked her for the advice, told her he will always lover her and closed his phone. Next, he turned to his second oldest friend, his Gibson guitar.

He was still in a lot of pain, so he spent the rest of the day sitting on his bed, wringing out his heart, page by page through every song in his song books. He'd had his mom and his guitar longer than his marriage. On lonely nights he slept with his guitar. 'Coco-Lani' had a woman's curves.

You are so pathetic brah, his inner shrink was an expert at self-sarcasm.

By sunset his chest bones still felt broken, but six hours of singing had him breathing in and out with less pain. Uncle fixed himself a rum and coke and drank it down while standing in the middle of the kitchen. He refilled it and this time he tossed in some ice and a chunk of pineapple. The floating fruit looked like a yellow life-jacket of sunshine, chilled and uncomfortable there among all that ice; about as miserable as he had been living back in 'neck-pain' Washington State. So he tipped the medicine back and squeezed the pineapple with his teeth. Uncle planned to squeeze the fun out of life too. That meant living in Hawaii without Tanya.

You're finally getting the picture dumb ass. He couldn't argue with his brain this time.

He embraced his guitar tenderly and walked outside. The almost-sunset-sky was beckoning him downhill to Kahana beach. Already, the sun was doing the limbo under low, western clouds the color of whip cream. Uncle smiled, wondering, *Jolly Ol' Sol, how low can you go?*

Maui sunsets are medicine for a broken heart. He wanted to feel happy again, so reaching his favorite sand dune, he yoga-ed down to a full lotus, with Coco-lani, ready to be healed by a sky full of color. But tonight, his great expectations were over too soon. A black-shroud of a cloud threw itself out from the eastern mountains and covered the beautiful sky. It was getting dark too fast, as if the sunset was passing out or quietly dying. Far away on the western horizon the last sails of red color dropped over the edge of the ocean. It was that quick. No magnificent healing, no green flash, no afterglow, it was an awful sunset of an awful day.

Ole played some Moody Blues chords on his guitar to match his loneliness. After one verse of, 'Nights in White Satin' it was full dark. Uncle could play in the dark so he started to sing without any real plan, just lost chords of this and that. Some of the dark clouds blew out to sea and evaporated with the music. A few shy stars peeked through the torn ribbons. They struck tiny flint-sparks of bright hope down from the gloom. It wasn't enough. Verses of hurt came limping up out of the trench where his heart used to be and he sent them stumbling along into the coming divorce battle with melancholy chords.

Time slowed down fast. A huddle of hours later, the stars had clocked themselves around the night sky and piled up in a rejected heap of diamonds west of the Big Dipper. It looked like the dipper was about to sweep them into its cup to be thrown away, among the millions of other starry-eyed love dreams that didn't come true. It reminded him of an astronomy class he took in college. The professor said that our entire, immense, galaxy of stars could fit inside those four stars of the big Dipper. That's how far apart those four stars really are. It was a dipper well named. That's how far he felt from Tanya.

Somewhere around the middle of the night, a man came walking in long strides down the beach. It wasn't that unusual to see someone out here alone at any hour. But this guy did not have that wandering beachcomber walk. He was on a mission. He marched with a determined pace and was headed right for where Uncle Ole was sitting. On guard for self-defense; the guitar player laid down his guitar.

As the stranger neared, he was talking in an excited voice,

"I see you playing the guitar brah, this is perfect."

Uncle had never seen this character before. He looked kind of scruffy but not dangerous. He was dressed like a haole surf-dude guy. Maybe he was another retired teacher from Seattle. The stranger was carrying a large backpack over one shoulder. He did not try to shake hands, he just said,

"I'm Len, howz it brah?"

"Hi Len, call me Ole."

"I'm gonna build a campfire on the beach tonight, might as well be here if that's okay with you?"

"Beach fires are illegal on Maui Len, they dirty up the beach with blackened ash and if you cover them with sand people burn their bare feet on the left-over coals, bad idea."

"No mess brah, no trouble, watch 'dis."

Len shut-up and went to work. He opened his backpack and pulled out three logs. Each one was a few inches in diameter and a couple feet long. He propped them up against each other in a small tripod. From where Ole sat, it looked like the Great Pyramid out on sands of Egypt, only smaller. Next Len pulled out a can of lighter fluid and soaked the pyramid for a couple of minutes with a fine spray. Then he lit it with a match.

"Shazam, instant campfire! Let's sing a song Ole."

Len was a clever scruffy dude or a wizard; they had a cheery campfire burning quietly in front of them in less than a minute.

"Wanna beer?" Len offered, reaching further into his pack.

"No thanks, I quit beer fourteen years ago. It was making me fat. Got any rum in there?"

"Sorry brah, let's sing."

The two new friends sang every verse of Dylan's 'Blowin' in the Wind. When they finished, the silence they had kept at bay, returned with a sigh. From behind them, they felt a soft land breeze begin to bend the flames out toward the ocean, so they sang it all over again. It sounded better the second time around, with more harmony in the wind, along with the answer. At the end of the song nothing more needed to be said. Dylan had said it all.

The campfire went out. Len got the can of lighter fluid and gave the three sticks another good soaking. He struck a second match and fire went twirling up the logs again. It burned through three more songs and died down to nothing. Len emptied the last of the lighter fluid on the logs and gave it one more match. They sang 'The Hour When the Ship Comes In' and 'Boots of Spanish Leather' and 'Hey Mr. Tambourine Man'.

The fire left the logs for the third time. The darkness was deep black for a few seconds, and then ancient starlight brought the world into pale focus. Len picked up the three logs and put them back in his pack. They didn't show any sign of burn, weren't even hot to touch. He gathered up his empty lighter fluid can, the three burnt match sticks and his two beer cans. He zipped shut his pack, shook Uncle's hand and said goodnight. With that same determined walk, he disappeared down the beach. Ole looked down at the sand, no ash, no coals, no mess.

"I like this island." He said out loud, for the tenth time this week. All the worry and heartache were forgotten. As soon as he admitted he felt better, he became happy again. Then like a karmic reward for getting over himself, a 'moon-bow' appeared in the clouds above Molokai island. He'd never seen one of these bright pastel-colored rainbows cast by moonlight. Hawaiians called this, 'Ulalena rain'. They say the only place it falls in all the world is on the islands of Maui, Molokai, Lanai and Kahoolawe. Ole felt like dancing so he tried a slow pirouette and sang out strong,

"Oh, I'll dance beneath my diamond sky, one foot in the sea, even if nobody needs me…"

He beamed free electrons like starlight; alive in a wonderful dream, hugging his guitar close to his side like a lover and waving one hand free.

53

Perjury Karma

Uncle Ole's new attorney did what he promised. His response to Tanya's broadside was officially stamped and entered in court the next morning along with Uncle's financial statement and tax returns. He did not have to fly back to Seattle.

He was instructed to call the courtroom on the day of the hearing, stay on the court's speaker phone and leave the defense to Burns.

Ole called at ten am exactly, on the appointed date. The court officer put him on speaker phone and Ole heard the judge talking to him.

"Good Morning Mr. Gold, I am Judge Wall. Can you hear me all right?"

"Yes, your honor, Good Morning."

Ole could hear papers shuffling as the judge said hello to Mrs. Tanya Gold and her attorney, Mr. Blackheart or Backstabber or something. Ole didn't hear his name very clearly. There was more paper noise before the judge spoke again.

"Mr. Gold is listening by phone this morning, his counsel Mr. Burns is present in court. Mrs. Gold, I have read your petition and financial declarations. Your husband's counsel has entered a financial statement of Mr. Gold's current monthly income in Hawaii. It is radically different than your claim. Mr. Gold states that his income is forty-one hundred dollars per month. That figure is supported by his current paycheck stubs of three to five-hundred dollars a week plus his fixed benefit retirement pension of twenty-one hundred dollars per month from the Washington State Teachers Employee Retirement Service. That is forty-one hundred dollars per month Mrs. Gold." The judge repeated. Then, his voice sounded a little more interested.

"In your financial statements, you claim that your husband is earning over seven-thousand-dollars-per-month. That would be eighty-four thousand per year. When I reviewed Mr. Gold's tax returns over the last three years, his income, working full time as a college teacher was sixty-five thousand dollars a year. That works out to five-thousand four-hundred dollars per month. So according to your claim, your husband is now making much more in his retirement years than he was making while he worked full time. Do you have evidence supporting your claim, Mrs. Gold?"

"Yes, your honor!" She spoke right up, clear and confident. It was the first time he had heard her voice in a long time. It warmed his heart for a half second before the ice-cold blade of her divorce dagger stabbed him in the back again, all the way to his heart.

Be careful brah, don't say a word. He listened to his inner caution coach. He had loved this woman long enough, she's out for his blood and his money. He kept his mouth shut.

"Please explain, Mrs. Gold."

"It's all right here your honor. This pamphlet I am holding published by the Washington State Family Support Commission has a table of earnings for men and women with and without college educations. Men in my husband's age group with a double master's degree, like Mr. Gold, should be earning at least seven-thousand dollars per month. The average *college* teacher however, with just one master's degree, in his age group, earns over eight-thousand three-hundred dollars per month. So, you see I was very conservative in my claim as to what my husband should be earning."

There was a long pause of at least a minute of silence. Then the judge asked,

"Besides a pamphlet of guidelines, do you have any other evidence of your husband's current income?"

"No, your honor, I felt this was..."

"I am not interested in how you feel Mrs. Gold. This is a court of law. I am bound by the laws of the state of Washington to consider only evidence. A pamphlet of guidelines is not evidence. Making false claims in court is called perjury, Mrs. Gold. You are hereby fined seven-hundred and fifty-dollars, payable to Mr. Gold, plus two-hundred and fifty-dollars court costs payable to King County Superior Court. Mrs. Gold, never come into my court room again unless you have sought divorce mediation first. If mediation does not provide a satisfactory settlement between you and your husband then you may bring your petition before this court. I advise you both to settle your case out of court. Next case bailiff, oh... you may hang up the phone now, Mr. Gold."

Uncle closed his cell phone and was about to cheer when his phone rang. It was his new attorney.

"Well, we won that one Mr. Gold."

"You never said a word, Mr. Burns."

"Right, but I filed the documents that won this battle and I was in the court room for you wearing my best wool suit from Brooks Brothers. Ha ha hah. I saved you a long flight to Seattle and back. Your wife is in the court records, fined for perjury. You should be happy. You gained seven-hundred and fifty dollars."

"What is your fee for this twenty-minute drama?" Uncle had to ask.

"Our firm charges a minimum of twelve-hundred dollars per hour of court room work, one minute to sixty, same fee."

Ole ground his teeth together.

"What is this phone call costing me?"

"When I call you, there is never a charge. When you call me, the fee is one-hundred and twenty-five dollars from one minute to thirty."

"Then while I have you on the phone, what do we do next?"

"We seek mediation as the judge advises. I will send her

attorney three family mediators I have had success with. I'll let you know when he responds. Don't worry about a thing."

"I've heard that before. Good bye Mr. Burns."

54

Don't Worry

Time changes tires when you retire. Ole was never in the fast lane as a college professor, but now he was in the bicycle lane. Which was a welcome accomplishment. To stay within his fifteen-dollar a day budget, he became fond of Subway sandwiches and water on his breakfast cereal. He didn't care much for milk anyway, it cost nine bucks a gallon at the store.

He bought a bicycle at a garage sale, so the Cadillac could save its energy for important stuff, like being a closet for his music gear and a limo on special dates. Hawaii was so expensive that living here without being a millionaire made every day a challenge and an accomplishment.

He woke up one morning in his beautiful room and watched the same three doves outside his window. They were just preening and cooing. Maybe all their hanky-panky was over for today. It was entertaining to watch them care for each other. He missed caring for someone. He had loved Tanya and taken care of her. He got a chill clear to his spleen and his stomach hurt remembering the short notice, 'take-all' hearings and perjury bomb she and her attorney had thrown at him. He wanted to know how the divorce was progressing. He wanted it over with. But if he called, it would to cost him another hundred and twenty-five-bucks. He was just putting the question out his mind when Mr. Burns, his attorney called.

How do eerie coincidences like this happen, brah? He's

stunned.

"Mr. Gold, I have news. Your wife will not agree to mediation with any of my suggested professionals. I asked her attorney to recommend some family mediators, and he did so. She would not meet with them either. I strongly suggest we set a final court date as soon as possible."

"How soon?"

"How soon can you fly over here?"

"I have to be there?"

"Do you want to come out of this with or without some of your pension?"

"Give me thirty days to book an airfare at a reasonable price."

"Ok, Mr. Gold I am looking at the judge's calendar for next month. Let's go with April 7th. You will be notified by the court of that date with a certified letter. I will need the month to prepare your defense. If you have any other documents you wish to fax me, do so as soon as possible."

"Fine, I'll be there the evening of April 6th, Mr. Burns, Thank you."

"See you in court Mr. Gold. Don't worry."

Uncle closed his phone. *Uh huh, don't worry. Just live on mantras and tofu for the next thirty days, that 'ought'ta help.* His inner voice sounded more facetious than usual.

Chapter 55

Don't Worry Beach

Uncle spent most of his evenings not worrying at the beach with the sun downers. There is something soothing about watching sunsets with a cold drink in one hand. Sometimes Ole would have a drink in both hands for the double-feature sunsets with 'broke 'da eyes' afterglows. Sunsets are the great-equalizer in Hawaii. You may be a bus driver or an investment banker, at sunset you are the same as your neighbors. It doesn't matter if you have thirty-million, two-million or ninety-one dollars, you're here in Hawaii, just another beach bum in a t-shirt watching the sunset.

These sun downers all loved music and a select few would pass around the ukulele as the sun slowly descended the treble clef of clouds lining the western sky. Ole liked to hear Captain Billy sing his songs of maritime poetry. Oliver also sang whaling and sailing songs. Ole and Billy were two of a kind, with years of sailing yarns to spin. Both had set their anchor on Maui and would most likely never go to sea again.

A.J. a retired US senator, was another sunset regular and a musician at heart. He did not play the ukulele, but he knew the words to every song you could think of. One evening A.J. explained a simple, truth to Ole.

"You know why I get to live here, Ole?"

"Because y'er rich?" answered Ole.

"Nope, well I get by, but I get to live here because I was nice to people for thirty years. These were people I worked with every day in Washington DC. Mean people, mean as scorpions. But I treated them all with kindness. Now I'm here, barefoot on warm winter nights, watching the sunset with happy people and they are still back there shoveling... snow and being mean to each other. It's karma man; it's all about how we treat each other." A.J. knows the two rules.

The sun was almost set. To the east, over A.J.'s shoulder there was a double rainbow from the sun's last dramatic spotlight. It was arching in a graceful final bow and landing at their feet. The pot of gold tonight was overflowing with friends. It was comforting to be around people who don't have to worry.

56

Settling out of Court

April 7th found Uncle Ole jet-lagged but on time in the Seattle court room. He was the first one to arrive. There wasn't even a bailiff or reporter present. He sat down at an empty table. He hoped it was the defendant's table. He was taking books out of his back pack when a slightly balding, hunched-over man wearing an expensive looking suit, walked into the court room. He was carrying a heavy briefcase.

"Oliver Gold, I am Michael Burns, of Anderson, Burns and Kellar. How was your flight?"

"It was just as uncomfortable as being in divorce court," he said, shaking the attorney's manicured hand.

"I'm at your service Mr. Gold, don't worry."

Do they learn to say that in law school? Ole wonders.

"What is the best and worst that can happen this morning?"

"I have discussed your case with my partners at the firm. We all agree that your best option is to settle out of court."

"How do we do that Mr. Burns?"

It was at that moment Tanya and her attorney arrived and dug their trench across the aisle. Even before he saw them out of the corner of his eye, Ole felt the presence of the Dream

Shark swim into the room. The fear in the room was colder than a few minutes ago. He had not seen his wife in a long time, but he didn't want to even look at her. He remembered her accusations one by one and stared at the pen he was taking apart with his fingers. Its little spring rolled across the table and over the edge. He didn't pick it up. *He abandoned me. He left me with all the family debt. He was a terrible father. He retired without me, making seven-thousand a month and I am just scrimping by. He can only see his daughter one week a year at his own expense. His pension should belong to me.* Mr. Burns leaned over and whispered in his ear,

"It's already done. Your wife's attorney and I have reached a settlement that I think you will agree is fair to both parties."

Just then the judge entered the court room from a side door. There was no, "All rise!" call from the bailiff. There was no bailiff. Instead of walking up on his elevated bench, the judge walked into the aisle between the tables and spoke in a firm, deep voice.

"Mr. and Mrs. Gold, I am Judge Taktuda Wall. I have not had time to review your case. Divorce trials are a waste of my time and your tax dollars. I do not know if you have sought mediation as I advised. I seriously urge you to come to your own terms concerning the dissolution of your marriage. If you cannot, I will bring in a court reporter and a bailiff then I alone will decide your case. I guarantee that neither of you will like my decision. Knock on my chamber door when you have come to your senses." He turned his back on everyone and disappeared into his inner sanctum.

Of course, Mr. Burns knew what to do. Lawyers do this dance five days a week. He and Tanya's attorney met in the middle of the room and exchanged courtesies. Uncle watched them as they shared the attorney, 'secret' handshake. He knew that they knew, they were the only winners in this room. They were each making over a thousand-bucks-an-hour. Ole could almost hear the unspoken words during the handshake,

This is gonna take at least two hours, ha, ha, hah maybe more, ha, ha, hah.

Mr. Burns led Tanya's attorney over to introduce him to Ole.

"Mr. Gold this is Vader Blackenedheart, Mrs. Gold's counsel."

Ole ignored him. He was preoccupied reading one of the books he had brought with him. He did not bother to even look at the man.

There were a few seconds of awkward silence, then Burns continued,

"The way to proceed this morning is the four of us, you and your wife and Vader and I will meet together in an adjoining private room and see if we can come to terms as the judge advised."

"Mr. Burns, I'm not going anywhere with those people. You talk to them. That's what I am paying you for. I'm staying right here."

"Alright Mr. Gold, but please reconsider. As your counsel, I would advise you to join us.

"No thank you Mr. Burns, I'll wait here."

Turning to Darth Vader, Burns said, "You and Mrs. Gold go on ahead. I need a moment with my client."

Tanya and Blackenedheart left the room. Her attorney did not have a thick brief case full of documents, just one thin paper folder which he gathered up and took with him. His table was now as empty as his soul. Mr. Burns waited until they had left the court room.

"What are you thinking, Mr. Gold? You heard the judge. We must try to hammer out a solution and settle out of court."

"What have you and Vader already hammered?"

"After a series of lengthy negotiations, we both think that sharing your pension 50/50 with your wife would be fair to both parties. Rounding it off you would pay your wife one-thousand and fifty-dollars a month for the rest of your life, half your current monthly pension. Any increase in the base monthly payment in the future will also be shared 50/50.

"Mr. Burns, that is a not negotiation that is a train wreck. What am I paying you for? This woman won't move to Maui with me, where its warm, so that I'm not in chronic neck pain. Our marriage counselor suggested we try Hawaii for one-year and Tanya flat out refused. After four years of trying to convince her that retiring with me and my pension would be a good idea, she found a boyfriend and has filed a slanderous

272

lawsuit against me to steal the pension she could be spending with me in Hawaii. So, *NO*, capital *N*, capital *O*, *NO* way, am I giving her half my pension. Think up a better plan quick. That's what I'm paying your for. I want this over with."

"I will do my best Mr. Gold. Will you accompany me to the conference room? They are waiting for us."

"I am staying here Mr. Burns. You're my attorney, go to bat for me."

Without another word, Burns turned and left the court room. Ole looked at his watch, wrote down the time, ten-thirteen, and went back to reading his book. *Don't worry,* he thought to himself.

Mr. Burns was gone for a long time. When you're earning over a thousand an hour why hurry? At noon he returned with a big smile on his unhappy-looking, pale face.

"Good news Mr. Gold. We have an out-of-court settlement that is good for everyone. Tanya will receive a set five-hundred dollars a month with no future increases required. I strongly suggest you agree Mr. Gold. This judge does not like contested divorce cases. He can be brutal. Attorneys in Seattle call Takuda Wall, Judge 'Wailing Wall' and trying to convince him of anything is like 'talk'-ing-'tuda'-wall. We should settle this amongst ourselves, now."

Ole was feeling more than he was thinking. All he wanted to do was get this nightmare over with and fly back to Maui. Mom had told him to be kind, be generous.

"Tell them I will agree to five-hundred-a-month starting May first."

"A wise decision Mr. Gold. We are done here. You will be receiving confirmation of this by mail from Mr. Blackenedheart who will arrange all the paperwork. Our law firm will send you a final statement for the balance owed. Thank you and good day." Burns shook Ole's hand very briefly but met Tanya's attorney with the secret, law-brotherhood, double-handshake that seemed to say, *Ha, ha-hah... that was perfect, two hours and five minutes! Three-thousand, six-hundred bucks apiece and we can still make our tee time at Indian Hills by one-fifteen. Shall we say fifty-bucks a hole on the front nine?*

57

Nami, the Cute Japanese Traveler

When Uncle got back to Hawaii he began in earnest, to find something or someone to fill the bombed-out hole in his chest called divorce. He saw the Chinese girls in Yu'layne's kitchen from time to time. They smiled, he smiled and that was as far as it ever went. Maybe they were all embarrassed about the full-moon fireworks. One evening the girls were out on the lanai having another candle-lit dinner. This time they were with two handsome young Chinese men. Uncle bowed and said hello and went to his room. He was bored and broken, but officially single again. It didn't feel good.

He opened his computer to check his in-box at the dating sites. It had been awhile, there were fourteen-hundred new friend requests and seven-hundred and ten new messages. Six-hundred and ninety-nine of these were from women under twenty years old. He ignored them and read the messages from women over the age of twenty-five.

One claimed to be a Chinese doctor and did not want to move to the USA. She wanted Ole to visit her in China. Her photos were really something. She was forty-five and beautiful of course. She had her own big home, surrounded by flowers and tropical trees. She had a new Toyota van. She said she was looking for a pen pal to help her with her English. Then someday she wanted a husband. He typed a question to her and asked why she needed help, her messages were all in perfect English. She admitted to paying to have her letters translated from Chinese. He stopped writing her. Ole did not want to live in China and he figured it's hard enough to understand a woman who speaks your own language. Double red flags.

The next cutest correspondent was a petite Japanese woman who owned a home in Tokyo, but she worked in Malaysia. Nami was her name and she was thirty-five and single. He always asked that marriage question now. His divorce was settled, he was an eligible bachelor. It should feel exciting. Instead it felt like his best friend had just kicked him in the stomach for six months and left him barely breathing. He would live, but he knew he was crippled emotionally and financially for years to come.

Nami's photos were nice. She was small, maybe ninety-five pounds, a real Japanese doll. She was fun to chat with online. Nami spoke English fairly, well. They sent friendly messages back and forth. Ole had learned some Japanese. A couple of weeks after his return from Seattle, Nami surprised him with a call to his cell phone. "Hi Ole, moshi-moshi, it's me Nami."

"Nami? Are you calling from Japan?"

"No, I vacation now in Hono'ru'ru."

"Cool, are you coming over to Maui?"

"You invite Nami?"

"Of course, I would like to meet you in person."

"Ok, when?"

"Whenever you like, today, tomorrow, you decide."

"Where I stay?"

"Well my place is just one room with one bed. If you are okay with that, you can stay here.

"Okay," there was no hesitation. "I make f'right for tomor'low. I text you my landing time; you pick Nami up?" This was not a cautious woman.

"Sure Nami, see you tomorrow."

Uncle went back to his laptop computer and re-read Nami's profile. She had traveled all over Europe, Asia and some of North America including the Caribbean and parts of Canada. Most of the photos of her, 'friends' were men. Her pictures were demure and pretty. She was too small to be glamorous. She did not wear make-up in any of her close-ups. She didn't need it, she looked like a very cute high school senior. Ole was hoping she wore deodorant.

58

Unsettled out of Court

The morning Nami was to arrive, Ole found a large manila envelope addressed to him in Yu'layne's mailbox. It was from Mr. Vader Blackenedheart, noted attorney for captured Nazi SS Officers, now practicing family law. Uncle had to read it twice, before his knees gave out. He dropped to the floor, shook his head and read it again.

Unbelievable. This guy was truly a dark-force, gangster-attorney from an evil Death Star. It was a court-ordered statement for seven-hundred and fifty-dollars, payable to Tanya Gold beginning May 10th and a payment book for the next forty-five years; payments all due on the 10th of the month. This was not what he had agreed to. He called his attorney right away.

"He did what?" Mr. Burns sounded only slightly surprised. "That's not what we agreed on."

"That's right Mr. Burns. I agreed to five-hundred. What can you do about it?" But at that instant he saw it for what it was. *It's just another dirty trick from the attorney handbook.* He guessed what Mr. Burns was about to say, *Oops, Tanya's lawyer has simply made a mistake. I'll fix it for you Mr. Gold. Of course, I'm going to have to operate on your wallet again and take out any of that left-over green stuff that's still in there, but don't you worry.*

Instead Mr. Burns said, "How could Vader make such a stupid mistake?"

They're on a first name basis, I knew they were golf buddies.

"Don't worry Mr. Gold, I'll send him a letter and get it all straightened out in a few days. In the meantime, ignore the payment book you received. I will go back to court and make double-sure the five-hundred-dollar payment is recorded correctly."

"No, Mr. Burns you will not... this deal is off. I have not signed anything yet. You will go back to court and set a new trial date and we will present our case, including this little 'mistake' of Vader's to the Judge."

"As you wish Mr. Gold. I will do it this afternoon and let you know when the new court date is set.

"Make it thirty days from now. Let me know right away so I can book another flight. Goodbye, Mr. Burns."

59

Can You Help Nami Travel?

At noon, Uncle was waiting at the little Kapalua airport on Maui's west side. The single engine Island Air commuter plane landed smoothly and rolled to a stop next to the terminal. Nami was the first one down the folding steps. She carried one travel bag and wore a stylish white safari outfit. She looked so fresh in her mid-thigh skirt. Her legs were bare, short but nicely shaped. Her petite size, white crew socks and brown shoes made her look like a sophomore from a Japanese high school. She had to hold on to her large fashionista hat because the trade winds were gusting as she walked from the plane to the airport terminal.

She opened her arms and gave Ole a big hug. It was a thrill for Uncle. She must wear deodorant, because she smelled good, like some kind of shampoo.

When Yu'layne met Nami, she looked surprised and a maybe a little jealous of her staying in Ole's room. Or maybe he was just reading that into her wistful expression. His landlady reminded him it would add ten dollars per night to the rent. Ole took Nami to the Sands restaurant for dinner. Dollar, the bartender, rolled his eyes and frowned when they walked in. Ole chose a table far away from the bar, overlooking the beach and the pool. The dinner was simple, Nachos and Calamari with rum and cokes. Ole had no big expectations this time, so he could not be disappointed again. They laughed and got lightly acquainted, but the chemistry was somehow cool between them. Nami did not project any free electrons or subtle sexual glances or even very much eye contact. She was funny and happy and that was good enough for Ole too. They planned a snorkel trip for the next day.

Back at Yu'layne's house, Nami did not seem to mind the cozy sleeping arrangements. When it was time to slip into bed, Nami wore a long t-shirt, no bra and short shorts. Uncle slept far to the other side. He tried not to think about her there in his bed. He did not try to even hold her hand that night. In five minutes, she was snoring and he was still wide awake. It was a restless night for Uncle. He must have awakened her with his tossing and turning.

"No touching below waist," she said, as she rolled over with her back to him and went back to snoring. He thought about that for ten minutes and finally fell asleep. The rules had been made perfectly clear.

In the morning when he awoke, she was snuggled up next to him, back to back. He remained perfectly still, enjoying the heat of her lovely cute body. When she awoke, she turned over and smiled up at him.

"No touching below waist."

The first words she said to him this morning were not romantic, just a repeat of the rules of her game. It came clear on Ole's mind screen.

So that's how she travels the world. She shacks up for free with her online men friends in all those countries and no touching below the waist. Very clever this one.

"Hey Nami, you snuggled over here next to me remember?" They both laughed.

What the hell brah, she's funny and cute, no wonder she can travel where ever she wants. Play nice. His wise inner coach almost always knows what to do.

The snorkel trip was aboard a forty-foot rigid bottom, inflatable raft with twin, two-hundred-horse, Honda outboards. It was a terrific boat, trimmed perfectly to cruise flat out and fast over the ocean's chop. They saw whales breach, and spinner dolphins leaping. But, the snorkeling was the best part. Right outside the entrance to Manele Bay there is a perfect snorkel reef. The coral is psychedelic with brilliant color and teeming with fish and turtles and eels and octopus. It was the best snorkel trip of Ole's entire life. Nami thought it was as good as Belize. Uncle smiled.

They swam together, but she made no accidental or intentional body contact with him. Uncle was very aware of the pretty Nami-fish that swam next to him. Her black bikini looked great on her petite figure. Maybe it was because she was so young, thirty-five compared to his fifty-five. There were just too many years between them for this to be the start of a serious relationship. Plus, she lived in Japan and worked in Malaysia. He wasn't moving out of Hawaii.

You don't have to marry the girl, brah. Don't make plans, just go with the flow. It is what it is. Live in the moment, show compassion. Buddha knew the two rules.

Ole reached out with love and held Nami's hand as they snorkeled along together. She squeezed his hand and held on tight. It was pleasant in a friendly, platonic, fatherly sort of disappointing way.

After the day swimming with the fish they were hungry for fish and chips. The Pioneer Inn was right there alongside the Lahaina harbor when they returned. They ate and laughed and looked at the photos Nami had shot with her expensive underwater camera. Gina, the best waitress in Lahaina, served them the drinks they ordered, quite a few drinks. Ole quit after three but Nami had two more and was seriously buzzed when Ole poured her into the big passenger seat of his Cadillac and buckled her seat belt around her. He might of, accidentally squeezed her breasts but it was all in the interest of safety. If she noticed she didn't object. He was pretty sure she didn't even notice. It gave him no thrill. By the time he shut off the engine at Yu'layne's house, pretty Nami was snoring again.

"Come on swimmer, let's get you up the stairs."

It wasn't too hard to support her light weight as she stumbled along. Uncle guided her to his room and when he laid her down on her side of the bed, she woke up and said,

"You ve'ly nice man O're-san. I 'rike you. You can below waist if... if, you can help me with some travel money." She smiled shyly. "Can you help Nami travel Ole? I make so nice for you."

Uncle stepped back and looked at the cute, drunk Japanese girl on his bed.

"How much, travel money, do you have in mind?

"I usual'ry ask five-hun'red-dolla, for nice fella like you, only ask three-hun'red."

He's so surprised he can't stand up anymore so he sits down next to her on the bed. *So, it's money not friendship that gets men 'below the waist.' What a waist brah, slim as a Japanese Barbie doll. That should be 'wasted' yah? So Nami is a hooker.*

You never hired a hooker in your whole life brah. Coach weighs into Oliver's thoughts. Now there's a willing, drunk one on your bed. All for you tonight, just pay special price, this week only, three-hun'red-dolla and then all you can eat, raw Nami-sashimi, peel and pig-out."

Uncle had eighty-bucks in his checking account to last him 'til the end of the month. He looked her up and all the way down. She was a sexy little fish and he started to harden just thinking about it. He was just wondering if she took credit cards when her eyes rolled back in her head and she fell sideways off the bed and slumped so hard onto the floor that her head bounced once before gravity won. She was so passed out she was a 'Hail-Mary-Pass' all the way to the end-zone. The end-zone of negotiations anyway. He had to laugh out loud it was so sad.

Nami had worn a sarong over her swim suit all day on the snorkel boat. He picked her up and unwrapped her. He pulled the covers off the bed and laid her back down on the cool sheets. Her bikini was still wet so he took off her top and let it fall on the floor; her petite boobs were small but would fill his hands. He didn't touch them. He left the bikini bottom on and covered her up nice and snug with the top sheet. It was too hot for the blanket. Uncle washed his face, brushed his teeth and climbed into the far side of the bed.

"Stinkin' booze," he whispered as he turned off the light. He lay there awake next to the half-naked little hooker. His inner voice was mighty quiet for a few minutes. The temptation to roll over on top of Nami was very strong. That's when the fight started.

What fun would that be? asks his karma coach. *You'd actually screw an unconscious drunk chick?*

"Thinkin' about it," he said out loud.

You're sick dude.

Yah, but here she is in my bed. Out cold, no still warm. No cost, free sample yah?

For-get-it brah, never, not even if she is a hooker. Remember the Two Rules. He knows that his coach is right. *Yah, but what if I broke the rules just this once? So, what? She's not gonna know. Would she suddenly jump up fully sober and holler 'No touching below 'der!' I don't think so. She's out like a boxer with a concussion.*

Stop it brah, be pono (righteous).

Ole had to listen to his inner Jiminy Cricket. If he hadn't had those three drinks with dinner, he wouldn't be arguing with himself. He would never consider doing any such thing.

"Stupid, stupid booze," he mumbled, mad at himself and

very tired. He rolled further away from Nami so he wouldn't even touch her above the waist. It had been a long day; he fell asleep in a Maui minute and flew into a dream. He saw pretty fish in the sky over his head. They were tropical cloud fish with white birds flying in them. He was one of the birds. They were all Jonathan Livingston Seagulls only with bigger wing spans, more like gliding albatross. He flew over the very top of a rainbow and banked steeply with the curve. His wings changed color as he floated lower and lower, red to orange, orange to yellow, yellow to green, green to blue, blue to purple, purple to ultra-violet. He rode the colors with his arm-wings outstretched like he was the Pope bestowing blessings and colors unto the whole world. Maybe he was Nami's papal guardian angel. Maybe he was a dumb, flying monkey.

The next morning Nami was up early.

"Wake up O're-san. It now seven o'crock, return f'right is at one o'crock. Still time for below waist... if you can help Nami travel? I make so nice for you. Nami make O're very happy man."

"What?" They had never discussed how long she would be on Maui. *So, that's how she travels all over the world. She takes advantage of lonely men, who provide her a few days shelter, snorkel trips or snow skiing, and nice dinners and lots of free drinks. All her internet guy-friends are hoping to get lucky with the little Japanese doll. For five-hun'red-dolla 'travel money' she will 'make nice' for them. What a clever way to see the world. The men who pay her fee, get lucky and get her to the airport the next day. Nami travels on forever, spending very little of her own money. She probably collected 'travel*

286

money' from a few guys in Hono'ruru before she flew to Maui. With just ten guys a month, she's making five-thousand bucks every thirty days and traveling the world for free.

Bet she doesn't have a job in Malaysia at all. She doesn't need one. No wonder she can afford a home in Tokyo. She's a brilliant con artist. Coach is impressed.

Nami steps out of the shower, fresh, ripe and wrapped only in a towel as small as she is. She smells like shampoo. His will power started to weaken then harden. But he jumps out of bed and starts pulling on his clothes.

"Get dressed," his only greeting of the morning. He does not offer to buy her breakfast like he had planned. This morning he's fully sober and remembers he's looking for a new soul mate not a hooker. He wants her out of his life right away.

Uncle drives straight to the airport, arriving five hours early. Without a word he opens the DeVille's big trunk, puts her one travel bag on the sidewalk and walks back to the driver's door. He's about to get in when the unexpected final act in her game totally surprises him. She runs over to him, puts her arms around his waist and squeezes him tight as her pretty arms can and starts to cry. Not just a little crying, but serious body shaking sobbing. She holds on, cries hard and won't stop. This was airport drama of the strangest kind. It felt completely staged. After a while standing there, listening to her sob Ole looked at his watch and waited quietly, saying nothing. Three whole minutes she played this out. That's a long time to have someone hugging you around the waist and crying hard. She was so short that her head was pressed up against his belly button and her round little boobs were rubbing back and forth below his belt and making things harder by the minute.

Finally, Nami stopped sobbing but she was still pouting and wheezing. She looked up at him with bloodshot brown eyes.

"I 'rove you, O're. I 'rove you. I 'rove you."

Uncle unwrapped her thin arms from around his waist and simply said, "All you love is traveling. Sayonara, Nami." He got in his Cadillac and drove away. When he glanced in his rear-view mirror. There was the cute Japanese girl in a mini-skirt, looking mad as hell, and giving him the middle-finger with both hands.

60

Death Trumps Divorce

Ole tried to sleep on the red-eye to Seattle, but he was too agitated. His heart was a chemistry lab full of emotions and his mind a magnetron of determination. He had to get this divorce drama behind him, but there would be no more negotiating with Mr. Vader Blackenedheart, chief attorney of the underworld. Uncle was going to let the judge see the facts and make the call. When he thought it through like that he felt less worried. That lasted about a whole minute until he remembered that judges were all attorneys before they became judges, and he started to worry again.

Oliver had run up another credit card with this flight and one night in a cheap hotel in Seattle's University District. It was close to downtown but without the downtown rates. He figured Coco would have put that in her budget travel guide. It made him smile remembering that day of kissing her in the breathing jungle valley. Once he was thinking of something pleasant he dropped into sleep for the last four hours of the flight.

It was 43 degrees and raining in Seattle. His neck and shoulders tightened and began limping down that old familiar trail of pain. He caught a taxi to the U district. When he was pulling his carry-on down the musty hotel hallway to his room and frowning, his phone rang. It was his attorney.

"Mr. Gold, this is Michael Burns, I have some bad news.

Judge Taktuda Wall's mother died today. He has cancelled his docket for the whole week."

"Oh? I… ah, I'm very saddened for the judge. That's terrible. Is another judge available?"

"Not possible, every judge is booked for weeks in advance. I can try for next month if you like or we can re-negotiate with your wife's attorney." He sounded too cheery, as if counting the additional hours, he could bill either way.

"Book another court date for mid-June and let me know ASAP."

"Yes sir, Mr. Gold, good day and …"

"Yah I know."

61

Tony the Hero of Ka'anapali Beach

Ole was still married. It angered him, but he shed his angst playing music in rest homes on Sunday evenings and at the PI two nights a week. He enjoyed selling Maui Jim sunglasses for KAM three days a week at the beautiful Embassy Suites. You couldn't be down-hearted at this amazing, happy resort. It was what you'd expected Hawaii to be. There were lots of vacation palms along the beach, and in the tremendous pools; safe, fun in the sun, everyone protected by expensive, 'Supremo' natural sun block. As if that weren't enough, there were two or three rainbows overhead every afternoon. 'Magic' wasn't a big enough word for this place. It 'broke da eyes' and eased the pain.

One rather slow afternoon in the towel cabana he and Tony were cleaning the rental snorkel masks and tubes in a barrel of water mixed with a little chlorine bleach. A honey moon couple had come up to the counter. You could always tell the honeymooners. No matter how old they were, they were always the happiest looking couples on Maui. Ole secretly envied them. He missed being in love. He missed caring for someone and being married.

"You still married brah," coach is right again, *you can't seem to get that over with.*

"Oh, look dawh-ling." The honeymoon wife exclaimed.

"They have Maui Jim's; the Lady Pilot Model and the Lady Sport Model. I want one of each my sweet meat, handsome maa...an." When a new bride makes that drawn out drawl, you know you've got a sale.

'Ka-ching.' Ole sold six-hundred-dollars-worth of sunglasses before noon, that would net two very fat, seventy-dollar commissions. Tony was so proud of Ole, he told him to take a break.

"Way to go, Ole-brah. Here, take a clean towel and go lay on the beach. Let me make some money today."

Uncle obeyed. He walked over to the coconut palms along the beach. There were bright yellow Hibiscus all over the place adding to the cheerfulness of the resort. He knew this was the Hawaii state flower. It used to be the red Hibiscus but during a week of nothing more important to do, the Hawaii legislature got a big new idea. Let's argue for days about changing the color of the state flower. The yellow party won. Hawaii tax-payers lost again.

Instead of turning toward the beach he decided it was close enough to noon he would head for the employee lunch room inside the hotel. The food was great, always buffet style and free for employees. He loved his job; he could count on at least one nutritious meal, three days a week. For a single (married) guy living alone on fifteen-bucks-a-day, that was a real plus. Bethany, at the rest home, still brought him one plate every Sunday evening after he played music. So, that was four meals a week with nutrition. The rest of the week it was soda crackers and Mangos, carrots, string cheese, grapes and cereal. Ole cut every stick of gum into three pieces. He lost his desire for rich food and with it, ten pounds of weight.

Ole wandered along the pathway lined with official yellow flowers, all the way around back to the employee entrance. He was just reaching for the door when he heard distant shouting; the kind of shouting that rings of distress. People were running toward the ocean. Uncle ran for the beach, someone was in trouble.

The first thing he saw was Tony with his shirt off, lying on his surf board, arm-paddling out to sea as fast as he could. Then the whole scene slapped him out of paradise. Shark attack! About a hundred feet off shore, a woman shrieked and thrashed in bloody terror. Her siren screams filling the sky with pain. Tony slid off his board and pulled the woman up on to it all in one quick motion. Ole called 911 with his cell phone. He was told that it had already been reported and to hang up. He did.

Tony was out there pounding his open hands on the water and yelling angry shouts at the shark. Ole could not make out what he was yelling but it was angry cussing for sure. His boss climbed up on the surf board, right on top of the woman's back and he started paddling for shore. Another surfer hand-paddled out in front of Tony and yelled to him,

"Grab my ankles brah, I tow you." And with incredible strength the lead surfer paddled like hell for the shore. Tony held on with both hands, still lying on the back of the injured woman on his board. Ole waded into the surf to help. They carried her up to the lawn. Together they got the bleeding slowed down with their bare hands until someone gave up a towel. A large piece of her back was torn off and missing. Her shoulder looked like fresh ground hamburger. The flesh under her right arm was hanging like a fillet. Watery looking blood ran down her side and back, and all over Tony's chest. It was a bloody nightmare right here in safe, happy vacation-land. The poor woman was crying and babbling words at the same time. Her swim goggles were still hung around her neck. Tony unsnapped the goggles but left the swim cap on her head. He reassured the frantic woman that the wound wasn't too bad, and she'd be Okay. He was lying like a politician. The poor woman was shredded. Ole nodded to Tony and took charge. In his calmest professional voice, he reassured her.

"We are both trained in First Aid. An ambulance has been called and will be here in a few minutes. I want you to sit here and lean back against Tony. This will keep the wound elevated and we are applying direct pressure to stop a little blood."

There was a lot of blood, but nothing arterial.

"Your job, young lady, is to relax and breathe very slowly. Breathe with me. Inhale, listen to my voice, deep breath, now let it all go. Stay with me, breathe in, slowly, in through the nose... that's it, stay with me. Exhale out the mouth. Good, you're safe now, you'll be okay."

"Are you okay Tony? Get bit too?"

"Nah, I'm fine."

They kept up the direct pressure on her wounds and watched for signs of shock to set in. She was an athlete of a woman. She got her breathing in sync with Ole and quit crying.

"I was training for a triathlon." She said in a gasping but firmer voice. "I actually ran into that shark. My arm swung down in a crawl stroke and I hit him on the back with my hand. Then my head rammed right into his side. It was like hitting a log. That's when he turned so fast and bit me!" Her voice rose in a frantic pitch. "He kept biting and biting me!" she couldn't help screaming again and again; she had to be hurting like hell.

"Believe me, it's over." Ole's professional voice cranked up louder to smoothly comfort her painful shrieks. "Breathe with me. Inhale with me, deep breath, again... again. You're gonna be okay."

It seemed to take a half hour but later they realized the first responders arrived in less than four minutes. The severely injured woman was carried in a hand gurney up to a wheeled one in the shade of a beach palm. Bandages were quickly applied, sedatives injected and an IV put into her good arm. Then the medics rolled her to the ambulance in the underground parking cave and she was gone.

The beach was now crowded with firemen clearing the area of tourists. Of course, there was no one in the ocean. Life guards on ski-dos were running back and forth on the water to chase away any sharks still in the area.

"Tony, that was very brave." Uncle gave him a pat on his bloody shoulder.

"Here's a clean towel, go shower off some of that blood."

"Just another day in paradise," grinned Tony but Ole could see he was exhausted and worried for the tri-athlete.

Uncle wasn't hungry anymore, he went back to work in the towel cabana. With everyone now in the swimming pools, he handed out more than two-hundred towels and pushed five heavy carts full of wet towels back into the hotel laundry. His body was gonna stay buff with this job.

Most days were not so exciting. Ole never again sold two pair of Maui Jim's at the same time. There were no more shark attacks. It was sunny days at a beautiful resort hanging out with happy people. He was a beach bum now. His pidgin-English was getting, 'da kine'. He met lots of people but Uncle was not meeting any rich widows or foolish young trust babes. He was lonely.

Whenever his thoughts returned to Tanya it was like someone suddenly threw shave ice in his face. After two flights to Seattle, the divorce was still not finalized. The attorneys were milking him *and* his wife like a couple of Holsteins. Michael burns, the 'milk-er' on his side of the dairy, had set a new court date for June seventeenth, and said, "don't worry."

What me worry? Ole felt like Alfred E. Neuman from Mad Magazine. Like Alfred, worrying was not Ole's style, but his style was changing with every expensive turn of the dharma wheel. Tanya and her paid assassin were Dream Sharks about to filet him and bite off his pension. His confidence was at low tide and every flood brought more worry. Uncertainty is built into the workings of the Universe. He worried about that too.

62

Evidence

Ole booked his third divorce airfare to arrive in Seattle early on the morning of the seventeenth, and return to Maui that same evening. He wanted this over and done with, all in one day. Once again, there was no one in the court room when he arrived so he sat down at the same table and tried to fortify himself with meditative breathing.

It's just a legal shark attack brah, no matter what happens today, she can't kill you. That would stop the bloody flow of your money. Fight back, don't cave in like last time. Coach gives him a pep talk before the big game. Uncle Ole felt the evil presence of his own attorney swimming up behind him.

"Good Morning Mr. Gold, how are you today?" Ole turned to see Mr. Burns grinning like he had a fish in his teeth. No doubt, calculating the money he was gonna chew up this morning.

"I'm not worried," Uncle lied. They shook a handshake because each knew they should at moments like this, but neither man felt any camaraderie toward the other. Tanya entered with Blackenedheart and the room temperature fell ten degrees. Ole got a chill up his spine that made his neck and shoulders hurt even more. Now the court room was a shark pit, three of them, four... counting Judge Wall and as Jimmy Buffet wrote in a song, Ole was the only 'bait' in town. It all had that underwater feeling of a dream. But when Judge Wall came out of his locker room at exactly ten am, it all became surgically real. Like any well-paid referee, he walked to the same center location on the fifty-yard line between the opposing teams. Ole could imagine him in a black and white striped shirt about to flip a coin to decide who gets to kick who, first. Mr. Burns pulled his chair closer to Uncle and whispered,

"Well Mr. Gold I assure you that whatever negotiations we enter into today will be recorded at the clerk's office properly. We will formally sign the agreement we make and there will be no misunderstanding of the terms like last time."

Ole had no time to reply, Judge Wall was blowing his whistle with the same warning speech about how he did not like divorce cases. They waste his time and the taxpayer's money. He repeated his requirement for mandatory mediation before he would hear a case and that neither party would like his ruling if they could not reach an agreement on their own.

"Knock on my door if you do not come to your senses." he challenged. It sounded like, "I double-dog-dare you to knock on my door."

Judge Wall signaled for the game clock to start. He turned and walked back through the heavy oak door, a mysterious place where winged-monkey-judge referees hang upside down like bats until disturbed by a knock on their door.

Mr. Burns turned to Ole and saw the stack of books on the table.

"What are all these books, Mr. Gold?"

298

"Evidence," he whispered. Ole counted down a stack of twenty-five thick books. "This judge likes evidence. I brought along twenty-five years of personal journals that I wrote during my marriage. I have documented the fun we had as a family. I can prove I was a loving, supportive father. I still am. I was a loving husband. I can prove I did not leave Tanya with all the family debt. I have copies of all our prior debts with receipts showing that I paid the bulk of them in full, before I retired to Hawaii. I have receipts that show I put up the first, last and deposit on the condo she has in Bellevue. She couldn't have gotten that place without me co-signing for her. She has bad credit from over-shopping and not paying on time. I have the receipt showing I paid for the Pontiac convertible she's driving. That, Mr. Burns is not abandonment."

"None of that will impress this judge," said Burns. "You heard him again this morning. He hates divorce cases. He's got a reputation for being a 'Wall'. Believe me Mr. Gold, I've seen him make absolute confetti out of the most reasonable appeals".

"Be sure to explain to Tanya and her paid thug what I just shared with you Mr. Burns, about the evidence I brought with me."

"I will, Mr. Gold," and he walked slowly toward the war room where his pension plan was hog-tied and about to be butchered alive.

Uncle Ole sighed. He looked up at the clock above the judge's pulpit and wrote down the time. Ten-ten. It was so quiet in the court room he could distinctly hear the clock ticking high above the judicial bench. Those distinct clicking sounds were meant to be seconds. But this morning he saw the hour and minute hands racing each other to see which one could spend the most money at a rate of twelve-hundred dollars an hour. Uncle pulled in deep breaths of air to calm his anger. In just a little under nine-hundred dollars, Mr. Burns came back into the court room, alone.

"Mr. Gold since we are starting all over again, Tanya will settle out of court for fifty-percent of your pension. That currently would be one-thousand and fifty dollars a month for the rest of your life. Do you agree to these terms?"

"No, I do not agree. Stop messing around Burns. Go back in there and tell them both that this is my third flight to Seattle, and I'm going to tell my story to the judge, today!" Ole almost shouted.

Mr. Burns did not say a word. He turned and slowly walked back to the very deliberately slow, 'no-progress' negotiations. The attorney meters were running full speed ahead without regard for credit card limits and without results. The court room clock was spinning into the Twilight Zone. When Burns finally returned, another fourteen-hundred dollars later, he was all smiles, the theatrical kine, no doubt learned in law school drama class.

"Well I did it Mr. Gold. I negotiated the same deal we had before. Tanya will settle out of court for five-hundred dollars a month and this time we will ink the deal before we …"

"You're not listening Burns," Ole interrupted. "Go back in there and tell them what I am about to say. Listen this time:

"Mrs. Gold has already lied to this judge. It's in the pending case record. I have a copy of the perjury decree with me. She has been fined seven-hundred and fifty-dollars. A penalty owed to me over sixty days, a fine that she has not yet paid. She knows that the rest of her petition is also based on lies and greed. I brought all the evidence I need to prove it. Remind them both that this judge rules only on evidence." Ole had to take a breath, he was trembling with pent up adrenalin turbo anger.

"She had to sign off on pre-trial documents, admitting that she refused to try mediation to resolve our case. I have a copy of this with me, also. Mediation is something this judge has reminded us twice now that he insists upon before divorce cases come before him."

Ole had to stop and breathe again. He couldn't risk a heart attack. All this angst was pumping up his confidence but also was making his left arm and chest ache. When he calmed his emotions down to a furious boil, he went on.

"No more back room bullshit Mr. Burns. I don't want to *settle* out of court today. That is another story for the judge. I settled out of court in good faith at five-hundred-a-month, only to be baited and switched by her lying attorney who upped the ante to seven-fifty as soon as I was out of state again. I am totally pissed off. You tell them I am presenting this case to the judge, today.

"Plus, you can tell them this: I am submitting a parenting plan that allows my daughter, 'our' daughter, visiting rights with her father for three months in Hawaii every Summer.

"Plus, I am so angry that I am back in Seattle for the third time because of the criminal obstruction of our agreed settlement by her attorney. I am going to ask Judge Wall to award me financial relief for all my attorney fees and travel expense to be paid for by Mrs. Tanya Gold."

"Slap!" Ole finished by slamming his hand loudly on the table. "Let's get on with it."

He must have gotten Burn's attention this time. He marched from the court room with renewed vigor, all his guns loaded and extra bandoliers of ammunition over each shoulder. But he was in no hurry to return. The hands of the clock were speeding around the money track like they were in the Indy-500. Eighteen-hundred-dollars later, Burns finally returned with an even bigger grin on his unhappy looking, dishonest face.

"Mr. Gold, you should be an attorney. You were right. Tanya does not want to face this judge again. If you will agree to forgive the seven-hundred and fifty-dollar fine, she will drop all claims to your pension and sign the divorce agreement and the amended parenting plan today."

He tried to shake Uncle's hand. Ole did not offer to return the gesture. Burns recovered quickly from the intentional slight. He was a professional hand-shaker and had probably been rebuffed many times before.

"You won this one, Mr. Gold. You kept throwing touchdown passes and she had no defensive line."

"So, does that mean I don't have to pay you, Mr. Burns?"

"Hah, very funny Mr. Gold, you hired me to represent you. I'm here with you, inside the courtroom and I'm wearing my best suit." He snickered at his own joke. Oliver didn't smile. Now, he understood how lawyers can afford those professional threads. By the time this is all over today, Burns will have run up another three-thousand plus dollars of attorney time to add to his already staggering bill.

"Tell her... are you listening?"

Of course, Mr. Gold."

"Tell her, I will forgive the perjury fine if this gets settled today, upon the terms you have just described." Burns wasn't smiling anymore, he was all business. "I'll be right back," and with that he turned on his very expensive, wing-tipped heels and slow-marched his way back to the war room to accept their surrender.

Oliver shouted at him as he walked away, "I want to be present when the ink dries on this mess. I'm catching a flight back to paradise this evening."

63

Forgiveness at 32,000 Feet

Uncle did not order any rum on the return flight from Seattle to Maui. He was emotionally beat up and his neck and shoulders were a mess of painful, nerve cables. The narrow, thin-cushioned hard-bottom, United Airline seat in economy class, with limited leg room, did not improve his mood.

He hurt like he had been hit by a truck, 'T-boned' with malice by his 'loving' wife just as hard and dirty as she could. Ole had won in court, but all he could count was his losses. His love for Tanya, their twenty-seven-year marriage and their future happiness that he'd always hoped for were all killed in the crash. Ole's heart was critically injured by this mash-up. He couldn't stop a few man-tears from squeezing out of his eyes. But, there were two rainbows still shining. His daughter, Brita would be spending summers with him, surfing in Hawaii and somehow his pension had survived intact, if only to pay his attorney fees for the next ten years. Burns had sent him a text with the final bill as Ole waited to board his return flight. One-hundred and fifty-six billed hours at two-hundred and fifty per hour plus the court room billings came to forty-eight thousand dollars plus or minus five-hundred. That didn't include the three round-trip airfares currently on two credit cards. Nobody wins, when attorneys are involved. *Why did it have to end this way?*

The information flat screen on the back of the seat in front of him showed airspeed of 550 mph, outside temperature of forty degrees below zero and an altitude of 32,000 feet. He looked out his window at the fluffy, mindless clouds passing below the jet. He could see a rainbow in the thick plastic window. He heard a sad piano étude being played in the empty concert hall of his musical mind. Madame Melancholy, one of the most famous pianists of all humanity was yearning the keys with trembling fingers and tears. She gave him more hurt than solace.

Uncle knew chemistry like he knew the alphabet. He weighed his sadness and his debt along with the anger he had felt in the court room. Their combined atomic mass added together, were absolutely. exponential, stomping up and down on one side of a painful equation. Label that side, 'Y.'

Why did it have to end like this? He kept wondering.

Guys like to fix things, so his mind went to work. To balance this equation, he needed an unknown equal weight of exponential value. Label that side, 'X.' If he could solve for, 'X' maybe he could find some happiness again.

Ole had learned in grade-school that Christianity taught forgiveness. He knew it was necessary, but how do you do it?

In college, Ole had signed up for a series of philosophy lectures. They included one called, Comparative World Religions. He was surprised to learn that many religions have a 'Savior.' They all support that savior with written legends of miracles, most written decades after their messiah had returned to heaven. They all promised, pie in the sky when you die, and they all claimed to be worth dying for. The similarities traveling down through time and on different sides of the planet were amazing. All of them rising out of the human 'psyche' providing an explanation for birth, suffering and death. He preferred science. Especially chemistry where there are the observable facts that describe chemical balance and energy release in measurable units. Ole wanted to shout at the world, "Wake up human primates! Take another look through the Hubble Telescope. How can you possibly package God and sell him under all these popular brand names? The answers are a little more complicated than we previously thought!"

Today with five more hours of jet flight ahead of him, he didn't have anything more important to think about than his quest for 'X' (forgiveness). He knew that when Buddha found enlightenment, he set aside his homeless, pan-handling, esoteric life and spent another fifty years teaching a path to enlightenment through compassion. *But, that wasn't forgiveness. Or was it? This stuff is so confusing. How do you measure forgiveness? How do the Christians forgive? How could any human person be the forgiver that Christ was? Maybe he was more than human. How do you forgive the people that are nailing your hands and feet to a cross? But he remembers that Jesus quote from the book of Luke:*

"Father, forgive them, for they know not what they do."

Ole felt nailed in place by the paralysis of anger and attorney debt. He physically couldn't move his arms, because he was scrunched tight between a huge Hawaiian wahine on his left and the jet's cold wall on his right. Clouds full of Hydrogen and Oxygen were all he could see outside the passenger jet's window. He imagined John Lennon was right about, try to imagine there's no heaven.

Wedged in like he was, he told himself he didn't need to move. He would practice stillness. He tried to meditate on the word, 'forgiveness'. In mere seconds, he lifted off the spiritual runway became sunlight reflecting on the smooth surface of a lake. But there were no trees to sketch, no ducks, no flies wearing car wax, just a lot of calm... nothing. Then suddenly the Dream Sharks of resentment broke the surface, their fins slicing toward him. He welcomed their anger, opened his heart and let them in. It hurt somethin' terrible. Staying hurt and angry wasn't solving anything.

His mind overflowed like the cartoon castle in the Sorcerer's Apprentice. He was that Mickey Mouse looking frantically down a flooding stairway and all he could see was brooms of pain and buckets of bitterness coming his way. When he was exhausted by the futility of it all, he pushed those mad sharks away with something he pulled out from under the burning car wreck of his heart. It was his once beautiful, 'love' for Tanya. How could he ever forget how much he had always loved her?

He began to feel better. He didn't have to own what she said or did with her life. He owned what he did with his life. He had loved her pure and simple. When he thought the thought again, his reward was a peaceful feeling.

He whispered the word, 'forgiveness' over and over like a mantra. The passengers near him must have wondered about the big man with his wet eyes closed, chanting softly,

"Forgive, forgive, forgive her, forgive me..." over and over, again.

"Why is that man crying mommy?" He heard a child's voice near the big Hawaiian woman.

"I don't know son, maybe he's afraid of flying."

"I'm not afraid, am I?" Said the boy.

"No son, you're very brave, we'll be home soon," she said this in a loud enough voice to reassure the crying man as well as her son.

The meditation, 'to forgive' became another flowing stream. He let it flood. He tried a conscious effort to say yes to forgiving Tanya. As Ole remembered loving her, he saw memories: Canoeing the Nooksack River with her, hiking the trails on Mt. Rainier, camping and campfires. He saw her at the helm of their sailboat out on Puget Sound with the wind messing her blonde hair. He saw her and their kids, sailing among pods of leaping Orca whales. Each happy memory made him feel a little better. There they were, laughing at dinner parties on the docks of the Seattle Yacht Club. He remembered quiet nights at anchor in Echo Bay on Sucia island. He played flute while she played guitar, the echoes bouncing back in the dark from the tree-lined cliffs. Ole began to feel much better. Maybe forgiveness was simply choosing to remember the good and not the bad. It wasn't gonna be easy. He would never forget how she tried to filet him in court. But he could still remember the good times. He could say yes to all the great years they had together and wish her happiness. He could do that.

He thought of the birth of each daughter and the amazing fun of raising three great children together... love goes on and on, even after the Titanic sinks. It won't cost anything extra to keep on loving the woman he had always loved. True, it would be another romance that didn't end with Walt Disney's 'happily-ever-after,' but love is the center hub of the eternal drama wheel. His memories of Tanya wouldn't have to end with, 'bitterly-ever-after.'

Ole's meditation swept along like a wild river to a sharp bend, the good years were running so strong that they flooded away the court room drama and made his heart a fertile valley, a valley flooded with a future.

But... there was still a staggering amount of personal guilt to deal with. He held that mirror up to himself. He's the one who wanted to move to Hawaii. It still felt like the right thing to do. He hoped Tanya could someday forgive him for chasing his dream with or without her.

Fault, schmalt, it's all history. Forgive yourself. Get on with your life brah. Father, priest-coach is waving benediction at him from inside the confessional of his mind.

When Oliver finally arrived home to Yu'layne's house he felt a whole lot better, but exhausted. He collapsed on top of his bed and had the best dream of his life, so far.

He was flying over jungle tree tops, spreading his arms and forgiving the people in the villages below. He was healing everyone too. Powerful as a hawk, he was gliding above them all. Maybe he was one of the good winged-monkeys sent from Oz to heal the hurt in this world. He saw cripples throwing down their crutches, the blind able to see, and his mother smiling up at him with pride, that sort of thing.

Uncle flew away from the village, soaring very high. He flew straight up, right through the colors of a rainbow arching over black clouds. On his back he now has a bunch of rockets and they kick in with a whip-lashing blast. The noise of the rocket pack is crazy loud and the heat is scorching the backs of his legs and his feet. His rocket speed must be ninety-thousand miles per hour. In the blink of both eyes, he's wearing a silver helmet, a space suit and some kind of super boots that protect him from his back-pack jet blast. The sky is losing its blue and going gray. Two more super-sonic minutes and Uncle is in lonely orbit around the sun. He's become the famous, elliptical Comet of Forgiveness.

To his right, way over there on the earth's curved-edge of planet and space, the moon looked back at him with tremendous guilt, ready to hide behind the planet. He waved a blessing and forgave the moon all the reckless romance that chunk of rock stirred in the foolish hearts of humans down on earth.

He was still waving one hand when he woke up starving. He'd forgiven the world and the moon for over fifteen hours.

Ole stretched for a while, his wings were a little sore. He headed for the kitchen, but there on the lanai table where he had dined with Ling and Liang, was a bunch of ripe apple bananas. While he sat down to a monkey-breakfast of peel and eat, he called his mom to tell her the good and bad news. He needed to hear the forgiveness in her voice.

64

The Pretty Japanese Millionaire

One Saturday morning Uncle drove his land yacht all the way to Kihei. It couldn't possibly be as bad as Los Angeles like everyone said. Kihei is only twenty miles away. It's a good-looking urban sprawl that covers a stretch of southwest Maui with residential homes and strip malls tossed together like a salad. There was obviously no planning or zoning done over the thirty years of the area's random development. But, the beaches are beautiful. He checked out parks called, Kamaole One, Two and T'ree. Kam 'T'ree' had the finest sand. He swam the ocean for a quarter mile keeping within one-hundred feet of the shore. Ole couldn't stop thinking of the young woman that swam into a shark. He tried to think of anything else, but with every up stroke he started, he imagined hitting a log of a shark on the down stroke. It worried him so much that he got out of the water before finishing the swim and walked the beach back to where he started. He was a working musician now, he needed his arms and his fingers.

After a beach shower he got into his dry clothes and cruised his Cadillac down Kihei's oceanfront drive. He stopped for lunch at Denny's which was up a flight of stairs in a strip mall. There are more upscale places to eat, but he'd just put six bucks in the gas tank, that left him nine more for lunch and an apple later, thanks to his well-dressed attorney.

After a good lunch, he did some window shopping. He couldn't afford to buy anything but he was curious. It might be a long time before he drove to Kihei again.

He stopped in front of a clothing store. All the stores look alike and sell the same stuff: tourist souvenirs, swimsuits and collectible Hawaiian clutter, made in China. But, this one had an advertisement taped on the inside of a window. There was a Willy Nelson concert coming up in about six weeks. He was wondering how he could afford to spend forty-bucks on a ticket, when a nice-looking Japanese lady came up and unlocked the front door of the store. She was slender, tall, well-dressed and very attractive. She smiled at Uncle and said good morning. It was about noon. The store hours printed on the door were nine to five.

"Kind a late aren't you?" He asked. She nodded yes in that double-triple nod way that Japanese women do.

"Don't worry, I won't tell the owner." Uncle thinks he is such a witty guy sometimes.

"I the owner," she smiled back pointing one finger proudly at her shapely chest.

She left the door propped open and went behind the counter and started fussing with the cash register. Uncle looked in the store. It was wall to wall the same as all the rest. There was nothing in here that he needed. But he was looking for some way to keep her talking to him. He walked to the counter and remarked on the first thing he saw. Lying there next to her store computer was a Bible.

"Are you a Christian?" Uncle asked pointing to the worn looking book.

"Yes. I go Japanese Christian Church."

"I go to church in Lahaina." It wasn't a total lie. Sometimes on a hot day he would stop by the beautiful Maria Lanakila Cathedral. It was an oasis from the Lahaina heat, always ten degrees cooler inside. He could cool down and meditate or pray there undisturbed. He liked quiet, spiritual moments, but right now he needed to say something, anything. The silence was getting awkward. She beat him to it,

"You 'rike go Japanese Church with me?" she asked.

"Ah, yes, I think I'd like that very much." He was kind of taken back by this invitation. This was the first time anyone on this island had invited him to attend church.

"Me, Suki," she smiled and offered her hand to shake American style.

He shook her hand. It was a long graceful hand. He did not want to let go and held it a little too long. She didn't let go either. It was an unspoken instant mutual infatuation. Or you might call it, love at first sight, if you were old fashioned. Uncle and Suki were about the same age and feeling old fashioned.

Dang, your Mojo is really working these days brah. His thoughts running away with Ling and Liang and Desiree and the dish and the spoon and the Coco that jumped over the moon.

Why do you feel so dizzy? It's just a hand shake.

"My name is Oliver, but friends call me Ole." He was feeling

313

braver now. Brave enough to tease her a bit.

"Where you been, Suki? I've been waiting here at your door since 9 am, It's almost noon. That's a bad way to treat your customers."

He sounded serious but his smile was giving him away. He tried to frown like Dollar the bartender. She was so cute, he couldn't do it.

"So s'olly customer-san," she knew he was kidding. She continued looking down demurely arranging things behind the counter.

"It was very important appointment I had this morning."

She was lovely. He folded his arms and casually leaned on her counter. She was about five-seven, with a great figure, slender legs and a nice tan; a few crows-feet showing at the eyes, some time has gone by, maybe forty-five years. It's hard to tell with Asians. She has the slim waist of a twenty-year-old. She must have felt him appraising her like a race horse.

"What you looking at?" she demanded.

"Pretty Japanese old lady."

"Hah. I too young for you, o'rd man." and she giggled like a school girl. Her right hand came up to cover her mouth. She was actually very beautiful no matter what her age.

"What was so important to make me wait out in the cold wind and rain all this time?" Anyone could see It was another eighty-three-degree, sunny day outside.

"You sure one snoopy customer; you buy something, yes?"

"Ok I want…" He looked around and picked up the first thing he saw, "this." He was holding up a folded t-shirt from a table with a big sign that read,

"Seven T-shirts for $20." She didn't even look up.

"Those for keiki. How many children you got?"

"Oh?" Was all Uncle could think of to say then he answered,

"Three."

"Only t'ree?" she looked shocked.

"Betta you buy seven shirts then you be 'leady when make more babies," she started laughing. Her hand came up and covered her nice smile.

Why do they always do that? He wondered again. He laughed with her.

"I would need a new wife." it seemed a clever thing to say at the time. She looked at him a long time, appraising, frowning.

"What you really want snoopy customer-san?"

"Just shopping," he innocently replied.

"Liar, everyone always shopping, shopping, shopping,

always shopping, you come here, you buy something."

"I'm an honest old man, not a liar. Ok, I wasn't here at 9 am, and I made up that stuff about the cold rain and I don't go to church very often. But, I really am just shopping, window shopping. I saw the Willy Nelson poster in your window. He's gonna play a live concert in Wailuku next month sometime."

Uncle looked at her hands, no rings. He was trying to think of more to say. He put the child size tee-shirt back on the table. He decided to prove he was shopping and started walking around aimlessly looking at everything on every shelf like he had seen so many people do. He disliked shopping. You feed your soul with desire, looking for things you don't need. What did Buddha say?

"Watch the tracks of your desires, for attachment and desire are the cause of all suffering."

She busied around doing stuff. He stole a glance at her from time to time. When he wasn't looking her way, she stared at him too.

Eventually, he found a man's t-shirt that read in whimsy-font letters, 'Live Aloha,' so he took it to Suki at the counter and studied her slim figure.

"This is stupid shirt," she announced.

Why would a store owner say something like that?

"Yah, it is, but I do try to live Aloha, so it fits."

"Not fit, this is a Small. You look like Medium."

He had not even looked at the size just the words and color.

"Actually, I am quite large, I mean I wear a large-size shirt." he was smiling at his own Freudian-slippa.

She was smiling too.

This is going well; his romance coach is happy.

"Pick another shirt," she said. "Here try this one."

It was a Large, same color, black. On the front was written

"I got lei'd in Hawaii." She winked at him.

"I think I like this woman." His thoughts are going back, forward and sideways.

"I'll take it," how much?

"Twenty-dolla."

"What-up wi' dat? Those shirts are seven for twenty dollars."

"Don't what-up me. Those shirts junk. This hun'elt-pe'cent cotton, no shrink. Good shirt, nice words on front, you buy."

"Okay... I'll give you ten dollars for this really, special shirt."

"You a very bad man, Mr. Snoopy-san, fifteen dollars for the shirt and no date tonight. You buy then you go."

"Deal." He gave her a twenty-dollar bill, the smallest he had, the only one he had left in his wallet. Uncle was attracted to this woman but she was nuts.

"What date tonight?" He was getting confused.

Why are the pretty ones always so crazy? Probably because they get hit on all the time and develop a kind of self-defense / offense. His coach was only guessing here.

She rang up the cash register. It came to fifteen-dollars and forty-nine cents. She started digging for the change.

"Keep it, call it a tip." He wasn't smiling anymore. She was only playing with him to sell a t-shirt. Without another word he turned to go.

"Okay, we go on date tonight," she snapped.

He didn't even turn around, just walked toward the still open door. She couldn't see his smile.

"What time do you close your store?"

"Five o'c'rock, I ready by ten after, don't be late."

Without saying another thing, he walked away. He didn't look back.

Let her wonder all afternoon if you're gonna show up or not, brah.

He thought this was a clever thing to do. It was. Suki thought about the handsome customer-san all afternoon. By

318

four-thirty she had changed her outfit three times from her store inventory. She settled on a white blouse open at the neck, a modest way down. She chose a black mini-skirt, one that made her shapely legs look long. They were long. She only had one pair of shoes, brown penny loafers that didn't match her skirt but she figured snoopy-san would not notice or care about her shoes. She tied a white ribbon into her hair above her right ear. She looked in her store mirror. She still had the slim good looks of a twenty-four-year old if she didn't study her face too long.

65

You Call This a Date?

Oliver arrived back at Suki's store at five-twenty.

"You late." She said.

"I'm lucky to get here so soon. Traffic out of Lahaina was a bear jam. I went home to shower and change clothes. That's a forty-mile round trip."

"Okay, I forgive you."

"My car is right over there." He pointed to his white Cadillac.

"Nice car. You take me to Union 76 now." She commanded.

Uncle Ole said nothing. He opened the passenger side for Suki to climb in.

"Ve'ly nice car."

"Domo arigato, Suki,"

"Oh, you speak Japanese?"

"I have learned a few things," he was thinking of the cute little travel hooker.

Betta 'vibes from this sophisticated lady, brah. His coach can

320

read 'vibes.'

"Now, who sounds like a hippie?" He said out loud.

"What say?" She asked.

"Nothing," Ole recovered his bearings. "Where is the Union 76?"

"Go that way. You find. On this side maybe tree, four b'rocks."

"Why are we going to a gas station?"

"They fix my car today. Remember my important appointment this morning? You so nosy about me, why I open store late."

"Yah, so?"

"I drop off car at Union 76. Then walk to work. So make late."

It was further than three or four blocks. More like a mile. Uncle pulled in to the only space available. The place was packed with cars of all makes. There were two gas pumps and one service bay. Tires, tools and parts lie scattered about like a mechanic's garage sale. Suki went in to claim her car.

She came walking out of the gas station like a runway model. She knew he would be watching. The swing of her hips sent mating signals to every man within stare range. Two mechanics came to the bay door and stood there wiping off wrenches and gazing at their hottest looking customer of the day.

She had her keys in one hand and she leaned into Uncle's driver-side window. Her face was near his face. The scent of her hair was a memory of flowers he forgot the names of long ago. Uncle tried not to look down the front of her open blouse. But he did and she noticed but before she could speak, Uncle scowled at her,

"You call this a date?" Am I just your taxi?"

"If Suki was surprised by his attack, she didn't show it. She simply said, "You wait here, then you fo'r'ow me. We take car home." With that, she turned and walked around the far side of the station. Uncle waited as told. *Sit boy. Stay. Roll over.* He would do just about anything she asked him to.

Uncle Ole's jaw went slack key when Suki came driving out of the back lot in a Mercedes convertible, fire-engine red, about mid-eighties vintage. She looked good in it too, like an Asian actress in a scene from a James Bond movie. Uncle followed her out onto the street in his eighteen-year old Cadillac. It was a two-car classic auto parade. She drove up hill to the by-pass highway and turned south for about four miles and then mauka (toward the mountains) into an area Uncle knew was called Maui Meadows. This is where the rich people live. Not the Mega-ultra-rich, but if you own a home on an acre or two or five anywhere in Hawaii, you are among the top 1.000000000721 percent of the wealthiest people on planet earth.

Here it got confusing. He stayed close on her tail, because she took so many turns. He was totally lost by the time she turned into a beautiful Beverley Hills looking estate with walls that looked like a Mediterranean villa. The high adobe bordered the long driveway all the way to a metal gate with a pineapple design across the bottom. Polished brass spear tips pointed up along the gate's top edge. It swung open quickly and they drove up a winding drive that led to a huge two-story mansion. But before they got there she turned to the right into thick jungle. A small Japanese style house was at the top of this driveway. Suki parked her Mercedes under a carved pillared Tori that looked like it was right out of a Tokyo movie set. She waved to Uncle to park where he was and motioned for him to come. *Come doggy. Of course, you will.* Coach figures that with enough training from this Japanese doll, he can be taught to obey simple commands. But the tremendous weight of '*Now... look at that*' held him in the driver's seat. There out his windshield, was a beautiful Asain wahine getting out of her Mercedes convertible in front of her house and waving him inside. She even owned a store. Okay it wasn't a liquor store, but it was a store. This moment left him literally choking on four-scoops of amazement. Suki waited for him by her front door.

"Shoes off p'rease,"

"Suki, I live here in Hawaii, I know this."

"How 'rong you 'rive Hawaii?" she asked.

"Almost nine months,"

"You still learning, o'rd man. What your name again?"

"My name is Gold, Oliver Gold, friends call me Ole." He

bowed his chin slightly as Nami had taught him. Men do not bow to a woman from the waist. He thought about Nami's slim waist and the night she passed out in his bed. Thanks to his semi-sober coach he could still look himself in the mirror for agreeing to abstain that night.

Suki's little cottage was exactly as he imagined a Japanese house to be: highly polished wood floor, a small ancestor shrine built into the entry wall, a low shelf for shoes. The main visiting room was uncluttered with a simple low table and pillows set on the floor. A slim vase with one pale flower stood off-center on the table. In one corner was the only modern touch, a black pole lamp with several lights shining softly on different walls of woven pandanus. A sleepy looking Buddha sat cross-legged on a low altar. Interior opaque shoji panels were partly slid open, revealing other rooms. Suki slid one open wide and disappeared inside.

"You sit O'river- san," she called from the next room. "I bring tea."

Sit doggy. Drink your tea water. Good doggy. Uncle's thinking what dogs must think every day. *I think I'm gonna bite somebody.* He thought about biting Suki and it made his tail start to pound on the floor.

Suki returned wearing a full-length kimono. It was a slinky silk wonder, light beige with golden embroidery along the seams. No dragons or such, it was simple and elegant. She placed two gold-rimmed cups on a woven mat on the table. The mat was adorned with black elephants sewn into the reed fabric. Her graceful movements hypnotized him. There was a hemmed slit up both sides of the kimono that revealed glimpses of her beautiful legs as she moved. This was a scene from his dream movie entitled, 'Perfect Asian Girlfriend Pours Tea for Oliver Gold.'

When she returned, she carried a man's kimono for Ole to wear. She helped him put it on over his clean polo. She tied the robe belt around his middle and off to his right side. He was enchanted by her personal attention. It was as if she appreciated having a man in the house.

"Is this your husband's Kimono?"

"Yes," ex-husband, ten years. He no-good bas'tad, but still friend. He 'rive one mile away. I bring tea now."

Suki returned through the shoji with a wooden tray holding a gold-glazed porcelain tea pot with a gold handle and small rice cakes on a gold-edged plate. She knelt at the table directly across from Uncle and bowed twice. Her hands moved slowly as she filled Uncle's small cup less than half full. Then she bowed again. Ole nodded and took a sip. Then he nodded again. Suki filled both cups this time, bowed once more and they sipped their tea in silence. She picked up the plate and offered the rice cakes to Ole. He took one, thought about it and then took another. Suki smiled, took one and spoke quietly.

"I call this, a date."

Uncle frowned. He nodded his reluctant acceptance of the less than perfect tea served with less than perfect grace. He had seen enough Japanese movies and read enough about their psychology to remember how a man behaves in these formal situations.

Suki must have been impressed. She blushed. Ole's eyes were boldly on every curve of her body and her every move. Quiet moments of Oolong tea ceremony, dressed in a kimono with lovely Suki felt like a dream. A fantasy that he wished for from the back seat of a taxi just nine months ago.

You amaze me brah, his romance coach is also impressed.

It was getting dark outside. She got up from the tea ceremony table and cleared away the cups.

"I think I should be going Suki." Uncle stood up to leave. He didn't want to go, but he wanted to start this relationship off right.

She must have felt the same caution; she didn't argue like he'd hoped she would. The free-electrons around them were combining in a careful, not a reckless way. They said good night with just a hug. But what a hug, her thin body felt wonderful in his arms. It was hard to let go. Suki had the same problem. They held a little too long but finally with a light squeeze, they broke the spell and released each other.

Ole drove back to Kahana with a lot to think about and a new song of hope in his heart.

They dated on and on without many days off, for the next two weeks. One night during a romantic dinner at Kimo's they sat side by side watching the sunset and listening to Willie K sing. The Maui sunset was melting crayons, making a beautiful mess all over the sky and ocean. Suki was beautiful too. Ole leaned closer to her face and she met him more than half way. It was their first kiss. Her soft lips were quivering with excitement. The sunset, the restaurant and the music vanished. He tasted steak and rum mixed with wine and eternity. He had not had a kiss like that in many years. That led to more kissing. But they both kept it sweet and old fashioned.

She drove her Mercedes to his gig at the PI a few times. She must like him, to drive so far to hear him sing. He sang to her with all his passion. He thought he might be falling in love again. Thinking of a possible future with Suki gave him great happiness. The chains of failed marriage linked around his heart, were falling off one by one.

They did go to her church service one Sunday. They sang the old Protestant hymns in Japanese. It lost a lot in translation. In fact, since it was all in Japanese, he kept falling asleep. Suki poked him when she heard him snore and said something angry in her language.

"Not nice to cuss in church," he scolded her.

"Keep round eyes open, bad manners man."

Sometimes they would put the top down on her Mercedes and cruise around the south side. They liked the Grand Wailea and other five-star hotels, where they would have a drink or dinner and walk those perfect beaches. They attended dinner parties and benefit art shows with the crispy, upper-crust of south Maui society. Suki had lived here for twenty years, she introduced Ole to many beautiful women, who were probably influential on the South end of the island; he only had eyes for

Suki.

Ole was surprised that he was dating someone clear down in Kihei; a long commute. But not as far away as the women he met on the Internet. He was going to enjoy this romantic karma as far as it could stretch. He believed in destiny, especially if you dream it up yourself, and it comes true. One evening after his lovely, rich, girlfriend paid for dinner at the Four Seasons Resort, Suki said, "We go to my other house."

66

On the Rocks

Motion sensor lights along her driveway welcomed them home. The Pineapple gate swung wide. She parked the Mercedes at her shoji house and Suki led Uncle up a narrow, flat-stone pathway through palms and ferns. There were Zen-like sculptures off to each side of the path. Each lit by subtle lighting. They came to a carport big enough for six cars but with nobody home.

The day was slipping into its evening kimono of late reds. There were no lights on in the house. Suki found a light switch and lit up the sweeping curve of a marble stairway to the front double doors. Purple Bougainvillea grew out of large urns along each side of the stone handrails. It was like entering a palace.

The top of the stairs opened onto a huge lanai with life-size Greek-looking statues, silhouetted by the pink sky.

Every day brah, there's new magic on this island. What an amazing woman and what a house!

Uncle's finally found an established Asian woman on Maui. He can't help thinking about what his dad said about rich women and falling in love. Maybe he was finally gonna take dad's advice.

Suki turned on the interior lights. The living room / dining

329

room were as big as Texas. There was one wide carpeted stairway going up and one wide, marble-tile stairway going down. The ceilings were so high you could hang the 'Spirit of St Louis' from the rafters and still have room for the 'Kitty Hawk' to hang over the kitchen. Uncle had to sit down. Of course, he was standing next to a black leather sofa right where he needed it. He eased down into its cool, expensive comfort.

"Who lives here Suki? This place is big enough for a family of twelve. Where is everybody?"

"I throw all renters out last week, make remodel, they all bad, all stupid, too loud.

"Why did you throw them out?" He had to ask.

"You bad 'ristener O'river-san. They loud and stupid and bad. I make remodel now."

"This place looks great. What's to remodel?"

"Come, I show you downstairs."

She led him down the marble stairway to a locked oak door big enough to drive a Volkswagen through. Suki found the right key from her ring of fifty. Inside this door was a lobby that would make the Ritz Carlton proud. There was a fountain in the center of the hall with a seven-foot-high bronze statue of 'Zorba' the Greek, misted by soft jets of water so it looked like he was dancing in the rain. Around the hall there were four more oak doors. One was a large private entryway with glass side panels looking out onto a swimming pool. It was movie star elegant, lit by underwater lamps and lights in the surrounding ferns. There were more Greek statues standing guard around the pool looking dignified and wise. He could see the pool house, another mansion just slightly smaller than the shoji house. Every detail was perfect.

Suki opened the oak door to her right and led Ole into a large, well-lit laundry room with two matching sets of those expensive washers and dryers that look like they're right out of Star-Wars.

Around the fountain to the left, Suki opened the last two oak doors. She reached inside for the light switches. There before them were two of the most grossly damaged apartments Ole had ever seen. The stink of old clothes and garbage was disgusting. Several holes in the wallboard looked intentional. There were, busted light bulbs and beer bottle glass scattered all over the filthy tiled floors. The place smelled like a college dormitory. Suki did not bother to walk into the rooms.

"How can renters be so mean?" Ole was shocked to see such destruction in such a beautiful home.

"Not your prob'rem, O'river-san. I fix up and find new renters easy." She closed the two apartment doors and they walked back upstairs.

At the far end of the kitchen there was a built-in, floor to ceiling pantry with teak doors that looked like they might have been hand-carved in Japan five centuries ago. Suki shook out a long, bronze key and unlocked the ancient doors to reveal dozens of bottles of booze, large racks of red wines, corked heads slanted down and the glass door of a refrigerated cooler for the white wines.

"Drink, O'river-san?"

He was speechless for a moment, but his head was nodding 'yes' with a formal, man bow.

She does own a liquor store. She locks it up in her kitchen.

In amongst all the expensive show-off brands of booze she had five bottles of Bacardi rum.

"That one, the gold rum," he pointed. "On the rocks."

She fixed his drink and opened a bottle of Merlot. It looked expensive and imported. She poured herself a healthy red splash. Both his glass and her long-stem were Swarovski crystal. Even at social gatherings at Stanford University, no one ever served him a drink in Swarovski crystal. He held it with both hands.

They walked for a half-mile across the living room to get outdoors to the lanai. It was the size of a parking lot. The Greek or Roman statues were standing around whispering amongst themselves about the positions of the stars and the circumference of a circle. Taking it all in, Ole felt like he was in Europe somewhere. It humbled him to be invited into this luxurious home. Everything was magnificent, like maybe it was a queen's winter home in Hawaii, away from her drafty Greek castle.

"Who designed all this? It's absolutely amazing." He could switch from pidgin to King's English when surrounded by opulence.

"My ex, he make design and build this place. Him perfection alla' time, everything must perfect, even me. But I too far from perfect, I just stupid 'peasant woman' he yell me."

Uncle shook his head no, no, no.

"Pretty and smart sez me," Ole offered. "You have your own store and this beautiful rental property. Too bad you are so old and skinny. If you were just younger and fatter, I might be interested in you."

Suki went from angry face about her husband to Japanese beauty queen in a lickity-split second. She smiled her most beautiful smile yet.

"You bad man O'river-san." She held Uncle's eyes with hers and made a toast,

"Here's to o'rd O'river, bad manners man." She sipped her wine and then returned her eyes to his. A proper toast in any language.

"And here's to an old Japanese lady that's too skinny but not too stupid." The nicest thing he could think of that would not sound schmoozy and romantic. *She's so beautiful she's heard a lifetime of nice compliments.* He guessed right and took a chance.

"What's upstairs?" He knew it had to be bedrooms. She knew, that he knew that it was bedrooms.

"I show you," Suki led the way.

The carpeted stairs came to a landing big enough to hold a regulation pool table. They turned to the left and climbed up three more broad stairs to a hallway about a mile long.

"All bed'looms up here, damage apartments down below."

"How many bedrooms are there?" Uncle was more than curious. It was so unusual to see a place this big in Hawaii that wasn't a museum or a Wal-Mart or something.

"Four bed'loom, on this level, two on main floor. Plus, each apartment is two-bed'loom so ten, total. She opened a door; it looked like the master bedroom. There were arched stone windows like in a castle, that looked out over her private jungle. He could see one small glimmer of a street light shining through the trees about a block away.

The four-poster bed was made of Koa wood. It was a huge California King, piled high with silk pillows.

"Bed's too small," said Uncle, "probably very uncomfortable."

"Bed comfortab're, I show you." She climbed up and walked to the firm center of the satin-covered mattress. She began to jump, bouncing up and down barefoot like a kid on a trampoline.

"That looks fun." Uncle's smiling a little too much; happy as a sixteen-year-old boy who just found a cute sixteen-year-old girl.

"You try," said Suki with a demure smile.

Uncle Ole climbed up on the huge bed with her. She grabbed his hands with hers and they started jumping together. Suki began to sing off key. "Two o'rd monkeys jumping on bed... One fall off... Break head... Go find doctor... doctor said... no more monkey's jumping on bed."

"Now, this is what I call a date," said Ole.

After the second verse it did not take long for them to fall. However, they did not fall off the bed. They fell, wrapped in each other's arms kissing with two-weeks-worth of built up hungry need.

Maui was squeezing the juice again; sixteen-hundred years of lovers had found this island before Ole and Suki. There is love here. Come to the islands to 'give' love and karma will let you stay. Uncle gave it his best that night. Around midnight, naked, exhausted Suki said he could stay.

In the morning, he woke with the daylight. Suki was wrapped around his body like a dream, his dream. Uncle's thoughts turned to Metaphysics.

Is this real brah? Or is she a sweet figment of your best dream so far? Are you real? Or are you just a winged monkey from Oz, dreaming you're inside her dream?

When he thought he saw the answer it glowed like a soap bubble with a woman inside, who looked like a Japanese Glinda the Good Witch. Then her face became a drop of water misting down like jungle rain with millions of other faces. The trade winds blew all the mist out over the sea where they gently bent some sunbeams into colors. The rainbow stretched out over an ocean filled with circling sharks…

"Hey you, O're monkey, wake up. I open store at nine, must go soon."

Pouf! the vision of rainbows and sharks was gone.

"Not if you have another important appointment." He reached out and pulled her back into bed. He wanted her slim body under him again. He rubbed his day-old stubble chin into her neck. She moaned a little but pushed him away.

"I make breakfast. You shower. Then come to small house in twenty minutes or you no eat."

Yes boss. Uncle only thought it. He said nothing, just a frown and one casual nod not even looking at her. She couldn't see the frown curve up into a smile at this Japanese game of male / female drama. Suki was a control freak by day but last night she was his submissive sex slave. It had been three long months since Ling and Liang had rocked his world with their one-night *menages a' trois.* He fell back into the sheets and watched Suki hurry away. She was butt naked beautiful and did not bother to dress for the run through the jungle to her shoji house. Ole was falling in love with the naked, Japanese Princess of Kihei.

Wow, there was no other thought in Ole's mind than, *Wow, Wow and Wow.*

"Bow-wow-wow-wow," he barked out loud, as he gathered

336

up his wrinkled clothes.

She's got you barking like a dog. Who knew that could ever happen? Now, you gonna be her dog forever. Dogs must think like that, with their heart. Good old faithful O'river. He stuck out his tongue and panted all the way to the marble master bathroom. There was a gold shower head and gold faucet handle of course. Oliver Gold felt right at home.

In exactly eighteen minutes, Uncle appeared at Suki's front door and knocked.

"Come... sit here," she commanded, pointing to the new settings at the same low table. Ole has been so independent since arriving on Maui that it felt good to have a wealthy Alpha dog tell him what to do. He sat there on his haunches on a silk doggy pillow and started scratching his ears.

He admired the craftsmanship of the low, ebony-wood table. His sense of smell was better than ever. He could smell the furniture polish. Breakfast smelled wonderful too, Miso soup and frying fish. From his embroidered pillow on the floor he could see his master though the open shoji panel. She was in a different kimono this morning. It was probably meant to be a jacket but she wore it like a mini-skirt. It revealed small glimpses of her perfect round butt and her skinny legs traveled for a long time down to her three-inch-high heels. The heels made the muscles of her calves plump out in come-hither ways as she balanced from one toe-tip to the other. She was singing something in Japanese and flipping fish.

"Hope you cook better than you sing."

"You, terrible man O'river-san. No wonder your wife left you."

"Hah," was all he said. It was enough.

The Miso was served in round gold-glazed bowls. Suki then set a square plate of lightly fried Salmon filets gracefully in front of Uncle. She knelt in her lovely way, and began to pray.

"Jesus-san, thank you for food and bad o'rd man find Suki. Amen."

"Amen," Uncle woofed. He was truly thankful for these past two weeks of magic with Suki. During breakfast, she told him the combination he would need to open the gate of her Villa. She was going to work but he could stay and enjoy the pool if he wanted to.

"I don't work at the hotel today so I could stay." Then added, "Maybe I could help clean up the apartments for you."

Suki looked at Uncle for a long minute of silence. "Maybe, you not such bad man O'river-san. I pay you. Insurance company will pay for repairs. How much you charge?"

Uncle could use some extra income. "Those apartments are gonna need a lot of work, twenty-dollars-an-hour would be enough to start. After the first thirty days I want full medical insurance, a cell phone and vacation pay plus a 401 K pension to support me when I get old."

"You a'ready o'rd. Twenty-dolla' too much, I pay ten-dolla-hour plus 'loom and board."

"I'll think about it." And he did. *Room and board?* Coach heard it too. Uncle Ole figured there must be wisps of smoke coming out his floppy ears from all the burning rubber his thoughts were leaving on the paved street of his mind. He wanted to chase her around the room. *Room and board? Was she serious? Live here in a private villa with a part-time job, and certain fringe benefits?* Ole's tail was wagging and his long tongue was hanging out one side of his lower jaw.

She could take us for a 'walk' every morning. Coach is wagging his tail.

He remembered his first day in Hawaii, riding in the taxi-cab. He wished he knew even one person on this island. *Like perhaps a beautiful Asian wahine, with a big house and a Mercedes convertible, someone really, cute with a flaming crush on him.* He realized he had stopped breathing. Ole closed his eyes and exhaled for as long as he could. His next deep breath refreshed him like rainbow shave ice.

Your power of visualization is strong Luke Sky-dreamer. Dream big, believe in your potential and you will prevail. His inner Yoda seems completely unsurprised by all of this.

Uncle Ole could not think of any reason not to accept her offer. When she returned from carrying the bowls into the kitchen he stood up like a man, but he could imagine his tail still wagging like crazy. He nodded to his new love with a slight bow.

"Fifteen-dollars-per-hour with a written contract and it's a deal."

"Okay, you make contract. I go now, sign paper later." And with that she did that little stumble-walk that Japanese women do when they're happy. She went up two low stairs, slid open a shoji and closed it behind her. Uncle heard water running in a shower. He imagined her slim naked body covered in streams of hot water and soap bubbles. He shook his head and howled a low wolf call, "Aaaooooooo." He was her dog now.

67

The Dharma Rainbow

The Zen of this moment was over-powering. Ole bent himself into downward dog yoga on his embroidered silk pillow and listened to the shower splash on Suki. He not only had a real live, sexy girlfriend, he had a magnificent home and a purpose. He would help her all he could. He opened his eyes and looked around the empty peaceful room. The Buddha in the corner would have been looking back at him if his eyes were open. The only sound was the shower and some morning birds calling in the surrounding jungle. Ole sat back down on his pillow next to the table. He felt secure there, right where she told him to sit and stay with 'loom and board.'

He lapped up the last of the Miso soup like a dog prince in a fairy tale. Suki was a gourmet cook. The soup was delicious. Life was delicious. He needed some paper and a pen. He looked around the uncluttered, peaceful room. The statue of Buddha meditated quietly, knowing all. He probably knew where she kept her pens and paper.

There was no sign of a desk but his eyes found a drawer on one side of the low table where breakfast had just been served. Somehow, he knew that inside this drawer was exactly what he needed. He was living in a science-fiction world or some other dimension where you merely envision what you want and it appears or happens. He slid open the perfectly crafted wooden drawer. Inside he found a short stack of monogrammed stationary with a gold-embossed 'L' at the top

341

and a gold plated, Schaefer, Century-Edition pen set. It looked like it had never been opened. He shook his big ears, then his back, then his tail. He began to write out a work agreement that specified his expectations and her promise. He left out the medical plan, cell phone and the pension stuff. He specified the fifteen-dollars-per-hour and the room and board clause. He made the term of the contract for six months, starting today. He wasn't going to move out of Yu'layne's house for less than that. He didn't want to move. He liked his room with a view. He laid the pen down and thought about it for a while. Suki turned off the shower. She was singing again. His sensitive ears could make out every word of the sweet song, 'Sukiyaki.'

He liked the people at Yu'layne's, especially Ling and Liang. The place was close to his job at the Embassy Resort and it was affordable. Should he give all that up? He'd only known Suki for two weeks but wasn't this what he wished for?

It's your destiny Scooby-Doo dumb ass, right here in front of you. Why don't you want to accept it? Debating this is ridiculous. Coach is already convinced.

Ole tried to weigh both options carefully, objectively, like the chemical scientist that he was. But his head coach was doing all the talking,

Pay six-hundred dollars-a-month to live alone in one small room in a million-dollar home or live rent-free in a five-million-dollar villa with an over-sexed, rich, Japanese babe who likes to cook? No contest brah.

He finished the short contract as Suki slid open a shoji

panel. She wore a black, high collar Asian dress of some kind, very sophisticated. It had a slit up one side that revealed a sexy peek at her leg and a row of buttons on one shoulder that he wanted to unbutton. Ole caught his breath. *What a doll.* With his passion loosely in check, he stayed on task.

"Contract done," he announced. "Needs your signature and I start today."

"What it say?" She took the paper and quickly read the two paragraphs.

"No, no... I no 'rike this part, stay for six months." She took Uncle's pen, rather, her pen, and scratched out the words 'six months.' Then In perfect English she carefully wrote,

"...as long as Oliver Gold wants to stay." Then she signed and dated it.

That's a commitment brah! Maybe you're her destiny, too.

Oliver's heart swelled to extra-large in his big chest. She does like him. She likes him a lot.

"Okay Suki, I'll make a photo copy for you today when I go home to get my things. Where will I sleep?"

"Put your things in same bed'loom" she said, "you s'reep with me."

"Hmph, you snore too much old woman."

"You snore too, bad manners o'rd man. Okay, I s'reep in small house. We meet in your 'loom sometimes. I teach you

343

how to do it four-hundred ways, Kama-Sutra style."

He was about to say something clever, but decided to let her have the last word on that promise. Suki slid open a rice paper door panel and did her model walk into the kitchen to pack her lunch. Ole sat up straight on his pillow panting like a faithful pet. He watched her, adoring her with his eyes. His long tongue hung out hoping for another pat on the head or a dog-biscuit.

He was starting to drool when his big ears heard rain tapping on the roof. He got up from his pillow, turning around his tail. He was kind a surprised to see himself walking on two legs. Ole trotted outside to press his nose into the fresh world of Hawaii rain. He was so happy he wanted run all over the place marking this territory, then jump in that big swimming pool out back. He was about to pee on the side of the house when he chanced to gaze out over the ocean and saw a rainbow curving across the sky. Ole went on point like a bird dog. The rainbow curved down into a pot of gold that looked a lot like Molokini Island. This was the first rainbow he had seen today, so he memorized it while he waited for Suki. Ole-doggy was wondering if this rainbow was one of the omens predicted by Lao Tzu. *"I see rainbows in your life. Like blessings, they lead you by day."*

"So... our dreams actually do become our fate?" He sort of wonder-woofed out loud with a shake of his furry head.

The answer appeared before him with a grand gesture. The rainbow lifted off the pot of gold like the finder above a Ouija board and traveled right on up into the sky, two-hundred feet above the ocean. It sparkled there in the morning sunlight, a spectacular hula-hoop, a full circle rainbow. He'd never seen anything like it; didn't know it was even possible. It shimmered there in Technicolor Alka-Seltzer radiance. He wanted to reach out and touch it, maybe spin it like the wheel of fortune at the county fair. This was the most amazing 'instant-relief' omen he could never, have imagined.

Now, that's a certified message, brah. You're home. What kind of an enchanted island is this anyway? Coach is blown away; humming like the wind in the rigging; heeled over, and racing toward his future.

Ole's dog ears went flat, like sails trimmed for an upwind tack, his new life speeding across the finish line ahead of all the other mutts in the fleet. He heard the air-horn blast from the committee boat, Ahauuuooooooooooom," he howled with gratitude.

Congratulations brah! Coach approves. *You just won first place in the 'Destiny in Hawaii Girlfriend Regatta.'* Coach is spraying a magnum of champagne all over the celebration in his mind.

Uncle thought back to his first day on Maui. He arrived just nine months ago, a lonely, drunken dreamer with a broken yet somehow hopeful heart. He remembered his plan for making the people already here a little happier. He would make Suki happy and help her all he could. Just as he thought about her, she came out to the carport and frowned sadly.

"I must go now O're-san, store open at nine."

As she passed by him it looked like she was going to give

345

him a kiss on the cheek, but when she got closer, her heart must have melted like a candy bar from the heat of victory radiating from his muscled chest. Suki looked up at Ole with a smile on her pretty, Japanese face. Ole put both hands on her shoulders and turned her around to see the full-circle rainbow hanging in the sky. She inhaled with a soft gasp and went as motionless as an unopened box of chocolates. She smelled good; he might have drooled a little on her hair. When she finally turned back to Ole, she pressed her lips full on his mouth like she was never going to stop. He tasted chocolate and sex-flavored eternity. Ole opened his good eye for another peek at the Dharma Wheel Rainbow. It was turning like a smile, *'Be careful what you wish for,'* spoke the wheel.

He closed his eyes and devoured her lips. She was a delicious kisser, hot and sticky as melting marshmallows. Their bodies stuck together like two Graham Crackers. She reached up and tore open his shirt. The buttons flew off like freed winged-monkeys. Wild as two teenagers in heat, they toppled over the fender and into the soft leather backseat of that red convertible, both desperately hungry for S'more.

The End of the Beginning

About the author:

 Oliver Gold moved to Maui in 2002. His faith in karma, optimism and visualization, guided him through a living theater of crazy women before someone very special found him.

 Ole teaches Hawaiian cultural crafts, guides botanical nature walks, and teaches Tai-chi at three west Maui resorts. He is a musician and singer for weddings and private parties and owns Aloha Singing Telegrams.com.

If you purchased this book from Amazon after October 7, 2018 you can download the Kindle version for free. Please encourage your friends to discover other novels by Oliver Gold. If you enjoyed this book, do me an act of random kindness, please post a short review on Amazon.com

Thanks for your support!

Oliver Gold,

A sample of Oliver Gold's second novel, ~ Maui Leis an' Lies ~

Chapter 1

Kafka on a Sunday Morning

Uncle Ole slammed the gear shift into 'Park' while the car was still moving. He didn't care if the transmission busted a few teeth jerking to a stop. He searched through the clutter in his glove box until he found his pint of rum. Uncle fondled the hard cap like it was his ex-girlfriend's nipple, but he didn't turn it. Digging deeper, under a road map and buried next to some

348

fuses that probably fit some other car, he struck gold. His wedding ring was right where he threw it a year ago. He wiped a man tear out of his eye. He wasn't a crier, but his emotions were caving in on his tough guy resolve.

Ole looked around and was surprised to find he'd stopped alongside a large graveyard and a church on some side street in Lahaina. He left the engine running. He wanted that cold air-conditioning blowing on his unshaved face even if he passed out. He felt used, thrown away, worthless and thirsty.

Uncle held his ex-wedding ring tenderly, and looked down at his fourth finger. There was no pale 'married line' there anymore, to show where that ring had meant something for twenty-seven years. It slid onto his now 'single' digit too easily; he'd lost weight.

He'd lost at love too. He spun the gold donut around his skinny finger and thought about Tanya again. After so many good years of marriage, she'd threatened to divorce him if he moved to Hawaii. Four years of marriage counseling didn't solve the impasse; he moved to Maui to live in the sunshine. Tanya stayed in Seattle and filed in Superior Court. Her scandalous petition threatened to stomp his retirement pension out of his future and into her own considerable pension. Since she wanted it all, karma defeated her greed. He'd legally survived the attack with his full pension, but the collateral damage was the forty-eight-thousand bucks he now owed his defense attorney. Ole shivered in the cold Cadillac air. It had been an expensive nightmare; and would be for years to come.

Okay move along brah, his brain cop was waving him through that well-worn synapse.

There's nothing to see here anymore buddy, ancient history, move along. Officer Brain and other voices in his head have been keeping him company, since the divorce.

Uncle had tried starting over. Imagine that, a fifty-something divorced guy, dating again on a shoestring budget in very-expensive Hawaii. To his surprise, it wasn't hopeless. He'd met some cute, crazy, loose and willing women on Maui. His body was ready, but his heart was still tattooed with Tanya ink; not yet comfortable in a new world of casual hookups.

Most women seemed normal until the second date, when he'd see their messy true colors of addictions to booze, grass or worse. Some were attractive old hippie-chicks, who found Maui years ago and still tie-dyed every beautiful day with sad, permanent-ink baggage from their past. Every woman he dated was looking for a 'Money Daddy' to take care of them. They would take a quick read on Uncle Ole's old car and move on. He'd had eleven 'start-over' chances, all failed due to the above list of disqualifications. He'd considered writing a book on his adventurous first year in Hawaii dating crazy women. He even had a title in mind, 'Maui on the Rocks.'

Maybe you were aiming a little too high brah, whispered the right half of his brain.

Ya think? Teased the left.

Oh ya, remember y 'er 'must have' shopping list? All you wanted was one cute, Asian wahine with a flaming crush on you and plenty of money. She should own a big house on Maui, drive a Mercedes convertible and own a liquor store. That's 'all' you wanted. Really?

Ya, seemed like enough at the time.

Nobody's brain could defend visualization more convincingly than Uncle Ole's. The reality of it all, was that six weeks ago he'd found just such a woman, Suki Loco'ino, a resident of south Maui. He had dated her, rode around in her Mercedes convertible and worked for her, doing handy man repairs on her big house. She liked him so much that she asked him to move in with her. Ta-dah!

Visualization works brah, why you so surprised? Asks the right.

Life is too full of surprises wise guy, says the left.

His brain is still reeling from this morning's stun-grenade disaster. He looked out the windshield of his Cadillac. There was a heat mirage doing the hula out there on the sunny side of the street. He revved the engine to keep that air-conditioning ice cold.

This morning at seven-o'clock everything was perfect, well...almost perfect. He awoke in his wing of Suki's sprawling mansion and limped to his yoga mat. Downward dog helped stretch the sex-kinks out of his back. Suki was younger than him and a double-jointed acrobat in bed.

By seven-thirty, his monkey-mind had wandered away from pure Yoga and was thinking of her delicious impure distractions. For almost two months, she had filled his life up like a helium balloon with sex and gifts. The two of them had even talked about marriage and the exciting years of senior assisted-living that lay ahead.

At eight-o'clock this morning, she'd turned his world upside down, dumping him out like yesterday's trash. She'd cut the string and let go the balloon. He was on his own, spinning up and away to nowhere. The imagery was so spot-on that he felt

351

his 'Helium-Spiritus' lifting through the roof of his car and up into the big shade tree overhead. It snagged on a limb and came to a sticky roost alongside other suicidal souls that haunt the shady under-branches of trees near churches and graveyards.

He'd been 'out of body' during meditations that went into overtime. His spirit shooting out like a champagne cork spraying rainbows of ectoplasm straight up, high above his motionless empty form below. Today, his soul was the color of lawn mower grease and it stuck like moss on a tree limb already burdened with grief.

"What 'er you... doin' up here?" mumbled the foggy, lead-colored light next to him.

"You first," Ole nudged him with his, ah... shoulder or elbow or something.

"No, you go... hmphh," the apparition grumbled in confusion, "You first...oh wha 'tha hell... Okay, almos' dead new guy, look down there. You see 'dat pile 'a rags under 'da h'biscus bushes?"

"Ya, I see it."

"Tha'zs me. I been a drug addict since my dad kick my lazy ass out'ta his house. 'Dat hurt brah. It was my fourteenth birthday. Today, I turn twenty-nine years old; homeless for fifteen years. I steal for a living so'z can buy my next load."

Uncle Ole's soul sniffed with that soul-sniffing sound that only the desperately depressed can hear. The sad birthday soul went on,

"Don't say it, ... I know wha 'chu thinkin', I heard it all before. It's all my fault. I keep making bad choices and t'ink things gonna get better? No way brah, 'dey get worse. I nev'a eat once since las' Monday when get release from jail. Now I sick brah, too sick fo' eat. I stink like a dog. At least in jail I got a shower. I face it, now. I'm junk. I deserve ta' die brah, soz' las' night I make one solemn vow, gonna lay 'der un'da 'dem bushes and look at yesta' day's flowers until I go mak'e (dead). No one gonna know; no one ev'a gonna care."

"What a spoiled whiner you are," boomed an older fizzle of pale light further up the dark branch of the tree.

"You lazy, stinking, meth head! You're young! You could still make a go of it. My wife and I lived up in Kapalua. We had a great life, married fifty years. She got some kind of cancer, dried her up like a leaf. For a while, I stayed above water with credit cards for flotation. When Sarah died, my world ended. The bank foreclosed on our house; I had to move out. My rich friends all forgot me. For a year I've slept in an abandoned car in a lot behind the same damn bank that took my home, bank of Aloha my ass."

Ole's spirit went a darker shade of mud green as the old soul peeled off his painful story scab by scab.

"Look inside that church down there. See that old fart in the back pew, that's me. I attend every Sunday because it's the only air-conditioned meetin' in town with a free lunch. Nobody ever speaks to me, nobody knows my name. They tolerate me eating brunch with them after all the hymn singing but they don't like me. I don't smell good like they do. I'm a walking dead man; always hot, hungry and tired of being alone. I miss my Sarah. After church today, I'm gonna step out in front of a truck on the highway an' I'm going straight to Hell. At least there I'll have plenty of company."

353

Ole's soul looked down into the Cadillac where his feelings were shooting back and forth at each other like spoiled children in an air-conditioned cowboy gunfight over a crazy Japanese woman.

"Gotta go guys, thanks,"

And just like Zeus throwing a lightning bolt, his spirit threw itself back into the depressed body in the driver's seat. Uncle shook his hairy head back and forth in the arctic wind of the dashboard vents. That cold air could freeze meat in a morgue. His eyebrows were frosting over. He stretched out one skinny finger and pushed a button. The four tinted windows opened at once; all the way down. Fresh air cleared his head with scorching waves of heat. December days are wicked hot in Lahaina, a Hawaiian name meaning 'Merciless Sun.'

It must be ninety-nine degrees out there today, brah. Have mercy, roll up the windows! It's another confusing message from his survival coach.

The Suki disaster was making his chest hurt as it thawed. He did the math; he'd failed at finding a new girlfriend an even dozen times in his first thirteen months on Maui. Now everything he owned, what little there was, fit in the trunk of his fifteen-hundred-dollar Maui cruiser. The back seat he'd kept clear so he'd have a place to sleep.

So, mister 'visualization-wise-guy,' did you see this picture...you, living in a car?

Ya, you should a known cousin. Suki was searching for 'Mr. Money Daddy.'

354

His brain was tag-teaming now, about to finish this wrestling match; both halves in the ring and kicking him while he's down. Ole leaned his icy forehead on the steering wheel and lowered his hands. The ring slipped off his finger and landed on the floor mat. He left it there. He hit the button and rolled up all the windows again.

Uncle thought he heard a viola playing something by Erik Satie. It came haunting its way down a time-swept cliff from far away in his un swept mind. It was bad enough being divorced and then passing up all those dangerous-dating second chances, but to lose Suki, the woman of his dreams, yikes that hurt. He tallied it all up again: she was cute, Asian, rich and had an obvious crush on him. She owned two houses and a swimming pool on several acres of Maui, the most expensive island in the world. She drove a Mercedes convertible and owned a retail store. Okay it wasn't a liquor store as per his original wish, but realizing seven out of eight specific visualizations was a dang good score. He nearly smiled, but instead another tear rolled down his nose. It started to freeze in the air-conditioned blizzard howling inside his built-in-Detroit igloo.

Brrrr.... open 'da window! Carbon-deadly monoxides in your lungs brah, you really wanna die? Coach is back to basic survival.

Hey cousin, ma 'be dying not so bad, just change from 'dis form to formless an' back into some otha' form. Ma 'be next time you gonna be a dolphin.

No way brah, that take a lot betta karma than y 'er packin'.

Sometimes, his left and right brains strained at each other like chained up guard dogs. Ole wasn't really trying to kill himself, but he was in a Kafka mood. He remembered reading

Franz K. in college and his writing struck a bell that never stopped ringing. Something about accepting responsibility for all you do, without ever being certain if it's right or wrong. That confused Kafka and was still messing with people's minds eighty years after his death. How could anyone be certain, if his actions were right or wrong, good or bad?

Say you rush into a busy street to save a child who has fallen in front of a speeding car. The car swerves and misses you both, so that was the right, good thing to do, ya? But because of your action, the braking, skidding car jumped the curb, came down on the sidewalk and killed three members of a Salvation Army Christmas Band. Trombones and bugles flew up into the grey sky and landed dented and broken in the snowy street along with the dead soldiers for Christ. The little red kettle with all the money did a double back flip and came down in the open truck bed of a drug lord's El Camino as he cruised past the carnage on his way to an all-night strip joint.

So, was saving the little child the wrong, bad thing to do? That's Kafka. *Does it matter what we do?* Franz taught that the whole meaning of life, was to die.

Why not today brah? Whispered the Kafka side.

Don't push me, I'm trying to think cousin, argued the right side.

Hah! This could take awhile

Shut up brain.

You shut up.

Kafka wanted all his books burned when he died. That never happened because he had pinched a nerve on the spine of humanity forever.

Dating on Maui certainly had a Kafkaesque kind of twist to it. How had his rather normal life turned into a mini-series of meaningless soap operas? What he really wanted was a second chance at romance with a rich, smart, good-looking, brunette or black-haired lady who wasn't addicted to cigarettes or drugs. Maybe she'd be a golf professional and teach him how to break a hundred. Or a musician who was personal friends with the Moody Blues and they'd record Ole's songs on their next album. Or maybe she'd be a Native Hawaiian princess whose family owns thousands of acres on Maui, or perhaps an entire island!

There you go over-wishing again brah...

Maui Leis an' Lies
© Oliver Gold 2016
Available in paperback from Amazon.com / e-book on Kindle

Made in the USA
San Bernardino, CA
18 October 2018